JAXON

HEROES AT HEART

MARYANN JORDAN

Jaxon (Heroes at Heart) Copyright 2018

ISBN ebook: 978-1-947214-24-8

ISBN print: 978-1-947214-25-5

❀ Created with Vellum

AUTHOR INFORMATION

USA TODAY BESTSELLING AND AWARD WINNING AUTHOR

I am an avid reader of romance novels, often joking that I cut my teeth on the historical romances. I have been reading and reviewing for years. In 2013, I finally gave into the characters in my head, screaming for their story to be told. From these musings, my first novel, Emma's Home, The Fairfield Series was born.

I was a high school counselor having worked in education for thirty years. I live in Virginia, having also lived in four states and two foreign countries. I have been married to a wonderfully patient man for thirty-seven years. When writing, my dog or one of my four cats can generally be found in the same room if not on my lap.

Please take the time to leave a review of this book.

Feel free to contact me, especially if you enjoyed my book. I love to hear from readers!

Facebook

Email

Website

As an adolescent counselor for over twenty-five years, I had the opportunity to work with many young people. One young man, upset over a poor choice he had made, came to me. As I listened to his story and his confession, I told him that the true measure of a man was not in the mistakes he made, but in how he handled those mistakes. I remember the look on his face when I told him I was sure he was going to be a good man.

So, this book is dedicated to all the students over the years who allowed me to be a part of their lives.

Jaxon stared at the water, his stomach in knots, forcing an *I got this* expression on his ten-year-old face. He glanced to the side at his identical twin, Jayden, who was bouncing up and down, radiating excitement. On the other side were his best friends and foster brothers, Zander, Rafe, Asher, and Cael, equally excited with huge smiles on their faces.

Twisting to look over his shoulder, he observed Miss Ethel, her sharp gaze resting on him. Her grey hair was twisted into a bun at the back of her head, her glasses perched on her nose. Wearing a shirtdress, neatly belted at the waist, stockings, and comfortable black shoes, she always made him feel secure. But, right now, even her presence did not stop the queasiness in his stomach.

Tossing her a lopsided grin that he hoped passed for enthusiasm, he turned back to look at the water in the pool. Other children were swimming, and their laughter rang out over the water. He watched as they moved with such ease, seeming to float along with no fear.

Looking down at the edge of the pool, staring at the depth marking painted on the concrete, he blew out a breath. Four Feet. *I'm four feet, six inches tall. Does that mean if my feet are on the bottom, then only my forehead and nose will stick out? What about my mouth?*

Before panic ensued, he felt a firm hand on his shoulder and Miss Ethel said, "Come on, boys. We're going to the end, down here."

She steered him toward the end of the pool and he sighed in relief at the words painted on the side, now reading Three Feet. Breathing easier, he listened to his brothers complain that it was the baby side, but one look from Miss Ethel had them quieting immediately.

Braver, now that he knew he would have his head out of the water, he watched as the others jumped in, whoops and yells calling out. Sitting on the side, he twisted his head up toward Miss Ethel once more and, with her encouraging smile, he clung to the side as he inched his body into the water. His grip became tighter until his feet hit bottom and his face broke out into a huge grin as he stood with his head and shoulders above water.

Turning, he splashed his arms around, careful not to leave the safety of the side of the pool.

"Come on, Jaxon," Cael called out, kicking his legs in the water to move faster.

"I'm good here," he replied, nervousness and envy warring inside.

"But—"

"He's good," Zander said. He was already twelve, making him the oldest, and he always looked out for his brothers, maintaining peace between them when needed and beating up on anyone on the outside who said anything derogatory about them.

Shooting him a grateful look, he continued to move along the side, keeping within grabbing range of the ledge. Cael, eleven, paddled up next to him, his face contrite.

"Sorry, Jax. Listen, if you want, I'll stay nearby and play."

"I'll be here," Jayden said, moving closer. Jaxon shared a look with his twin.

"It's okay," he said, feeling more confident, bouncing up and down on his feet. As his brothers moved away slightly, each enjoying the pool, he noticed a tiny, red-headed girl walk to the edge and dive straight into the water. Stunned, he had never seen anyone dive before, other than on TV. He waited to see what would happen, holding his breath as she was under the water.

Just as he was about to call Miss Ethel for help, the little girl broke the surface and began to swim to the deep end. He was amazed, not only for her diving and swimming skill, but that she had to be only about five or six years old. Losing sight of her, he noticed a man standing on the edge of the pool, yelling at the little girl to swim harder.

Looking back at Miss Ethel, he observed her pursed lips, the expression she had when she was irritated. Grateful that she rarely used it with them, he none-theless knew that she was not happy with that man.

"Children should be allowed to play," she mumbled before looking back down at him. Her lips curved into a smile again, and she said, "Take your time to get used to the water and just have a good time, Jaxon."

Relieved, he continued to bob up and down, moving slightly away from the edge as he became more confident. Blocking out the sounds of the man yelling, he played with his brothers, making sure to keep his head above the water.

Miss Ethel settled into a pool chair, placing her knitting bag on the table next to her. Able to knit and keep her eyes on her boys at the same time, she smiled as they continued to play.

"Miss Ethel?"

She looked up and saw a man standing nearby. His swim trunks and t-shirt with the pool logo on it identified him as one of the instructors. "Yes?"

"I'm Jimmy, the pool manager. We spoke on the phone?"

"Yes, please have a seat."

He sat across her from, his friendly gaze moving to the pool where her group of boys played. "Those your boys?"

Her face, always at ease when talking about her charges, broke into a smile. "Yes. I have six right now that are permanent with me and others that come and go as their needs change."

"You know, we have group classes that are less

expensive than private lessons." He threw his hand up and assured, "Not that I wouldn't like the business. I just wanted you to know you had choices. When the social worker first called me on your behalf, I told her I could let you know what options we offered."

"Thank you," she said, but nodded toward the pool and continued, "But those boys are all special and need all the individual attention I can give them. They have lots of socialization at school, but for something as important as learning how to swim and how to be safe in the water, I would prefer private lessons."

He nodded, and they sat in silence, watching the boys for several minutes. "You know," Jimmy began, "they all look pretty comfortable in the water, except for that one." He pointed to Jaxon and continued, "He might be the only one who needs individual lessons."

She smiled, her indulgent gaze landing fondly on her boys. "He might be the only one who needs the individual attention, but they will all have lessons from you." She caught Jimmy's questioning gaze as he swung his head back toward her.

"You see, each of my boys came to me with different needs...different backgrounds...different experiences. It's my honor to bring them together as a family, learning to function as one." She nodded to Zander and said, "My oldest came to me from an impoverished background. He may be unused to the water, but he was on his own for a while and learned to be self-sufficient. He's a quick learner and will watch after the others."

Indicating Rafe and Cael, she said, "Those two came from good families, but each one lost their parents at an early age. Both of them have been in the water before and know the rudiments of swimming. They'll be able to take on a leadership role and help the others as well."

They watched the boys splash as Jaxon continued to stay near the edge of the pool, occasionally reaching over to hang on to its side.

"The youngest, Asher," she chuckled, "he's the quiet one. I never know what to expect from him but, like Zander, he's fearless. He'll watch and learn."

She looked back down at her knitting needles for a few seconds, tying off the end of the yarn before choosing a new color. "Now, my twins, Jayden and Jaxon, are so much alike...identical in many ways. They even finish each other's sentences sometimes. But, while Jayden is the quieter one and Jaxon is the delightful mischievous one, there is a fear of water for Jaxon."

He looked at her, his brow wrinkled. "Fear?"

Nodding, she said, "I didn't know where it stemmed from, but in the beginning he was terrified of taking a bath, insisting on a shower, even at the age of seven. I finally asked his aunt, who had custody for a couple of years. She said that after their mother died, her mom had custody of the boys, but she had a heart attack and passed on unexpectedly. When the boys had been dropped off at her doorstep, the policeman told her that Jaxon had been left in the tub full of running water. He was unable to get out and nearly drowned."

"Jesus," Jimmy breathed, looking back at the boys, newfound respect in his eyes.

She watched him carefully, her lips curving in satisfaction. "You'll be a good teacher for them, I can tell.

You need to understand their needs and understand how to best help them."

"Yes, ma'am," he assured. "They can start next week."

"That would be lovely," she replied, her eyes leaving him and returning to the pool to follow the boys, a proud smile playing on her lips. "I'll make sure they're here on time and ready."

After about thirty minutes of splashing about, Jaxon watched as his brothers ventured a little deeper into the water, managing to stay afloat by kicking and using their arms. Determined to follow their lead, he tried to ignore the pounding of his heartbeat as he bounced on his toes toward deeper water, still keeping his head above the surface.

Suddenly, his feet slipped, and his head went under. Panicked, he flailed his arms and opened his eyes in fear. Uncertain what to do, he managed to get his feet under him but before he could move, he saw the red-haired little girl swimming toward him under the water. For an instant, he thought of the mermaid stories that Zander read to them. The hair that had escaped her ponytail flowed about her face as her blue eyes remained pinned on his.

She grabbed his hand and slid her body underneath his armpit, tugging him upward. His head broke the surface and he gulped in air. Too scared to be embarrassed, he grabbed onto her, holding tightly as she maneuvered his body through the water to the side.

Clinging to the edge with his elbows, he sputtered and coughed for a few seconds, using his hand to wipe the water from his eyes. Chest heaving, he looked at her as she smiled up at him.

"Th...thank you," he gasped, looking at her slicked-back hair and the light freckles that crossed her cheeks.

"It's okay," she said. "You should stay near the side for a while. Just until you learn to float."

"How old are you?" he blurted between deep breaths.

She giggled and replied, "I'm six."

"But...but...you're such a good swimmer."

"I swim a lot," she replied, her wide smile showing a missing front tooth.

"Jaxon," Miss Ethel called out. "Are you okay?"

Before he had a chance to answer, the little girl asked, "Who's that?"

"That's Miss Ethel." He saw her tilt her head to the side in question. "She's our mom."

Eyes wide, she looked back at the other boys still splashing and asked, "All of you?"

"She's our—"

"Morgan! Get over here!"

The little girl startled and rolled her eyes as the man on the other side of the pool yelled again, before she dove under the water, coming up a few feet away. Calling out, "Stay safe!", she dove back under and swam like a mermaid to the other end.

Still clinging to the side, he watched in awe. Even though she was a lot younger, he liked talking to her. Licking the drops of water off his lips, he looked up, seeing Miss Ethel walking toward him, concern etched in her face. Tossing her a sheepish grin, he said, "I'm okay."

She stared for a moment and he knew she had to see for herself that he was indeed okay. She finally nodded, and called out, "Boys, time to go. Come on out."

The first one out, he walked over and accepted the towel she wrapped around his shoulders. As he followed the others away from the pool, he cast his gaze back toward the water and winced as the man appeared to be yelling more orders to the little girl as she swam back and forth. Just as he was about to leave, he watched her make it to the deep end, look his way and toss her hand up in a little wave before she began swimming once more.

2

Dinner, as usual, was a lively event that night. Miss Ethel had taught the boys table manners, so while laughter abounded, decorum was still maintained. As she stood at the end, she looked down the table and asked, "Whose night is it to help clean?"

Scooping the last of his chocolate pudding from the cup, Jaxon swallowed quickly and replied, "Me."

Smiling, she nodded and they all jumped up to take their plates to the kitchen sink. As the others headed to the living room, he stood at the sink and rinsed the dishes before placing them in the dishwasher. Miss Ethel wrapped the leftovers in plastic wrap, humming as she worked.

"How did you like the pool today?" she asked.

"It was okay…kinda cool…kinda scary," he admitted.

"I didn't learn to swim until I was a young woman," she said. "We didn't have access to a pool when I was a child, but my husband insisted I learn."

His eyes grew wide as he looked over his shoulder at her. "You were already grown up when you learned?"

Nodding, she said, "Yes. I was terribly afraid of the water at first."

He remained quiet as he continued to rinse off the silverware. Finally, he asked, "Did you see that little girl? The one who was swimming all over the place?"

"Yes, I did," she replied. "Quite the little mermaid, wasn't she?" Placing her hand on his shoulder, she said, "She helped you when you went under."

Blushing, he had wondered if she had actually seen him do that, since she had not said anything. Covering, he said with false bravado, "Augh, it was nothin'. I was just playing."

"Well, it was nice to see her talk to you anyway."

"She said she practices all the time...she was really good."

"Hmmm," she hummed.

"I'm pretty good at some stuff, but not like her."

Miss Ethel turned to face him, placing her hands on his shoulders. "We all have different talents, different gifts. You are a good ball player, a good student with math, a good brother, and you make me laugh more than I've ever laughed in my life."

He grinned up at her, his smile infectious. She pulled him in for a hug and kissed the top of his head. "But, mostly, sweet boy, I want you happy. Whatever you're doing, I want you to do it because it makes you happy, not because someone else is forcing you to do it."

His smile slid off his lips as he leaned back to peer up at her face. "Did you hear that man yelling at her?"

With a pat on his back, she nodded. "Now, head into the living room and you can watch some TV before bedtime."

With a whoop, he turned and ran out of the kitchen, her eyes following him all the way.

That night, Jaxon finished brushing his teeth and ran into the older boys' bedroom. Miss Ethel's house had three bedrooms upstairs. Two of them held twin beds and bunk beds, allowing three boys each. Zander, Cael, and Rafe all slept in one room, while Jayden and Asher shared his room. They all shared a large bathroom at the end of the hall.

A smaller bedroom held a single bed with a small bathroom attached, but she kept that room available in case she had to take in another boy for a short period of time.

He grinned as he jumped onto Cael's bed, ready for story time. Each night, Zander would read to the rest of them. Sometimes he read modern stories, but he often read from a large, unabridged book of fairy tales.

"What do y'all want tonight?" Zander asked.

"Little Mermaid," he called out, his smile bright with anticipation. His eyes were trained on the Disney book lying on the shelf, but as Zander picked up the larger book, he asked, "It's in there too?"

Before Zander had a chance to respond, Miss Ethel walked in, sitting in the wooden, straight-back chair next to one of the bunk beds. "I think most fairy tales are in Zander's big book," she answered. "They are classics."

His brow crinkled, he said, "But I like the Disney version. The cartoon movie made them look like they were really under the water."

"Yes, and those are fine. But, all boys and girls should read the classic versions as well," she said, smiling at the six pairs of eyes pinned on her.

"How come?" Jayden asked, sitting cross-legged on the bed next to him, their poses identical.

"Many of the old fairy tales did not end as happily as we would like, but they served their purpose at the time."

They all quieted, each scrunching their faces as they tried to understand.

Smiling, she continued, "The original stories often taught moral lessons that are lost in the Disney versions. Moral lessons were given in story form, to teach us to think about our lives. In the classic version, Hans Christian Andersen didn't have the mermaid marry a prince. Instead of focusing on happily ever after, he used the story to warn us that our actions have consequences." Nodding toward Zander, she said, "You may start, dear," then moved over to the twin bed in the corner, settling down next to Jaxon as he listened.

The story told of a young mermaid who desperately fell for the prince but had to make a deal with the sea to gain legs. Dancing for the prince caused horrible pain, but she loved him so much, she suffered the agony to make him happy. He fell for a princess and married her, breaking the little mermaid's heart. The only way she could become a mermaid again was to kill the prince, but she refused and died, becoming sea foam.

As Zander finished the story, Jaxon's face crumpled, his heart heavy at the unhappy ending. "I don't like that story," he complained, looking up into Miss Ethel's face.

She wrapped her arms around him and pulled him into her embrace for a hug. "But, think. She loved him so much that she was willing to sacrifice her voice and take on great pain, just to be with him. And in the end, she was willing to give all for her love. So, while the story is tragic, it exemplifies her love."

"Did you give up everything to love us?" Asher asked, his young voice small, but his eyes holding emotion way beyond his years.

She leaned over to engulf him in her arms as well. "Oh, my dear boys. I gave up nothing and gained everything. Having all of you gave me exactly what I needed in life after my dear husband died. The house is full of life and energy, laughter and fun."

Still pouting, he slumped down and said, "I still like the Disney version better. I like that the prince and princess get together in the end."

Laughing, she said, "Nothing wrong with that, my dear. Moral lessons have their place, but happily ever after does too. They teach us that forever love can happen. The Disney version gives us a great chance to learn to take risks. Sometimes, they are absolutely worth everything."

Later that night, tucked into his own bed, he

dreamed about the little girl in the water and how easily she swam. It seemed to him that she took big risks for so small a person as she dove into the deep end of the pool. *If she can take such risks, I wonder what I can do.*

3

EIGHTEEN YEARS LATER

The ambulance raced down the street, the siren blaring as Jaxon cursed at the vehicles not moving out of the way. Finally, gaining a break, he drove through the cars parting like the Red Sea and pressed on the accelerator, turning onto the road leading to the hospital.

"ETA two minutes," he called into the radio.

"Jesus, how do you deal with the drivers who don't get the fuck outta the way?" Bob Sisco, the newest rookie, asked him.

"Gotta stay cool, keep your eyes on the road. You can press through, but you don't want to cause another accident." What he did not mention was that, as a medic driving an armored ambulance in Afghanistan when he was in the Marines, he had learned to drive in all manner of conditions—and staying alert was the difference between life and death for all involved.

He heard Mary Bibby, the attending paramedic in the back, radio the updated stats of the patient they carried to the hospital just as he turned into the ER ambulance lane. Stopping at the entrance, he recognized several of the staff that were awaiting their transfer.

He jumped out and rushed around to the back, meeting Bob at the doors that the hospital staff had now opened. As the patient was rolled out, they assisted Mary as she alighted, keeping the IV and EKG lines untangled. Running along, they made it to the ER bay before relinquishing the patient.

Mary stood with the ER nurse, giving her report, while Bob and he unhooked their monitors as the hospital hooked the patient up with their own. As Mary finished, he and Bob walked out of the bay and moved to the nurses' station, ready to fill out the paperwork required.

"Always paperwork," Bob said, taking the tablet that he handed to him.

"It's a lot better than the old days when we had to do all the paperwork and then the hospital staff had to try to enter it all. It's a lot faster and more accurate now."

"Hey, Jaxie."

He recognized that voice but had hoped to make it in and out of the hospital without hearing it today. Turning, he gifted a smile to the pretty nurse beaming up at him. He knew the look in her eye, the one that said she was pissed he had not called and that she was offering him a redemptive way back into her good graces with a date ending in a tumble at her place.

Her finger raked down his arm and she leaned in, just enough to brush her breasts against his side. "Been missing me?"

"You know me, Susie, busy as always."

Her eyes narrowed slightly, but she maintained the sugary voice. "But, you used to always have time for me. Don't tell me you've forgotten."

Handing his tablet back to the receptionist he looked over Susie's head and watched as Mary walked toward him, a raised eyebrow and smirk combo on her face.

"Sorry, Susie, I'm just not...um...I'm getting...married."

Blinking, she reared back. "M...married? You must be joking?"

Ignoring Mary's chortle and Bob's wide-eyed, mouth hanging open expression, he said, "Yeah. Tomorrow. So, uh...gotta go."

With that he turned, grabbed their equipment and hustled out the door. Climbing into the driver's seat, he started the ambulance, calling in their location and ETA for arriving back at the station.

"Married? That's the best you could come up with to get rid of Miss I-can-have-sex-in-any-position-you-want?" Mary cackled.

"Oh, shut up," he grumbled, focusing on driving and not on the jocularity from the back.

"I didn't know you were getting married tomorrow," Bob said, his brows drawn down.

Mary's laughter reached epic proportions and he bit out, "I'm not! Jeez. I just needed to shut her down."

Bob's head swiveled to look at Mary, still laughing, before going back to his profile. "But why? She's hot!"

Patting him on the shoulder, Mary quipped, "Oh, little grasshopper, you have a lot to learn."

"Grasshopper?"

"She's referring to Kung Fu," he groused.

"Huh?" Bob questioned, the look of confusion still on his face.

"Jesus, man. Kung Fu? Probably the greatest western show on TV back in the 1970's."

Bob jerked his head around. "I wasn't born then."

Mary slapped his shoulder, saying, "What the hell do you think the Classic TV channel is for?"

Shrugging, Bob said, "I never watch it. I figured that was for old people. Anyway, what does that have to do with that hot nurse?"

By this time, his eyes had rolled in his head so many times, he wondered how he stayed on the road. Sucking in a deep breath through his nose before letting it out slowly, he said, "Bob, let me put it plainly so you can get it. I fu—uh, spent some time with her one night. She likes to party and at one time I was dumb enough to shit where I work." Seeing Bob's eyes widening again and assuming he still was not getting it, he clarified, "That means I slept with a woman that I see at work. Not a good idea. Especially since it was just fun for me and she'd like to keep things going. So now, I have no interest in her, but I still have to see her around. Ergo, an awkward situation." Taking his eyes off the road for an instant to glance at his rookie partner, he growled, "Does that make it clear to you?"

Mary leaned back, still chuckling to herself, and Bob nodded. "Sure, I get it. Sorry, man."

"No problem. Now if we can leave my sex life outta this conversation, let's get back to the station."

Bob, quiet for another minute, piped up and said, "But what happens when she finds out you're not married?"

He cursed under his breath and Mary's laughter rang out once more. Pinching his lips, he refused to answer, having no idea what he would say when the persistent nurse found out.

Grateful to pull into the station, he stayed busy as they repacked the ambulance and he moved to fill out the reports needed for the Captain.

Bob stayed out of his hair until another call came out. Hustling back into the ambulance, he glared at the rookie, who threw up his hands and said, "I'm learning. No personal questions!"

"Thank fuck," he said, and they pulled out into the street.

Carrying their equipment into the sports arena, they followed one of the managers toward the locker room outside the pool where an older man lay on the floor. According to a witness, he had left the pool and headed into the sauna. He came out several minutes later, stumbling, holding his chest, and his breathing was erratic.

Jaxon nodded, noting the man's color was flushed, but he was conscious. Kneeling, he immediately began talking to the man in a quiet voice, asking him his name, age, and what happened. Glad the man was responsive and able to answer the questions, he nodded to Mary as she hooked him up to the EKG.

Bob inserted an IV line into his hand and wrapped the blood pressure cuff around his other arm. As the results came in, Mary radioed in the man's vital signs. Working together, they moved him onto the stretcher. Stepping back, he knew it was time to give Bob more responsibility, so he allowed him to go out with the patient while he quickly packed up their equipment.

A splash caught his attention and he looked through the doorway into the pool. A single woman was swimming laps, her long body and powerful shoulders cutting through the water. Her movements were graceful as well as strong and he was mesmerized. As he was staring, she hauled herself out of the water and jerked her swim cap off her head while pulling off her goggles.

Water droplets cascaded down her body, tanned skin tight over lean muscles. Her long hair fell over her shoulders and the color caught the bright florescent lights over the pool. Her deep russet hair glowed, but he noted there were lighter streaks of red as well.

He stood, rooted to the spot, unable to take his eyes off her, when she lifted her head. Her blue eyes hit him and he was struck by her beauty. He watched her gaze drift from his head to his boots and back up.

"Chapman!" Mary called, jerking his attention back to his task at hand. Bending, he grabbed the portable equipment and with a nod toward the beautiful swimmer, he hustled out of the building and into the cab of the squad.

Bob was in the back with Mary, working with her as he drove to the hospital. Never having lost focus when on a call before, he was glad for the emptiness in the front of the cab. Shaking his head, he wondered what had just happened.

"Morgan!"

Morgan dropped her head for a moment, still standing near the window of the pool with a towel in her hands, wiping her face. Staring out the window, she watched as the handsome EMT climbed into the cab of the ambulance and drove away. His dark hair, long since needing a haircut, curled over his ears. His body filled out the navy pants and short sleeved polo with the city rescue service logo on the pocket. His muscles bulged at the sleeves and caused the material to pull slightly over his chest.

"What are you doing?" her dad barked.

Sighing, she fought not to roll her eyes. She had heard that particular bark every day for her entire twenty-four years of life. "I was just taking a breather while they finished on Mr. Carson—"

"Who? Who's Mr. Carson?"

Turning, she looked at her dad standing with his hands on his hips in his usual uniform of shorts, t-shirt, and gym shoes, with a whistle and stopwatch hanging around his neck. His formerly red hair was now interspersed with grey and his ruddy cheeks were just as red. His eyes, still blue and sharp, were shooting fireworks toward her.

"Mr. Carson. The older man who is in here almost

every day during lunchtime?" She saw no recognition in his eyes. Huffing, she waved her hand to the left and continued, "He swims laps in that lane for about thirty minutes?"

Still no response. "Jesus, Dad, you might want to take a look around sometime and see what else is in the world. Or, say, even what is going on in this facility."

"Maybe when you shave another half-second off your time I'll be able to do just that," he bit back, his face unsmiling.

Pinching her lips together, she bent to the table, snatched her goggles and cap up in her hand, and walked back to the pool. He stopped her with a hand on her arm, forcing her attention back to him.

"You want this. You've wanted this your whole life. I'm just making sure you get a chance to have your dreams come true."

With a curt nod at his words, she dove into the water. Not even a minute passed before she could hear her father shouting orders and directions to her from above. The water had always been a refuge...and a prison.

She loved the feeling of gliding through the water like a fish, moving easily from one end to the other. But, for as long as she could remember, her father dominated her every movement. She needed to be faster, stronger, better than anyone else. It did not seem to matter to him how many trophies and ribbons she won, there was always another goal to work toward.

"Get up here!" the next shout came, drawing her out

of her musings. She swam to the side and looked up at her father, seeing the anger building.

"What the hell are you doing, Morgan? It's like you're down there daydreaming," he accused.

"Dad, I'm just off my game today. It's fine. I'm fine. I just got distracted earlier."

Standing there, frustration rolling off him, he finally said, "Get out. Hit the weights for the rest of the afternoon and get your mind back on the goal. I want you here for another three hours—"

"Dad, I've got a class tonight."

He pursed his lips tightly and said, "Your mother and I agreed that you could keep up with your graduate studies on a part-time basis as long as it did not interfere with your swimming."

"It's the last class of the semester. The final is next week and then I'm finished for the summer. It's one friggin' class, Dad."

"It may be the last class you take if you can't make your goals. Do you understand me?"

Blowing out her breath slowly, she nodded. "Perfectly, Dad."

He turned and walked out of the pool area and she sucked in a huge breath. With nothing else to say and no one to say it to, she walked to the locker room.

4

With the motorcycle roaring underneath him, Jaxon turned onto the residential lane. The neighborhood had managed to retain its appeal over the years, the houses still neat, young families buying the older ones and renovating them. Large, mature trees filled yards, many with picket fences surrounding the perimeters.

Bicycles and tricycles lined the driveways, some with basketball hoops set up over garage doors. He pulled up to the house at the end. The two-story wooden house was freshly painted, thanks to him and his brothers who worked to keep Miss Ethel's house in tip-top shape. The white planks with the dark green shutters and door, looked inviting as always.

Unable to keep the smile from his face whenever he neared, he remembered when he and Jayden had come to live with her. They had just celebrated their sixth birthday with the only mom they had known, their Aunt Louise. She had kept them from the age of two, only saying that their mom and grandmother had both died. For the last two years that she took care of them, Aunt Louise had been dating a man that neither he nor Jayden liked very much because whenever he was around he told Louise to put them to bed. So, they spent a lot of time in their room. And when she was gone to visit him, she dropped them off at various friends. Never in one place too long, they had become preschool vagabonds, always on the move.

The day after their sixth birthday, after they celebrated with cake and icecream, she loaded both them and their belongings into her car and drove down this very road. Curious, he and Jayden sat in the back while she got out to talk to a tall, thin woman with grey hair pulled back in a bun, and another woman with a large briefcase. They watched her aunt sign papers before she walked back to the car and said, "It's time to get out, boys."

Used to staying with her friends, they dutifully climbed out and followed her to the front porch. He spied two little boys' faces peering out from the door and he grinned. He elbowed Jayden to look as well. They particularly liked to stay with friends of their aunt who had kids to play with.

Aunt Louise turned and introduced them. "This is Jaxon and this is Jayden. Boys, say hello to Miss Ethel." She bent to give both of them a tearful hug. "I'm sorry. It's just, Harry doesn't want to start out as a dad."

He looked at Jayden, but his face showed confusion as well. They stood together and watched her jog down the porch to her car and take out their suitcases. Setting them on the porch, she hurried to the car and backed out. He had no idea it would be the last time they saw her as she drove down the street.

"Zander. Rafe. Run and help these two boys with their suitcases, please," the older woman, Miss Ethel, called out, and he watched as two big boys from inside the house came charging out, grinning as they grabbed the two suitcases. Zander and Rafe looked up to the older woman.

She smiled and asked the other boys to play outside for a little while, promising that the two new boys would be along to play soon.

"How come they look alike?" one of them asked.

"They're brothers, and they're also twins. Now go on and let me talk to them first." Doing her bidding, they left, and the two women led he and his brother inside.

He looked to the right, seeing a large dining room table, much larger than any he had ever seen. Moving past it, they walked into a living room, comfortably furnished with a dark green sofa with colorful throw pillows against the back. The wooden end tables were covered in white, crocheted lace. A thick rug covered the center of the wooden floor. Two, deep cushioned chairs sat facing the sofa, one with a bag of yarn on the floor nearby. The walls on either side of the fireplace held bookshelves, filled with children's books.

He and Jayden settled on the sofa, their legs swinging in time with each other. The woman with the briefcase smiled at them as she introduced herself as Ms. Carswell.

"Jaxon, Jayden, your aunt is unable to keep you anymore and she has signed her rights over to the state.

As your social worker, I am having you come to this lovely home and having Miss Ethel take care of you."

Staring, unspeaking, he cocked his head and asked, "Are we staying here for a few days?"

"Sometimes Aunt Louise has us stay with some of her friends," Jayden finished.

"Well, this isn't going to be a temporary stay," Ms. Carswell began, but Miss Ethel interrupted.

"Boys," she said, her smile warm as she focused on them, "I have a big house with a big yard that is just begging to have little boys who like to play. I'll introduce you to my other boys in a bit. You see, I have the special honor of taking care of boys who need someone to look after them. You'll stay with me for as long as you can."

He glanced to the side, seeing Jayden turn his head as well. They did not speak but, then, they rarely needed to. Understanding passed between them and he looked back to Miss Ethel and said, "We stay here? We won't go back to Aunt Louise?"

She nodded, her hands resting on her knees. "Yes, that's right. Ms. Carswell will continue to check on you and if we find that you are completely unhappy with me, or with living here, then we can talk to her about it. But, it is my dearest wish that you will be happy."

"What's that smell?" he asked, sniffing appreciatively.

"Chocolate cookies I baked this morning," she said, her blue eyes twinkling. "All my boys like my cookies. Would you like to have some?"

As he nodded enthusiastically she stood and, turning to Ms. Carswell, said, "I think that for now, we're fine."

He watched as Ms. Carswell smiled and said, "I'll be back next week to check on everybody."

Miss Ethel walked her to the door and then turned back to him and Jayden. "Come. Let's go into the kitchen."

Before she had a chance to move, the other two boys came barreling into the house. "We saw her leave. Can we play with them now?"

Laughing, Miss Ethel said, "Let's get the introductions complete first." She walked over to the tallest, the one with blond hair, and said, "This is my oldest, Zander. He is nine." With her hand on the other, dark-haired boy, she said, "And this is Rafe. He's eight and has been with me for just a few months."

She lifted her hand to Jaxon's shoulder and said, "This is Jaxon—"

"Uh uh," he said quickly. "That's Jaxon and I'm Jayden."

She raised her eyebrow. "Now Jaxon, don't try to pull the wool over my eyes. I can already tell you apart."

He and Jayden looked at each other before starring up at her in awe. Even Aunt Louise could not always tell them apart.

"I value honesty, boys. Please don't feel like you have to lie in this house. I never want you to be anything other than what you are."

"Sorry," he mumbled, truly hoping she was not angry.

She patted his shoulder and said, "Now, I think it's time for cookies and milk."

At that, he followed her eagerly into the dining room

where he and Jayden and the other boys settled quickly around the table. In a moment, she entered with a platter piled high with homemade cookies and five glasses of milk.

By that evening, he and Jayden were snugly ensconced in a bedroom with Zander and Rafe across the hall. Before bed, they had been allowed to sit in the older boys' room and listen as Zander read a story to them. Aunt Louise had never had time for such indulgences and they loved listening to fairy tales.

Once in bed, Miss Ethel came in to tuck them in. Sitting on his bed, she said, "I'm so glad you came to live with me." She smiled as she added, "Your names are so meaningful. Your mother must have loved having you."

Scrunching his face, he said, "We didn't know our mother. Aunt Louise never talked about her and the man she's marrying said she wasn't a nice person."

Jayden added, "He called her a crack wh—"

"Oh my," Miss Ethel hurried and said, her eyes wide. "You just forget all about what he said. Whatever problems your mother may have had, she gave you beautiful names." Her face softened, and she explained, "Jaxon, your name means *God is gracious*, and Jayden, your name means *thankful*. I think she knew that God had given her two precious gifts and she, in turn, gifted you with those names. And now, I get the honor to have you live with me. Aren't I lucky?"

Jaxon snuggled under the covers, strangely warm, thinking that Miss Ethel seemed to mean what she had said. He had never had someone tell him that they were lucky to have him. After she kissed their foreheads, she left the room, leaving the door cracked so the nightlight in the bathroom could guide them if necessary.

With a full belly, he and Jayden did not talk long that night, as sleep claimed them quickly. It was the first night he felt truly cared for.

Now, as he pulled the motorcycle behind Jayden's in the driveway, he saw the other cars parked on the street. His brothers had all joined the military when it was their turn to leave Miss Ethel's house at the end of high school, but each came back, considering her a mother and each other the brothers they would always have. Zeke had come to Miss Ethel when they were teens and stayed with her as well while they all finished off high school. There were a few others that were also younger than them that stayed for a bit, but it was Zeke who stayed the longest, eventually graduating while still under her roof. She built familial ties that were unbreakable...along with frying the best chicken he had ever had.

Grinning, he hopped off and strolled into the house. He was hit with the scent of her signature dish, his mouth immediately watering. Hearing the commotion from the kitchen, he walked past the empty dining room, knowing the gathering would be in the back. Stepping from the hall into the large kitchen, he observed Miss Ethel, her hair, now white, still pulled back in a bun, standing at the stove. Her tall, thin frame was covered in a striped, blue shirtdress with a slender belt. Her eyes, now more grey than blue, were just as sharp as ever. She was placing the freshly fried chicken from the pan onto a platter.

Looking out the back door, the guys were in the back yard, placing chairs around the large picnic table. His gaze landed on the women that now increased their family. Zander's wife, Rosalie, a high school English teacher, was mixing a salad. Eleanor was carrying a tray of drinks, handing them off to her husband, Rafe, to place on the table. And Cael's fiancé , Regina, had her head thrown back in laughter, cuddling Zander and Rosalie's new baby girl, Charity, in her arms.

As soon as they saw him, they called out greetings, but before he could head outside Miss Ethel left the chicken and moved to him. He wrapped her in his arms, pulling her in for a hug, feeling the thinness of her frame even more. She patted his back and he leaned down so that she could place a kiss on his cheek.

"My boy, how are you?"

"Doing well, Miss Ethel."

"Saving lives as usual?" she asked, her voice gentle.

Chuckling, he said, "As many as I can, but none as pretty as you."

Slapping him playfully, she clucked as she moved away. "Get on out, you rascal, and hang with your brothers. We'll call you when we need help taking the food out."

Nodding, he moved through the back door, passing Eleanor and smiling at her as she headed back inside. Smiles and handshakes greeted him, but it was Charity he really wanted to see. Just four months old and she already had them all wrapped around her finger.

It did not take long for the gathering to settle around the table, food being passed around. Miss Ethel had instilled table manners in her young charges, something that they maintained as adults. Making sure everyone had food on their plate, they sat, heads bowed as she prayed a blessing. With Amens all around, the eating and talking ensued, the group happy to be sharing a meal as they caught up on each other's lives.

Usually the loudest member of the band of brothers, he found himself watching the couples carefully. Zander, normally taciturn, smiled more often as his eyes drifted to Rosalie holding Charity in her arms, affection evident in every glance. Rafe's attention was riveted on Eleanor, never noticing the burn scars that covered one side of her face from her time in the military. And Cael's face gentled when he smiled at Regina, whose reddish-gold hair was growing back from her previous chemo treatment. She once more glowed with a healthy aura.

Normally joking, words stuck in his throat staring at the three women who had become sisters to the group of close brothers, which was not an easy feat. But, simply by being themselves, they had managed to become as important to them all as the other members of their family.

"You coming to Grimm's this weekend?" Jayden asked, drawing his attention back to his brother.

Nodding, he replied, "Yeah, time to blow off a little steam before the long week hits. I've got five straight days on duty."

Once the picnic was cleared away, he drifted into the kitchen, seeing Miss Ethel pulling out plastic containers filled with homemade chocolate chip cookies.

She turned and smiled, handing one to him. Patting his shoulder, she said, "You know, I'm so proud of you. I never doubted you would find your place in the world as someone who saves others."

He stared into her warm eyes. "I don't know how you figured that. I seem to remember our high school principal taking bets on whether Jayden or I would end up in trouble first."

Laughing, she agreed, "Oh, you did used to give Mr. Tolliver fits, didn't you? But you were never bad, just fun loving." Her mirth slowly faded, and she added, "One day, you'll meet the right one, but until then, have your fun."

Shaking his head, he said, "You know me so well. Thank God you never gave up on me."

"It was your names, remember? God is gracious and thankful. That says everything about you to me."

Pulling her into his embrace, he kissed her soft cheek before heading out for the evening.

5

Morgan walked into her parents' house, knowing her dad was not there, hoping to spend a few minutes with her mother and grab some things from her old room.

"Hey sweetie," her mother called out from the kitchen. "Do you need a protein drink?"

"No, Mom, I'm good." She walked into the large, sunny room, and breathed in the scent of brownies, fresh from the oven. "But one of those I will have."

She reached for one on top of the pile and immediately felt the sting of her mother's hand slapping hers. "Mom! What the—seriously? I'm twenty-four years old."

"Yes, and you're a swimmer that does not need the empty calories while in training."

Her hands clutched the edge of the kitchen counter so tightly her knuckles were white. Her mother, tall with an athletic build honed from daily tennis practice, was dressed in yoga pants that fit her frame perfectly paired with a designer shirt with little embellishment. Her hair, sleek and neat, hung in a chin-length bob.

Her mother turned her gaze toward her and said, "What?"

Sighing heavily, she shook her head. "Nothing. I just came by to say hello and to grab a couple of things from my old room."

With narrowed eyes, her mother perused her from head to toe. "Are you getting enough rest? Your father is concerned about your time—"

"My time is fine, Mom. I'd just like to do something occasionally besides swim."

"Honey, you know I'm just concerned."

"I know, I know," she interrupted. Seeing her mother's hurt expression, she walked over and offered her a hug. "I'm good, Mom. I've got somewhere to be tonight, so I'll pop up into my room and then head on out."

Leaving the kitchen before her mother had a chance to offer a rebuttal, she hurried back down the hall and up the stairs to her former bedroom. Raised in a large home in a nice residential area, she had shocked her parents when she moved out after college, but she could not wait to get out on her own.

It had taken her five years to get her undergraduate degree because of swimming on the university team as well as on her own. Now, finishing up the first part of her master's degree in education, she had managed to score a cheap apartment, sharing it with a roommate. Pinching her lips together, she knew with her roommate getting married, she needed to find another person to share the cost. Blowing out her breath, she pushed those thoughts from her head.

At the top of the stairs, she moved to the door on the

left, opening it and sucking in a fortifying breath before she entered. Despite her protestations that her parents update the room and turn it into a guest room, they left it as a shrine. A shrine to her. Well, her and swimming.

The shelves were filled with trophies, medals, and ribbons. So many it was hard to distinguish one from the other. Silver, gold, bronze, glass—all shiny trinkets of days gone by. Posters of Olympic swimmers from previous years adorned her walls.

She walked over to her dresser and stared at more trophies. Freestyle. Breaststroke. Butterfly. Relays. Backstroke. She whirled around, her gaze drifting over the entire room. Plopping down on the bed, she remembered the few times she was allowed to have a sleepover with a friend and how amazed she was at their rooms.

They were real childhood rooms filled with stuffed animals, dolls, books and toys. Pre-teen rooms covered in boy-band posters. Adolescent rooms filled with clothes, makeup, and even one friend's room filled with political activism posters. She would go around and touch the various items, marveling at the difference between their simple bedrooms and her own. She had envied each and every one of them, longing for a day when she could break free and live her own life.

But that was not to be. At least not now. At least not fully.

Moving to her closet, she dug through a few old photo albums and found the pictures she was looking for. Her roommate, and oldest friend, was getting married to her high school boyfriend and she wanted to give her copies of an old photograph of their first date that she had taken. She had never told Cindy that, for the homecoming dance, she had snuck out of the house and walked to the school to watch the couples going in.

She had been asked, but her father had refused to allow her to go since there was a swim meet that weekend. They had argued, but her father insisted she follow his rules, as father and as coach.

She had watched the girls, dressed in their long dresses with corsages pinned to their bodices or adorning their wrists, hanging on the arm of their dates, dressed in suits. Everyone looked so different, so grownup. She had snapped a picture of Cindy and Chuck as they walked through the flowered pergola, keeping the photograph to remind herself of what she could have had. Now, it was just an old picture and should be given to the couple getting married.

With a last look around the room, she hurried and closed the door.

Jaxon threw open the door to Zander's business, Grimm's Bar and Grille. Zander had been convinced that all he wanted was a bar and nothing else. Not a nightclub. Not a restaurant. But, over time, a jukebox had made its way toward the back where a few tables had been moved to the side so that patrons could dance if they wanted. And Zeke now worked with Zander, working in the expanded kitchen that they had opened up when the store next to Grimm's went out of business. They bought it together and Zeke now ran the grille, providing a basic menu of wings, burgers, fries, and nachos. Simple, but good, food that Zander found kept the drinks flowing.

Walking toward the bar, he nodded toward Joe, one of the bartenders, as he slid onto a stool. Thanking him as a beer was placed in front of him, he turned to check out the action.

The bar ran along the left side of the long room, ending at the hall leading to the bathrooms, office, and stockroom toward the back. Mismatched bar stools lined the old, wooden counter. Zander never polished it, allowing the rustic look to show through.

Round, wooden tables filled most of the space, sturdy wooden chairs circling each one. The walls held little adornment. People came to Grimm's to drink and socialize, not look at decorations. The sound of clinking bottles against glass rang out as the two bartenders worked efficiently, filling orders while the waitresses hustled to keep up with the demand. The servers dressed in jeans and t-shirts, nothing too revealing. Zander had said himself he was not desperate enough for money to use sex to sell drinks and was determined to keep the assholes who wanted to hit on waitresses out of his bar.

Most of the tables were filled, groups laughing and talking amongst themselves. What appeared to be a bachelorette party near the back was in full swing, with a few of the women dancing. The one wearing a tiara looked happy, although he was sure the smile was somewhat alcohol-induced if the number of shot glasses on the table in front of her was any indication. As his gaze roved through the others at the table, they landed on the deep russet hair hanging down the back of one of the women. Unable to see her face, he leaned back slightly to see if he could gain a better view.

A hand clapped him on his shoulder and he jerked, looking at Zander. "Hey man, looks like you have a good crowd here tonight."

"Yeah, perfect for profits if I can keep the assholes out. But, we haven't had any fights lately, so my bouncers are getting soft."

He looked over at Roscoe and Demetrius, laughing at their size and intimidating expressions. "I can see where that's a problem."

The door opened and Jayden walked in, heading over and hauling up onto the stool next to him. With a chin lift, Zander headed down the hall toward his office. Someone called out Jayden's name and they turned to see some of the mechanics that worked in his auto shop sitting at a table. Accepting the wave over, they weaved through the crowd and settled into two empty chairs.

Glancing to the side, he noted they were right next to the bachelorette party...and his chair backed to the woman with the long, red hair.

"What'll it be, fellas?"

He looked up at Lynn, one of Grimm's longtime waitresses, and smiled. A young mother, she worked evenings while her husband watched their daughter. She was a hard worker and her smile gained her extra tips.

"Hey darlin'," he greeted. "How's the little one?"

She blew out a breath, the puff lifting her bangs. "Who knew toddlers could wreak such havoc? They make working this place on a busy Saturday night seem like a walk in the park!"

Laughing, he ordered another beer before joining the conversation at the table once more. As the evening wore on, the shots continued to be delivered to the table next to them while the beers flowed for his group.

"Can't believe you're still here and not on the dance floor picking out tonight's flavor," Bill, one of their tablemates, said.

"Hell, I'm not that bad," he grumbled, strangely unhappy with the analogy. "Maybe I've played the field for the past couple of years, but that's gotten kinda old."

"Played the field?" Bill laughed and the others, except for Jayden, joined in. "Jax, man, you've played with anything you could get your hands on."

Wanting to argue, but deciding it was a debate he would not win, he settled quietly, feeling Jayden's gaze on him.

As the others talked and watched a game on the mounted TV, Jayden leaned over. "You okay?"

Sighing heavily before letting it out, he nodded. "Guess I deserved that." Holding his brother's gaze, he added, "But I've never left any broken hearts behind. Everyone always knew what the deal was."

"Hey, you don't have to convince me. I think you're doing more than just having a good time. I think you're searching."

"Searching?"

Nodding while taking another gulp of beer, he

stated, "Yep. And when you find it, you'll know it and won't have to search anymore. Nor fill your time with empty one-nighters."

"And you, bro? You searchin'?"

Chuckling, Jayden deflected, "This ain't about me, Jax. I figure I'll know it when it hits me."

"Well for it to hit you, you gotta be out there looking!" His eyes drifted to the side, where the red hair caught his attention once more.

While Jayden chuckled and joined the others watching the game, he kept an eye on the woman near him.

She scooted her chair back to stand and, in the process, bumped his chair. Looking up, he got a front view of her heart-shaped face with a sprinkling of freckles across her nose. She looked down at him and her blue eyes landed right on his face. Her pink lips curved into a smile and her eyes widened as though in recognition.

He grinned in return before realizing it was not one of his practiced panty-dropping smiles, but one that simply came from within.

"Sorry," she said, her soft voice melodious. "I didn't mean to bump into your chair."

Before he had a chance to speak, she scooted her ass around the table and walked toward the bathrooms with one of the other ladies she was with.

"Damn," Sean said. "What a fine piece."

Nodding his agreement, he kept drinking but watched for her return. He was not disappointed at the front view of her walking back toward the tables a few minutes later. Her tall, long-limbed, extremely toned body was showcased in tight jeans, boots, and a blue knit top that had little flounces over the shoulders. It was obvious she worked out and an image of them working out horizontally together ran through his mind. Her hair, unadorned, falling in what appeared to be natural waves, flowed over her shoulders.

Several of the women at the table next to them intercepted her and they all moved to the dance floor. With music pouring from the jukebox, they laughed and danced with each other, capturing the attention of most of the men around.

"Gonna join 'em?" Jayden asked, his chin lifting toward the women as he his attention returned from the game to his brother.

He sat for a moment, spellbound by her as she threw her head back in laughter with her friends, but was uncertain if he wanted to interrupt her joy. Just then, he watched as another man approached, placing his hands on her waist from behind.

She whirled around and moved quickly from his grasp. Jaxon was on his feet in a second, moving between people to get to her. The man had taken his hands away, but the desire to make sure he stayed away filled him.

"Sweetheart, sorry I'm late," he said, moving straight to the red-head. Getting close, without touching her, he locked eyes with her and smiled widely.

She stared for only a second before her smile matched his. "Um…Honey…you're here," she cooed, throwing her arms around his neck and moving in for a hug.

Wrapping his arms around her, he was struck by how her body lined up perfectly with his. Leaning back, she planted her lips on his and his eyes popped open in shock, until instinct kicked in, and he angled her head for maximum contact.

"Sorry, man," he heard a male voice say, but continued to focus only on her lips. She tasted of lemon drops, sweet and tart.

Hearing a cross between a sigh and a moan, he took over, plundering her mouth as all other thoughts fled his mind. His fingers pressed against her back, pulling her tighter to his chest, and barely aware of her fingers trailing through his hair.

Her tongue tangled with his and he felt the electricity straight to his cock. The bar noise fell away, leaving only the two of them in the universe. Nothing existed but the feel of her soft lips against his, her body in his arms, and the taste of sweet lemons on her tongue.

After a long, wet kiss, she finally mumbled against his lips, "Ih heh gah?"

Brow lowering, he tried to clear the lust-fog before looking into her eyes. "Huh?"

Giggling, she sucked in her kiss-swollen lips as an adorable blush covered her face. "Is he gone?" she enunciated, her voice as soft as a whisper.

Shifting his gaze from side to side, he nodded, but kept his arms wrapped tightly. "Yeah."

"Um...you want to let me go now?" she asked, her arms still clutching his shoulders.

"Not particularly," he replied, a grin curving his lips.

"Good. Let's dance," she laughed, stepping back slightly as she began to sway back and forth.

Never willing to turn down a dance partner, he placed his hands on her hips, checking her face to see if it was wanted and with another smile from her, moved her body along with his.

The beat of the music blared around them, but he felt cocooned with her, as though no one else was around. Now that he was close, he could see the shades of blue in her eyes, indigo near the pupil and sky blue toward the outer rim. Her light freckles did indeed cross her cheeks and over her nose. Her cheekbones were high and her mouth full. And as he focused on her mouth once more, he leaned back down, unable to keep from tasting her again. Definitely lemon drops.

6

The lights in Grimm's were low and Jaxon led Morgan slightly to the side of the dance floor to add to the illusion of privacy amongst the packed room. The song changed to a slow tempo and their bodies moved as one, still swaying, her front plastered to his. The crowd around them fell away as he focused on the warm body in his arms.

"What's your name?" he whispered, his lips close to her ear.

"Morgan. Morgan McAlister." Laughing, she said, "I know, I know. How Scottish can I be, right?" Biting her bottom lip, she stared up into his eyes and asked, "And you?"

"Jaxon. Jaxon Chapman."

"Jaxon…I like that—"

Her words were cut off as he kissed her again. "You taste like lemon drops," he mumbled. "Is that your favorite drink?"

"I normally don't drink. This was a special occasion. Bachelorette party."

"Your friend?"

She nodded and added, "They suggested lemon drops and guess what? I discovered they're awesome!"

Laughing, he held her close once more, his hand caressing her back through the thin material of her shirt.

She jerked in his arms and he separated slightly, looking down at her. "Are you okay?"

"Um…yeah. What…what do you do for a living?"

"Checking me out?" he asked with another grin. "If you're looking for a rich man, I'll have to disappoint. I'm a rescue worker for the city—EMT."

She seemed to relax in his arms again and she asked, "And that handsome man that's sitting at your table? The one who looks just like you?"

Chuckling, he looked over his shoulder at Jayden and asked, "Is that your way of telling me I'm handsome?"

"Oh, I don't think you need me to stroke your ego!" She shifted her gaze to the side and then back. "Well?"

"That's my twin, Jayden, and before you begin thinking that you'd like to dance with him, I'll tell you that I'm the much better twin."

Laughing, she said, "Better at what?"

"Uh, let's see. In third grade, I won a spelling bee. And, in fifth grade, I ran the hundred-yard dash faster than he did."

"Oh, my, the competition grows," she grinned.

"And, in eleventh grade, I dated the homecoming queen. Well, for a couple of weeks."

"Yes, but who got the prom queen? Him?"

"No, some prick named Gerald."

Her giggles rang out and her eyes widened. "You're joking."

"Okay, you got me. Maybe it *was* Jayden."

"Is he an EMT also?"

"Nah, he's a mechanic. Owns his own business. If you're looking for the richer of the two, then it's him." Holding her gaze, he said, "But I'll fight him for the right to dance with you."

She stared into his eyes, her hands moving up and down his shoulders and back, saying, "No, I'm dancing with the one I want." Shaking her head, she added, "That must be so cool to have a twin."

Shrugging, he replied, "Never knew anything else. But, yeah, I guess you could say it was cool."

"I'm an only child, so not only do I not have something as cool as a twin, I've got no siblings at all."

They danced for another moment until a loud peal of laughter rang out from the bachelorette table. He sighed. "I don't want to lose you, so I can't believe I'm asking this question, but do you need to rejoin your party?"

She glanced over and grinned. "Nah, the party has just about broken up and the bride's got to get home soon. Her fiancé just showed up to be her designated driver. Looks like he's ready to haul her out."

Looking over at his table, he noticed Zander and Rosalie had joined Jayden. Staring back down at

Morgan, he said, "Would you like to meet a couple of my friends?"

Her smile beamed as she said, "Sure!"

He took her hand and they weaved back through the tables. She tossed a wave at her friends, some who were still drinking. Stopping to hug the bachelorette, she turned back to him.

"Jaxon?"

He turned and grimaced at the shrill voice, seeing Susie standing nearby, her gaze jumping between him and Morgan.

"I thought you were getting married?" Susie bit out, her hip cocked, tapping her foot, her eyes now shooting daggers.

Morgan quickly looked at Jaxon's face and without hesitation, slid her arm around his waist and smiled. "He did. I'm his wife."

Susie's eyes narrowed as she pinched her lips in a tight line. She glared at Morgan before looking back to him. Without saying a word, she flounced away and he let out a sigh of relief.

"Was that okay?" Morgan asked, her eyes wide as she stared at him.

Dropping his chin to his chest, he nodded, before lifting his gaze to the worried look on her face. Giving her waist a squeeze, he nodded. "So sorry about that. And yes, you were perfect."

"You gonna introduce us to your *wife?*"

He and Morgan turned in unison to look down at the table filled with his group of friends, all battling laughter. Chuckling, he made the introductions before they slid into chairs.

Rosalie's eyes were as huge as her smile as she stared at him. "Well, I had no idea you were so serious," she quipped, her mirth evident.

He could not remember the last time he had blushed and found the heat on his face disconcerting. "Well, that's what I get for making shit up," he mumbled.

Laughing, Jayden clapped him on the back and said, "God, the look on your face was priceless." Turning to Morgan, he said, "And it's nice to meet someone who's got my brother's back."

"So, Jayden," she said, her grin matching the others. "Jaxon was just telling me that he's the better twin. I hear there was a fierce third-grade spelling bee that he crushed you in."

Jayden pursed his lips in mock outrage, shaking his head. "Yeah, well, did he tell you that in fourth grade, I won the Most Library Books Read award?"

Placing her hand on her chest, she exclaimed, "No! He left out that tidbit."

His arm had been on the back of her chair but at her declaration, he slid his hand to her shoulder and gently pulled her back to his side. "Don't believe all awards are equal, Morgan. He checked out a lot more books than he actually read, just to get the award."

"Dream on," Zander said, leaning back in his chair. "No one read as many books as I did."

"That's true," he admitted, looking down at Morgan. "Zander was our resident storyteller for years."

The group was laughing when Zeke walked over and placed a large platter of wings on the table.

"Kitchen's ready to close, so I thought I'd get these out here."

Jaxon introduced her to Zeke and Morgan observed the looks shared among the others and wondered the reason. Shifting her gaze back to him, she caught him staring at her. Ducking her head, she reached over to grab a wing before they were all gone.

"Good for you, Morgan," Rosalie said, grabbing one herself. "With these guys, they have super manners, are sweet as can be, but when it comes to food, you better go for it quick or it'll all be gone."

Once the wings were decimated, leaving only a pile of bones, she leaned back against his side. Strangely comfortable with a man she just met, and with his friends, she felt at peace even in the loud, crowded bar.

"So, what do you do, Morgan?" Rosalie asked, still licking her fingers from the barbeque sauce.

"I'm a graduate student."

Jaxon realized that he had not attempted to find out anything about the woman he had been kissing and felt a stab of regret. With a look of chagrin, he admitted, "I should know these things. After all, we're married now."

She snorted and elbowed him in the side, before explaining. "It took me five years to get my undergraduate and now I'm working on my Master's Degree in Education."

Rosalie perked up, her eyes bright. "Me too. I'm an English teacher at Hamilton High School."

She nodded as she wiped her hands on the napkins provided and said, "I know of that school. I'm getting certified in kinesiology and hope to work as a coach or athletic trainer, but I'll take whatever job I get offered."

He listened with interest as she and Rosalie chatted for a few minutes about their shared career goals and realized it was the first time in a long time he was interested in what a woman was doing with her life. The shallowness of that thought sobered him and he shifted uncomfortably.

She noticed and glanced at him, saying, "I'm sorry. This is probably boring you—"

"Actually no," he interrupted, his gaze roaming over her face, mesmerized with her startling clear eyes. "I'm interested, really."

Suddenly, she bolted upright and cocked her head to the side, listening. "Ohh, I love this song. It's been so long since I've heard it," she declared.

"Then let's dance," he said, scooting his chair back and linking his fingers with hers. This time, there was no awkwardness on the dance floor as they swayed together, their bodies in sync as the music swirled around them.

He nuzzled her hair and she buried her cheek against his chest. She sighed heavily, and he murmured, "You okay?"

Nodding, her face still pressed against his heartbeat, she answered, "Yeah. I haven't had this much fun in a really long time."

Before he could reply, she leaned forward, lifting on her toes to call out over the music, "You want to get out of here?"

Surprised at her suggestion, he asked, "Whatcha got in mind?"

She licked her lips and said, "How about a little diversion?"

His grin matched hers as he said, "You lead, I'll follow, Morgan."

Laughing, she slid her hand down his arm and linked fingers with him. Weaving between tables, she made her way to her table, where she bent down to snag her purse from the chair.

One of her friends whispered into her ear and she grinned and shrugged in reply. Looking back at him, she nodded, "I'm ready."

He tossed a chin lift to Jayden, who rolled his eyes in response, then led her out into the cool night air. As soon as the door closed behind them, the noise from the bar faded away, leaving them alone under a street lamp.

"What did your friend say to you?" he asked, curious.

"She told me to be careful. That you're a known player."

It was on the tip of his tongue to throw out his usual line of, 'I'll be your player for a night only, babe,' but the words halted. Instead, he said, "For the right woman, I'll no longer be a player."

He caught her wide-eyed look of surprise and wondered where the hell those words came from. Unwilling to think on them anymore, he placed his hand on the small of her back and escorted her through the parking lot.

Morgan glanced to the man at her side as they neared his Jeep, her heart beating out of her chest. Her back burned where his fingers lay softly as he guided her along. His words should have sounded cheesy, but, the look in his eyes and the tone of his voice said something else. He sounded as though he really meant it and unexpected, tiny butterflies whirled in her stomach.

Opening the door he took her hand, assisting her up into the seat. She remembered seeing him at the sports arena and thinking he might actually make her feel short. She was not disappointed—he actually was as tall as she as imagined. His dark hair was long, but unlike his brother's long, messy ponytail, his was shorter and she had a desire to run her fingers through the shoulder-length curls.

She had never dated anyone with long hair—*wait, this is no date!* She knew exactly why they were leaving the bar. A quick fuck and then it would be over. The release of pent-up hormones for her and a chance for him to get off. From what her friend had said, he did that a lot.

Pickups were not usually her thing, but a girl had needs and with her swimming competition schedule, she hardly had time for a relationship.

All these thoughts were swirling in her mind until he climbed into the driver's seat and twisted his body to spear her with his grin.

"So, where to, Morgan?"

Suddenly unsure, she wondered what to say. *My little apartment? Even if Cindy stays out late after her party, my room only has a twin-sized bed. His? Do women ask to go to his place?*

Her uncertainty must have shown because he leaned across the console and cupped her jaw. "Hey, don't think so hard. We'll only do what you want and go where you want. If you want to go home alone, I can take you there—"

"Your place. Can we go to your place?" she rushed, deciding to take charge.

He tilted his head to the side and stared.

Blushing, she amended, "Sorry, that was probably weird...or stalkerish. It's just that my place is small, and I only have a twin bed and my roommate—"

He shushed her with his fingers on her lips. She felt his eyes boring into hers before he slowly nodded and said, "It's absolutely fine. My place it is."

With another grin sent her way, he started the Jeep and they rumbled out of the parking lot, heading down the street.

As the wind from the open window blew her hair, she let out a huge sigh. Practice tomorrow, a trial meet the day after, and tonight? Casting a glance at the man driving, she smiled. *Finally, some fun!*

7

Jaxon kept his hand on Morgan's lower back as he escorted her from the Jeep parked on the ground floor and up the elevator to the fourth floor of the old, revamped warehouse. Not located in the best part of town, it was definitely on the edge of the ongoing revitalization of the downtown area.

They exited the elevator and his fingers continued to guide her down the hall to his door. Unlocking it, he suddenly found himself nervous. It had been a long time since he had brought a woman to his loft, preferring the ability to leave when he was ready, which was usually long before the morning light shone through the windows. In fact, as he thought back, it had been almost two years since he had had a woman here and the memory of having to almost bodily remove her the next morning sent a shiver down his spine.

Glancing at Morgan, he got the vibe that clingy was not going to be a problem with her. He watched as she entered and immediately moved to the large windows on one side of the living room. He held back, wondering what she thought of his place. The furniture was somewhat plain. A large, black, sectional sofa curved around an impressive flat-screened TV mounted on the wall. Two matching chairs, equally as comfortable, sat on either side with oak end tables and a coffee table.

He had only bought the tables to give his friends a place to put their beer and chips when over watching a game.

She turned and smiled. "This is a great view."

He laughed, saying, "In the daytime, I can barely see the river from here, and the view is kinda industrial. But, you're right, at night, the lights from the area buildings give it a cool vibe."

He stood awkwardly for a moment, unable to think of what to say or do. Most of the time, when he entered a woman's apartment, the last thing he was interested in was making conversation. But with Morgan, he found that he wanted to know what she was thinking. Before he had a chance to speak, she moved around to check out the living room.

A couple of pictures were mounted on the wall, hung by Rosalie, Eleanor, and Regina. They had determined that all Miss Ethel's boys needed pictures of everyone. Morgan made her way over to them, peering closely at each one.

"Are all these your brothers?" she asked, surprise in her voice. Her blue eyes found his as she turned to look over her shoulder.

"Yes...and no," he replied. Seeing her face scrunched

in confusion, he explained, "Jayden, of course, is my twin. The others are my brothers, just not of blood."

Morgan nodded slowly and turned back to the photographs, perusing them carefully. One was when the boys were children, standing on the front porch of a house with a tall, thin woman behind them, arms stretched out, encompassing them all. The other was more recent and appeared to be at an informal picnic. Besides Zander and Rosalie, she saw that two of the other men had women with them as well. The older woman was in that picture, too, sitting in a chair in front of the others, her face turned to the side as she laughed at something one of them was saying.

She could not help but smile at the obvious affection, but sighed slightly when she tried to think of the last impromptu gathering she had with her parents that did not involve swimming...and came up empty.

Jaxon watched as Morgan stared at the pictures for another moment, but if she had other questions, she kept them to herself.

Next, she moved to the DVD collection piled haphazardly next to his large-screen TV. Cocking her head to the side, she asked, "Old horror film buff?"

"You expectin' car chases and action flicks?"

She knelt down to get a better view. Twisting her head up to peer at him, she asked, "Who made a better Dracula? Bela Lugosi, Peter Cushing, Lon Chaney, Jr—"

"Seriously? You know these movies?" He could not keep the incredulity from his voice.

"My Nonnie, uh, my grandmother, and I used to watch all the old horror flicks. Personally, I love Bela

Lugosi but, I swear, Christopher Lee starred in a lot of them."

"Your grandmother watched horror movies?" he asked, his wide smile matching hers.

Laughing, she nodded. "Not the gory new stuff, but yeah, the old classics. Frankenstein, especially with Boris Karloff. The Wolfman—oh, and she loved The Invisible Man with Claude Rains. She thought he was handsome."

She looked back down at his collection and asked, "What about you? How'd you get started watching these?"

"The lady that raised me believed in us reading classical books and watching classic movies. One of my brothers, Cael, loved the old film noir movies, like Hitchcock's. Jayden and I were fascinated with the old horror movies."

"Lady?"

"Miss Ethel. My foster mom." He waited for the continued questions or expression of curious surprise, but they never came. She just nodded, her smile still in place, and looked back down at the movies. He normally avoided talking about his upbringing with anyone, but with her, it felt easy.

"Oh, my God," she exclaimed, twisting to look up at him again, a DVD clutched in her hand. "You have Abbot and Costello Meet the Killer Boris Karloff? I haven't seen this in forever! My Nonnie loved Abbot and Costello."

"You want to watch it?" As soon as the words were out of his mouth, he wondered what had come over him. *I'm just supposed to want sex, right?* Looking at her bright smile and sparkling eyes, he suddenly wanted nothing more than to settle with her on the sofa.

She ducked her head and nodded. "You don't mind?"

He bent to kiss her forehead and replied, "Just wanna spend time with you, however we do that."

He popped the movie in as she sat in the middle of the sofa. He moved to sit next to her, pleased when she immediately leaned in to cuddle with him. Wrapping his arm around her shoulders, he pulled her in tight and breathed in her delicate scent. The opening credits rolled and he forced his eyes to the TV, but his cock stayed at attention with her sweet body snuggled against his.

"You know, it's true that Abbott and Costello didn't get along. They were always professional but by the end of their acting together, they did not speak to each other off camera."

"I had heard that but didn't know if it were true."

She nodded and said, "That seems so sad, doesn't it? Two people, who were so funny together and very professional when working, actually couldn't stand each other."

"At least they weren't related. Can you imagine how awkward family gatherings would be if they had a hard time being together?" he laughed.

She remained quiet, almost sad, and he wondered if he had touched on a difficult subject. After a few minutes, she relaxed again and they laughed throughout the movie.

Walking into the kitchen when it was done, he asked, "You want a beer?"

She followed him but shook her head. "I think I've definitely hit my alcohol limit for the night. For the whole year, actually," she laughed. "But, could I please have some water? I want to avoid dehydration."

He blinked, not sure he had ever had a woman ask for water. Another drink or even some hangover food, sure, but water? "Yeah, let me get some that's cold."

Her lips curved as she smiled and slid onto one of his bar stools while he reached into the refrigerator for a bottle. He poured the water into a glass and handed it to her. Glancing to the side after taking a long drink, she said, "No table? You just eat here?"

Chuckling, he said, "I know this seems like a typical bachelor pad, but I never have people over that need to sit at a table. I eat at the bar and when my friends are over, we pile up on the sofa."

Nodding, she said, "I like this place. It's huge and has got personality."

"And your place?"

Rolling her eyes, taking another huge gulp of water, she confessed, "Graduate school poor. I've got a little part-time income coming in and student loans that help cover some costs. But, just one more semester, and I can go to work full-time and make some money."

They were silent for a moment as she finished her water. Placing the glass on the counter, she smiled again. "Thanks. Um...in the light of full disclosure," she began, drawing his instant attention. "I saw you the other day. At the sports arena on Layfayette Street. I was in the pool and watched you work on Mr. Carson, the man who had collapsed."

Eyes widening, he said, "That's why you were wondering about my job and my twin!"

Laughing, she said, "Guilty. I was so impressed with what you were doing and when I saw you tonight, I really wanted to meet you. Then I saw him and wondered if I had the right brother."

He rounded the bar and walked directly to her, moving his thighs between hers where she sat on the stool. Placing his hands on the counter behind her, effectively trapping her, he watched her pupils dilate and her breath hitch as he moved closer. "Oh, you've got the right brother, all right. You've definitely got the right man."

He moved in for a kiss, her lips just as delectable as he remembered from the bar but, now that he could hear the little moans escaping, he much preferred the privacy of his apartment. He felt the instant she yielded, her breasts pressing into his chest and her fingers clutching his hair. As his hands caressed her back, he was now fully aware of the taut muscles in her body. She tightened her thighs around his as he moved closer between her legs and again, he felt her strength.

Leaning back, he held her lust-filled gaze, and said, "Swimmer?"

"Mmm hmmm," she mumbled moving back in for more of his lips.

Devouring her lips, he finally pulled back. "I can tell you're strong," he admitted.

"You should see what I can do with my thighs," she grinned, her eyes sparkling.

"Oh, damn girl, you've just upped the game," he laughed, pulling her closer. Standing, feeling her thighs wrap around his waist, he walked toward the sofa, then hesitated. She must have noticed his hesitation because she cocked her head to the side in confusion.

"Would it be okay for me to take this to the bedroom?" he asked, wanting to make sure the direction they were going with the evening's activities was what she wanted.

"Have the sheets been washed since the last woman you've had here?" she quipped, her eyes twinkling.

He pretended to glare, then replied, "Honestly? I haven't had a woman here in about two years." Hearing her gasp, he stared into her wide eyes and quickly added, "I'm no monk, but just not here."

She bit her lip for a moment, thoughts moving behind her eyes before asking, "So you had an easy escape?"

Feeling the heat of uncomfortable honesty moving through him, he nodded. "Yeah...I...uh...yeah."

"That makes sense. It keeps someone from assuming too much and as long as everyone understands what it is, then there's no hard feelings and no awkwardness."

Surprised at her acquiescence, he wondered what she thought about him. "I always made that clear, but found that a few women who came to my place decided that the evening would include something ongoing that I didn't feel. I guess hearing that out loud makes me sound pretty smarmy—"

"Smarmy?" she laughed. "I'm not sure I've heard that term outside of a historical romance novel." She squealed as he dropped her a few inches before holding her tight again.

"Hey," he grumbled, "I thought that sounded better than saying that it made me look like some player asshole."

She grinned, bringing her hands up to his face, cupping his jaw. "It's okay, Jaxon. I know the score. This is tonight. A chance for both of us to let go and have fun with no strings attached. Anyway, my life's kind of crazy right now and there's no room for anything but a little fun." She kissed him lightly before asking, "But, why me? Why bring me here?"

He shook his head. "I have no idea. I just know that I feel a pull to be with you."

"Well, then, I'm flattered."

He leaned forward but stopped a whisper away. "I'm the one who's flattered you're here with me."

A slight sigh escaped her lips at his words and he moved in, his mouth moving over hers, the electricity between them jolting through his body. She yielded and he pressed her body into his, feeling her arms wind around his neck, holding tight.

8

With his lips latched onto hers, Jaxon moved down the hall toward the bedroom, stopping just as they reached the bed. He allowed Morgan's body to slide down so that her feet landed on the floor. She was tall, but even in her boots she was still inches below him. He moved his hands to the little buttons on her shirt, stunned to find them shaking.

His usual one-night flings found he and the woman throwing clothes off willy-nilly, but with Morgan, he wanted to take it slow, unveil her a little at a time. Finally getting to the last button, he drew the shirt down her arms and let it fall to the floor. His gaze dropped to her breasts, the mounds plump over the top of her lacy bra. Not overly large, they filled his hands as he palmed the pliant flesh before sliding the straps over her shoulders. "You're beautiful," he breathed, as her breasts were freed and the bra floated away.

She licked her lips nervously and glanced down at

his hands. "Sometimes I feel like I'm more muscle than...um...curves."

"It's all the swimming," he surmised correctly. "And it's fucking gorgeous."

As her bra fell away he bent to take a nipple in his mouth, the delicate bud taut, and sucked hard as he moved his hands to her jeans zipper. At the same time, she fumbled with the bottom of his t-shirt, trying to lift it over his abs and head.

He assisted by grabbing it and, with a jerk, sent it flying across the room. Her gaze raked over his naked chest and her lungs inflated as she sucked in a deep breath. He knew women lusted after his body, and he was not above flaunting it when getting naked, but her heated gaze was different. Less predatory. More appreciative.

"You work out," she breathed. "But, then, I bet with your job you have to stay in shape, don't you?" she asked, her eyes still roving over his shoulders, biceps, chest, and abs with her fingers trailing along the muscle ridges.

"Required physical training," he responded, pleased that she recognized the hard work.

She pushed back slightly and sat on the edge of the bed. Lifting her foot, she pulled off one boot, letting it drop to the floor before pulling off the second one. As he watched, he jolted into action, toeing off his own boots, kicking them into the pile with hers.

He placed his hands on her shoulders and gently pushed her backward. She landed against the soft, plush comforter, a grin wide on her face. He leaned over and moved her hands out of the way, unzipping her jeans. Sliding them down her long legs, he hooked his thumbs in her panties at the same time, divesting her of all clothing.

Standing, he stared in awe, looking down at the perfect female form lying on his bed. Natural beauty. Athletic. Curves and muscles in all the right places. Swallowing deeply, he scanned her from head to toe.

"Aren't you a little overdressed?" she asked, her smile wide as she grinned up at him.

"Oh, yeah," he agreed, shucking his jeans and boxers faster than he had ever undressed, fisting his cock.

Staring at the perfect vision of masculinity standing before her, Morgan could not tear her eyes away from his cock, jutting out from his body, long and thick, with veins bulging from the sides and pre-cum beading from the head. She dragged a ragged breath into her lungs, realizing she had never just stared at a man's cock before. It had always been put to quick use, but not admired.

He grinned as he bent over, snagging his wallet from his jeans on the floor, and pulled out a long strip of condoms, tossing them to the bed beside her.

She twisted her neck to the side and looked at the packets lined up next to her head. Quirking an eyebrow as she looked back up at him, she asked, "Feeling extra lucky tonight?"

Kneeling on the floor, his head disappearing between her knees, he said, "Just having the honor of you in my bed makes me all kinds of lucky already."

Jaxon's hands went to her bent knees, opening her

up to him while at the same time, aligning her just as he needed. Her legs fell open and one of his hands slid up to her belly, his fingers spread wide, pressing into the flesh while he nuzzled her sex. The scent of arousal filled his nostrils and his cock twitched in impatience.

Morgan gasped as he delved in, licking her folds before plunging his tongue in. "Oh…" she groaned, unable to come up with a better response as her fingers clutched the material underneath her. She lifted her head, seeing moonlight through the blinds sending spears of light across his face as he peered up at her.

She finally managed to snake her fingers through his hair, gently scratching his scalp, which caused the curls to stand on end. Loving the feel, she lost hold as he latched onto her clit and all thoughts of her hands in his hair flew from her mind, her entire being centered on what was happening between her legs. It had been a while since she had last had a boyfriend and she shied away from casual sexual partners, so her body was primed and ready to explode. The coils tightened and her breaths came in pants as his ministrations continued.

The taste of her was nectar and Jaxon inhaled deeply as he continued to swirl his tongue around her folds, inserting a finger deep inside her sex. Tweaking at just the right angle, he felt her orgasm as she cried out.

He slowly eased away from her intoxicating sex and trailed kisses along her hip bone to her tummy, to her breasts, where he lavished attention on each one. Moving upward, he continued to lick and kiss his way to her mouth.

Morgan's hands clutched his shoulders, fingers digging into the flesh. "Wow," she breathed, her voice hoarse with need. She had never flown apart with such abandon. She tasted herself on his tongue as it tangled with hers and the unfamiliar scent was heady.

He lifted up on his knees, his legs straddling her body, and hesitated. "I want you, Morgan. I can't remember the last time I wanted something...or someone, so much. I've got no idea what it is about you, but I want you...but only if you're sure. If not, then we stop right here, and I'll consider myself to be lucky to have been gifted with what you've given me so far."

Her chest heaved with emotion as her lips curved into a smile. Lifting her hands, she gripped his thick thighs, saying, "I want this. I want you. Please."

His smile matched hers as he rolled the condom over his cock and, leaning forward, placed his hands on the mattress behind her head. With his face suspended, almost nose to nose, he held her gaze and said, "A beauty like you should never beg. This is all my pleasure." Lining up the tip to her entrance, he plunged in swiftly, settling to the core in one thrust.

The tightness rocked him, and Jaxon sucked in a shuddering breath, unsure if he was about to be unmanned and go off like a teenager. Her eyes had closed as she bit her bottom lip and he was glad she was not staring at him as he attempted to gain control over his over-eager dick.

As he held himself steady, her eyes popped open and even in the dim light he could see the blueness, holding him captive.

"Are you okay?" she asked, and he heard the nervousness in her shaky voice.

"Yeah," he managed to say. Clearing his throat, he added, "Just needed a moment...this is too fuckin' perfect to rush it through."

Once more, a beautiful smile spread across her face.

Sliding out slowly, he plunged back into her heat, then began a steady rhythm, rocking her body. He linked fingers with hers, keeping their hands pinned next to her head as they stared into each other's eyes. The intimate act of clasped hands felt unfamiliar and yet, it made him feel more connected to this woman than he had ever felt to anyone before. The comparison with the typical physical-only fucks he experienced shocked him. For the first time, he realized what Zander, Rafe, and Cael must have felt when they connected to the women in their lives.

He kissed her forehead before sliding his lips over her closed eyes, cheeks, and down to the pulse point at her neck, reveling in her petal soft skin and the shivers that he felt against his lips.

Emotions slid through Morgan, surprising in their depths. A quick fuck, a fun night, a chance to blow off sexual steam. That was what this was supposed to be about. But as she drowned in his dark chocolate eyes, her sex alive with vibration and the heat of friction, she wondered how she would ever have casual sex again. If it was possible for nonexistent bells to ring, she heard them. He was ruining her for any other man.

Refusing to give in to the urge to tell him all her

thoughts, she concentrated on the physical connection as his body connected with hers. The electricity that snapped deep inside her core seemed to permeate the room until nothing else existed but the two of them. Lifting her legs higher, she dug her heels into his ass and squeezed her thighs together around his waist. Seeing his eyes widen, she grinned. "Told you my legs were strong."

Jaxon bent his head to take her lips, his tongue mimicking the movements of his cock. Tasting, delving, exploring. He stole her breath, feeling her sex tighten, and mumbled, "You close?"

As she nodded, he unlatched her fingers from his left hand and slid it over her breast, down her tummy, and to the area pressed between them. Tweaking her swollen bud, he felt her go over the edge, her inner muscles grabbing his cock as she cried out his name.

Following her, he lifted his head, the cords in his neck tight as he roared out his orgasm, pumping until there was nothing left. It felt as though his soul had left his body and had floated somewhere above as he crashed next to her.

Barely managing to shift to the side, he kept one thigh thrown over hers, one arm draped across her chest, and his face nuzzled into her neck. Not sure if he could move, he came to the realization that he did not have a desire to move...and certainly did not have a desire for her to leave.

Morgan lay, partially underneath him, his heavy body feeling warm and comforting, not sweaty and irritating. The urge to figure out when it would be socially acceptable to get dressed and leave was nowhere to be found. All she wanted was to lay, sated, wrapped in this man's arms. And she knew this was dangerous. Her life had no room for a complication like Jaxon Chapman.

Before she had a chance to speak, he lifted his head and stared into her eyes, a smile playing about his lips. "Jesus, baby, that was amazing."

A giggle slipped out and she said, "Glad I wasn't a disappointment."

"Fuck, no way could you disappoint."

"Uh…" she said, hesitantly, "should I…uh…get ready to—"

His whole body jerked as he bit out, "No way. This was only the beginning of the night. I want you here for round two and three." Seeing her lifted eyebrows, he grinned. "Maybe we'll stop after three. We'll have to see how much you wear me out."

"Then it's a good thing I've got great stamina," she laughed.

Jaxon bent to kiss her lips, memorizing the feel of the soft satin against his. Touching the tip of his tongue to hers, he said, "Oh, yeah. Great stamina, among other things."

The early morning dawn was streaking faint light across the bed when Morgan opened her eyes. Turning her head, she stared at the utterly male specimen she was pressed next to. From his hair, now standing on end from the night's activities and her hands constantly tugging at the curls, to his muscular biceps, chest, and abs that were on display, as the sheet had managed to slip to his waist. Even though she could not see them, she knew his thighs were drool-worthy and the cock that rested between would make most grown women weep with joy.

Sleep had been elusive with their antics during the night, but she felt rested and sated. Her muscles were relaxed and energy she did not know she possessed ran through her. But, now, it was a day of practice. And her father.

Slipping from his bed, she stood and stared. *He said he never brought women here and, yet, he did not hesitate with me.* The idea that it might be because she could be someone special in his life hit her, but that thought was dismissed quickly. Even if she desired it, it was not meant to be. Not now. Not with everything going on in her life.

Quietly dressing, she kept an eye on Jaxon, but he did not stir. Unable to keep the grin from her face, she watched as his face twitched slightly, as though he were dreaming. He looked like such a little boy when he slept.

That thought had her cross over the living room to stare at the photograph on the wall once more. She wondered about his foster upbringing and the other boys. *"The others are my brothers, if not of blood."* Remembering his words from the night before, she sighed. Unable to presume the significance, she nonetheless felt peace seeing the huge, happy smiles on all their faces. *Was I ever that happy as a child?* Unwilling to let her mind slide down that path, she walked to the door and quietly opened it.

With one last look behind at the large, loft apartment, she sighed. *What would it be like to stay and be a part of his world?* Closing the door behind her, she headed to the street, calling for a taxi.

9

Jaxon stood at his kitchen counter drinking a cup of coffee, his heart heavy. He had awoken to the memory of a night like he had never had before, paired with an empty bed. He could not believe he had slept so soundly. *I'm usually the one who is up early, leaving before things get complicated.*

He spent a moment trying to convince himself that it was better she had left, but quickly dismissed that thought. The truth staring him in the face was that he really liked her...wanted to be with her more. She was not a one-and-done.

Sighing, he tossed back the rest of his now luke-warm coffee and headed to the shower. He had five days on shift and no time to stay at home moping about her walking out. Looking into the mirror after taking a swipe at the condensation, he stared at his body. Tiny marks left by fingernails, scratched on his chest and shoulders, were visible. His cock jumped at the memory. He hurried to dress, but the vision of her clothes tossed on the floor, tangled with his, hit him as he walked through the bedroom.

A flash of silver caught his eye and he looked down at the rug. Bending down, he spied a tiny silver earring, a mermaid dangling from the hoop. Picking it up, he held it in his palm for a moment before closing his fingers around it.

Thirty minutes later he closed his door, the idea of a trip to the sports arena sliding through his mind. *Just to return the earring.* With that thought, he grinned as he headed to his Jeep.

"Ma'am, just put a towel over you and we can come in," Jaxon shouted through the door. Looking at Bob, he heaved a sigh. Twisting his head, he watched Mary climb the steps. "Think you'd better go in first, Mary. She's screaming that she's naked and we can't come in yet."

Mary nodded, then knocked on the door and said, "Female coming in." She opened the door and hustled through, but he could hear sputtering of "close the door!" coming from the woman.

"Do we get many calls like this?" Bob asked, his eyebrows hitting his hairline.

"More than I'd like to remember," he replied. The 9-1-1 call had come from the woman's child who had heard her mother screaming. While taking a bath, she had stuck her toe in the faucet and it had become stuck. Unable to get it out, she was floundering in the bathwater, although not in danger of drowning. She managed to open the plug, so the water had drained, but she was nonetheless trapped.

Mary opened the door and waved for them to come in. The woman was partially covered with a floral housecoat and had a pair of panties pulled up one leg in a desperate attempt to salvage her modesty.

As Phil, a fireman, came into the small room, Mary slipped to the side, not needed but providing female support to the horrified woman.

"Hey, Mrs. Walker," he said, kneeling at her head and putting a blood pressure cuff on her arm. "While Phil here takes a look at getting your toe free, I'll check you out to make sure everything else is okay."

Within a few minutes, he ascertained that her blood pressure and heart rate were only slightly elevated, so Bob moved back with Mary while he looked to the fireman.

"It's wedged in tight," Phil said. "I'm gonna have to cut the faucet from the tub so we'll have more leverage to grease it down to get her loose."

Covering her foot, as well as the rest of her body, he watched as Phil and another fireman expertly cut the metal faucet. Once free from the tub, they moved to lift the woman from her enamel prison.

Setting her on the toilet seat, they knelt and placed lubricant tubes at the cut end of the faucet, squirting the slick gel as deeply around her toe as they could.

The woman winced but held back her tears. "What if it doesn't work?"

"Don't worry, Mrs. Walker, I've never seen Phil not be able to get someone unstuck from anything."

"Cora!" a scream came from downstairs. The clomp of boots on the stairs indicated more people were approaching.

Twisting his head around, he growled to Mary, "What now? Who's with the daughter?"

"Policewoman is downstairs with her. Don't know who's coming up."

Rounding the top of the stairs, a portly man, his cheeks red, pushed his way to the bathroom door. "Cora, what the hell did you do?"

Her face crumpled in tears as she said, "Nothing. I was just taking a bath."

"Then how the hell did you end up with your toe stuck, my tub ruined, and all these people in our goddamn bathroom?"

Standing, he faced a man who was clearly Mr. Walker and said, "Sir, at this moment, we need your wife calm and cooperating."

Mr. Walker snapped his mouth closed but planted himself right next to Mary in the crowded space, watching the proceedings.

After a few minutes of gently wiggling the cut faucet on her toe to work the lubricant further, it finally slipped off. Kneeling again at her feet, he looked at the swollen, bluish digit. "Ma'am, I would have that x-rayed, if I were you. I'm unable to tell if it is broken without one."

She nodded and peered up at her husband. His face

still red, he nodded. "I'll get you dressed and then we'll head to the ER."

With thanks all around, they packed up and headed back down the stairs, glad to be out of the tight confines of the bathroom, but happier that the call had a satisfactory conclusion.

"What was that you used?" Bob asked Phil as they made their way outside to the trucks.

Phil shared a look with him and grinned. Holding out his hand, he showed a tube of K-Y Jelly.

Mouth open, Bob said, "You used pussy-lube on her toe?"

"Jesus, you moron," Mary called out. "K-Y Jelly is a surgical lubricant, not just for women."

The others laughed as Bob grimaced, stowing the gear back into the ambulance. Climbing into the driver's seat, he looked at the time, seeing the shift was half over. Before he had a chance for more planning on how and when to see Morgan again, another call came in.

Flipping on the siren, they headed down the road. This time, the situation was serious. A child had been climbing a tree and while still on a lower limb, had fallen onto a fence and the spike had pierced his upper arm.

The child's mother was screaming and, while a policewoman gained control of her, he and the others raced to the back yard where the child's father was supporting him.

The man's expression was ragged as he said, "I can't get him off. I'm afraid I'll make it worse—"

"We've got it now, sir," he said, his voice calm. "What's his name?"

"Brad."

Looking into the boy's wide eyes, tears streaming down his face, he said, "Hey, Brad. I'm Jaxon and we're gonna take care of you now."

Continuing to speak to him softly, he held Brad's body high enough for the firemen to cut the fence spike below his arm. Mary and Bob stood behind the child, assessing the wound and what would need to happen once he was free.

"Looks like it went through muscle, not bone," Mary said in a quiet voice, gaining a nod from him.

Once the boy was free from the fence, he knelt on the ground with Brad's body carefully tucked into his. Allowing the firemen to now be at the child's head, he talked softly to Brad as the firemen sliced the top of the spike close to his arm.

Making the decision to get him to the hospital before chancing removal of the metal that was still embedded, he placed him onto the stretcher. Rolling him passed the white-faced father and still hysterical mother, he nodded to the policewoman. As they lifted him into the back of the ambulance, she was giving them the instructions to follow.

"Bob, stay in the back with Mary. You know what to do. You've got this."

With a curt nod, Bob followed the gurney and climbed into the back while he hauled himself up into the cab. Calling in their location and ETA, he flipped on the siren and pulled onto the road.

Once at the hospital, they transferred Brad to the surgeon and staff, and he bent over the child, saying, "You're a brave boy. These people will take care of you and you'll be just fine."

Watching them roll him down the hall, surrounded by medical personnel, he turned back to Bob and Mary, who were packing up the equipment. The boy's parents rushed through the door and Mary took them by the arm and escorted them to the ER receptionist, who hurried them back to the bay.

Bob looked at him and said, "That could have been so much worse."

He nodded, his mind having taken that turn as well. "Yeah. As it is, he'll have stitches and a helluva scar to impress his friends with, but a few more inches to the side and he could have pierced his chest."

Mary returned, saying, "His parents are with him. You got the report done?"

He was working on the tablet, finishing the last entry. Walking to the reception desk, he handed it to the attendant and turned to follow Mary and Bob out the door.

With five more calls out that day, he gratefully clocked out at the end of the shift, but realized it was too late to get to the arena.

It wasn't until the next day that Jaxon was afforded the opportunity to leave work on time. Changed into a clean t-shirt and jeans, he drove to the sports arena, hoping Morgan would be there. If not, he would need to do a little searching to find her. *After all, she probably wants her earring returned.*

After parking, he walked inside and headed straight to the pool area. He had been surprised at the crowded parking lot and had to drive around twice before finding a space. Walking past the receptionist, he noticed she turned her attention to him, a smile curving her face. She blatantly dropped her gaze slowly from his head to his toes and back again, her tongue slipping out to lick her lips. "Anything I can help you with?"

Ignoring the innuendo, he asked, "What's happening today?"

Her eyes widened and she bent over the counter, maximizing the appeal of her sports bra. "Oh, the women's swim trials are going on. You know, for the Olympics? The winner here will be able to advance onward and if she keeps doing well, then she'll make the Olympic team."

"Wow," he replied, keeping his eyes away from her exposed décolletage and wondering how he would ever be able to see if Morgan was present amongst all the spectators. Turning back suddenly, he asked, "Do you know if Morgan McAlister is here today?"

The receptionist threw her head back in laughter. Cackling, she said, "Oh, yeah, I'd say she's here today. Just check the pool."

Brows lowered at her strange sense of amusement, he turned and headed into the massive pool arena. Spectators were in the stands and it appeared that there were reporters at one end. The scent of chlorine filled his nostrils and his eyes watered slightly.

The screams and shouts were ear-splitting, but he continued to make his way to the end of the stands near the finish line and searched the pool. With each female swimmer wearing a cap and goggles, their bodies encased in tight swimsuits, it was impossible for him to discern which one might be Morgan.

"Morgan!" a man's shout came from the sidelines.

His eyes darted to the woman the man was yelling at and he realized the swimmer that was in the lead must be her.

"Morgan!" the man screamed again.

Suddenly, a long-forgotten memory slammed into him and it dawned on him where he had heard that voice before. A public pool and an intense man coaching his daughter—the little red-headed girl who swam like a mermaid from when he was a child. The one who had lifted him up after his head had slipped under the water.

Pulling himself back to the present, he watched as she deftly flipped at the end, gaining an even bigger lead. His heartbeat began racing in his chest. Leaning forward, he cheered for her with the rest of the crowd.

10

Morgan's head broke the surface of the water, her turn executed perfectly, and she shot down the lane. Her father's voice was in the background, but she did not need to hear him call out times to know that she was in line for a personal best.

He had reamed her out when she first showed up at the gym yesterday, angry that she had been out late the night before. She had not told him that she had stayed out all night, knowing he would have become apoplectic as well. She was determined to live her own life. Plus, the night with Jaxon was her own memory to cherish, leaving her energized and ready to take on the world. For a brief second that morning, she had considered waking him up to see if he could come today to watch her swim. But, considering his reputation, she had forgone that line of thinking.

Now, arms and legs in absolute synchrony glided her body along. Every stroke ensured that her head was fully submerged to reduce drag, but she heard the cheers when she lifted her head to breathe. Executing another perfect turn, she kicked off the side and powered back down the lane, aware that no one to either side was close to her.

Focusing only on the prize at the end, she stretched her arms out, not slowing for a second. Her fingers touched the edge of the pool and she heard the cheering of the people who had gathered to see her. Screams and shouts echoed in the swim complex and she held on to the rope, trying to see the time on the clock. She clung to the side, her lungs burning as she gulped in air. Pulling her goggles down around her neck, she swiped her eyes and saw her father's exuberant face.

"Finally, girl. You got your act together, listened to me, and did what you needed to do." She watched as he stood, puffing out his chest.

She felt a hug from behind and turned to wrap her arms around one of her competitors. A few others swam over the ropes to offer congratulations as well. Hauling her body out of the water, she sucked in a deep breath, her smile genuine. Her gaze drifted to her father, who had moved over to the bank of reporters, all there to discuss her Olympic dream.

Swiping her hand over her face, she pulled her cap from her head and shook out her hair. Accepting a towel from one of the gym employees, she wiped down before walking to her chair to grab her jacket. Staring at the bank of reporters, she sucked in a deep, fortifying breath, before walking over.

"Ms. McAlister, how does it feel to make the next level of qualifications for the Olympics?"

"What did you think of your time today?"

"Ms. McAlister, who do you think your major competition will be at the next trials?"

"Do you have plans to stay in the area to continue training or will you be moving on?"

The camera lights were blinding and the questions came at her fast and furious. Trying to answer one at a time, her father continually jumped in to elaborate on her responses.

"Her time will improve now that she's in top physical condition. We've got two more coaches on board her team now and expect her to shave even more time off her personal best…"

As he continued to drone on, she smiled for the cameras and, with a jaunty wave, moved back to her gym bag, grabbing her sweatpants. She sat in the chair to dry off her legs before pulling on the pants. Zipping up her jacket, she stood, turned, and ran into a hard body.

"Oh, I'm sorry—" Her eyes widened as her apology caught in her throat. "Jaxon?"

He smiled at her, his gaze penetrating. "I had no idea. No idea you swam at this level of competition. You were amazing out there."

"You saw me?"

"Well, I got here near the end, so I saw the finish." He looked around, his gaze moving toward the crowd, and stuck his hands in his pockets. "I'm really impressed, Morgan. I had no idea that you did this. I mean, the Olympics…fuck, that's…that's…well," chuckling, he added, "I don't even know how to say how awesome that is."

She nodded, her smile for the cameras still firmly in place. "Thanks. That's been the goal all along. To reach that level." Her eyes darted behind him, where her father was still holding court. When she shifted her gaze back to him, she observed him stepping back slightly.

"Well, I need to let you get back to your adoring fans," he joked, but the smile did not reach his eyes.

"Why did you come here today? Was there a special reason?" she asked, more curt than she intended. She was surprised he had shown up and did not want to assume the reason. He looked even more nervous at her questioning and she hated she had given the wrong impression. In truth, she battled the desire to throw her arms around him.

He pulled his hand out of his pocket, opening his fingers as he held it out. Resting on his palm was her lost mermaid earring. "I found this on the floor and wanted to return it."

She gasped and her practiced smile fell away, leaving a natural smile that lit her face. "Oh, Jaxon, you found it." She reached out to take the jewelry, holding it reverently in her hand. "My Nonnie gave these earrings to me and I couldn't believe I had lost one. I figured it might be at the bar and I'd never find it."

"Then I'm glad I could give it to you." He stepped back even further, jamming his hands into his pockets. "Well, I should go. It looks like you've got some people who want to talk to you."

"Wait," she said, her hand darting out to rest on his arm.

He stared at her hand for a second, before lifting his gaze back to her face, his head tilted in silent question.

"I wanted to thank you for the other night." Blushing, she said, "I suppose that sounds rather lame. It was…well…it was special."

His lips curved slightly, and he nodded. Chuckling, he said, "Yeah, it was. I hated that you were gone the next morning."

Biting her lip, she ducked her head. "I thought, well, I thought it was best. I knew I needed to get to practice since I had the meet today. And I didn't want to be seen as one of those girls you think get too clingy."

He covered her hand with his, hers cool underneath his much warmer one. She loved the feel of his skin on hers.

With his other hand, he reached up to tuck a strand of wet hair behind her ear. "I'd never think that about you, Morgan. I actually missed you when I woke up alone."

As they stood, staring at each other, the rest of the swim arena's noise faded away. Her fingers twitched to link with his, the desire to step closer overwhelming.

Taking a chance, he began, "I wondered if you would perhaps like to—"

"Morgan!"

Her father's voice interrupted Jaxon's invitation and she grimaced when he jerked his hand back as her father neared.

"Morgan, come on. We've got an interview with the

TV station in an hour and then the magazine spread first thing in the morning."

Dropping her hand, she said, "I'll be there in a moment, Dad."

"I want—"

"Dad. I said *in a moment*," she emphasized, standing her ground. Her father bristled but with reporters still around, he stalked away.

Jaxon stepped backward but she reached out to touch him again. "What was it you were about to say?" she asked, her eyes pinned hopefully on his.

Hesitating, Jaxon looked to the side before stepping closer. "Just to say that I'm glad we met, Morgan. I wish you all the best and I'll be rooting for you." He bent forward to place a kiss on her cheek, the silky skin cool to his lips.

Closing his eyes for a few seconds, he opened his mouth to say more, but just offered another smile, one Morgan could have sworn was tinged with sadness. With a parting squeeze on her hand, he stepped back, allowing her to be engulfed in well-wishers.

Her heart ached as she watched him walk away, the desire to race after him filling her soul. Before she could act on her instinct, her father took her arm and escorted her to the side.

"Who was that man?" he barked.

"Just someone I met," she replied, jerking her arm from his grip. Seeing her father's pinched lips, she added, "I lost an earring and he was returning it."

"Hmph," he grumbled, then held her gaze. "Just remember, Morgan, you have no time for distractions.

Eyes on the prize. Always keep your eyes on the prize." Seeing someone else he wanted to talk to, he straightened and smiled, hailing them as he walked along.

She breathed out a long, slow sigh. She was no longer able to see Jaxon's head amongst the crowd and she battled the threat of tears. "Yeah," she said aloud to no one but her own heart. "Eyes on the prize." Walking away, she slipped her mermaid earring into her earlobe and wondered if she even knew what the prize was anymore.

Jaxon sat in his Jeep, still parked in the lot of the gym, and wondered why his heart ached. *It's not like I know her very well. We just met. She's got her life, I've got mine. She's going places and I'm...well, my life is here.*

Giving his head a shake, he started the vehicle, pulling out and driving down the street. In one night, he had begun to lose his heart to Morgan, an Olympic hopeful swimmer who had no room in her world for him.

Morgan walked into the nursing home, smiling and accepting congratulations from the staff at the reception and nurses' desk. She continued down the hall, her sneaker covered feet padding softly on the white tiled floor. The walls were painted a soft rose color with framed pictures of flower gardens, seascapes, and mountains.

Arriving at the door she was looking for, she knocked on the doorframe before entering, a smile spreading across her face as she spied the familiar figure sitting in a chair by the window, looking out over a courtyard garden.

"Nonnie?"

The room's occupant turned her head, her wrinkled face unmoving for a few seconds before sight and memory allowed her to recognize her visitor. Then, her smile settled into the creases. "Morgan, my girl. Come in, come in."

She flew toward her grandmother, landing at her feet and throwing her arms around her. Her grandmother's plump body, soft white hair, and the delicate whiff of a rose-scented perfume were all familiar and comforting. She felt arms encircle her and as she pressed her face into her grandmother's lap it was as though the cares of the world fell away.

"My, my, what an exuberant greeting," Nonnie said, patting her back.

Leaning back, she smiled and said, "Just like when I was little, right?"

"Oh, yes. You always had so much energy. Racing around. Throwing yourself into everything you wanted to do."

"How did you stand me?" she laughed.

"Oh, the young always have so much energy and fun. You wanted to swim, dance, climb trees, run races. Until your father harnessed all that enthusiasm into swimming, I thought you'd do a little bit of everything."

Her grandmother's words caused her smile to slip slightly, but Nonnie continued, "And from watching TV last night, it seems that congratulations are in order, my sweet girl. An Olympic hopeful. My goodness."

"Yeah…just what we always wanted."

Nonnie's sharp eyes held her face for a moment, before she said, "We?"

Blinking, she nodded. "You know, Dad, Mom…me."

Lifting her hand to cup her face, she said, "Is it still your dream? Or are you living your father's dream?"

Sucking in a quick breath, she swallowed deeply. "Of course it's my dream. Believe me, you can't get far in athletics if it's not your dream."

"I'm sure," Nonnie agreed. "But I also know that dreams can change. What was the dream at fifteen can change when you are twenty. And change again at twenty-five. My dear, even at eighty-three, I can tell you that my dreams have changed each decade and then some!"

Moving back to sit on the chair near her, she felt the need to put a little space between herself and the woman that held her heart and could seemingly peer into her soul. Clasping her hands in front of her, she looked around at the pleasantly decorated room and smiled. "You've got a new painting over your bed."

"I've been trying my hand at watercolors and flowers seem to be the thing that I can paint. I tried a landscape, but it looked more like a green river."

Laughing, she shook her head. "I can't believe you

created that beautiful picture, although, you have always been so talented. But to take up painting when you turned eighty!"

"Life is too short to not try to do all the things you ever wanted to do. New goals. New hobbies. New vocations. Remember child, you are never too old to try something new."

A smile settled on her face, now resting in the love she had for her grandmother. "Well, I really should be going. I just wanted to pop in and say hello before the new round of practices began."

"Tell me, Morgan, dear. Do you have a young man in your life?"

Hesitating for a moment, she said, "Uh…no."

"Hmm, that sounds suspicious."

Rolling her eyes, she blushed and admitted, "I did meet someone."

With a clap of her hands, Nonnie's eyes brightened and she begged, "Oh, tell me about him."

"It's nothing really. I mean, it sounds so cliché. We met in a bar and spent…um…some time together—"

"Oh posh, girl. You slept with him, didn't you?"

"Nonnie!"

"I'm not a prude and don't expect you to act like one around me. I'm too old for guessing games, so just tell me about this prince."

"Prince?" A giggle slipped out and she admitted, "Okay, he does seem perfect. Great manners—"

"You didn't sleep with his manners, Morgan. I'm glad he had manners and treated you well, but I'd like to get to the good stuff."

Throwing up her hands, she laughed. "Okay, he's really built. Great body. Super nice. We talked, and it was so nice to talk to someone about things that had nothing to do with swimming. It was like we connected on a level that I haven't felt in a really long time."

Leaning forward to clutch at her hands, Nonnie said, "Oh, honey, that sounds lovely. Do you think you'll keep seeing him?"

She shook her head, unable to keep her smile from falling away and her heart from aching. "No. How could I? I'm leaving soon for the next trials and you know what Dad's like when we're in the final stretch of something so important."

"I know what your father's like. But what do you want?"

She opened her mouth to speak but the words caught in her throat. Staring into the blue eyes that had not faded with age and now seemed to be forcing their way deep inside of her, she stammered. "I...I...no, no, Nonnie. I have to keep my eyes on the prize—"

"I call bullshit." Leaning closer, Nonnie said, "What do you want?"

Swallowing audibly, she shook her head sadly, "I don't know. I don't know." Sitting up straighter, she continued, "That's not true. I know that what I've been working all my life for is right at my fingertips and I owe it to myself to give it my all. When it's over, then I'll see."

"Then you'll find your life outside of swimming. And believe me, sweet girl, there is a life after the Olympics."

The statement was simple but jolted right through

her as thoughts of Jaxon flew through her mind. *Maybe he'll still be around when it is all over. Maybe.*

She spoke, voice soft as a whisper, "I know there's a world outside of swimming, Nonnie. I've glimpsed it. I...I want it. I just don't know how to get it, or even think I can, until this is all over."

"Your dad..."

Nodding, she said, "Dad's worked for this my whole life. He's poured his time and money into it. He wants me to live this dream and do it his way. And I know sometimes it doesn't seem like it, but it's my dream, too, even if, if I had my way, I might go about it a little differently."

Nonnie said nothing for a moment, sitting back in her chair. A small smile settled on her face and she said, "Then live your dream, my dear. And when this dream is over, find a new one."

With a final kiss, she walked down the hall, passing another older woman walking in the opposite direction, tall and thin, with her white hair pulled up in a bun. The scent of rose water drifted by, reminding her of Nonnie. A strange sensation filled her but as she looked over her shoulder, the woman had turned the corner and was no longer in sight.

Sighing, she walked out of the building, her steps less sure and her heart less happy.

11

As Jaxon looked around at the gathering, he couldn't help but notice how crowded the table was getting. "Miss Ethel, what are you going to do if our family gets bigger? We won't be able to make it into the dining room!"

She peered at him from the other end of the table, where she always sat in the place of honor at the head. "Instead of being insulted that you don't think I can find ways to fit more and more people at our table," she quipped, "I think I shall focus on the possibility that you have mentioned this because you have someone you would like to join with us."

At that, all eyes turned toward him, and he felt his face grow hot.

"I think it was that red-headed beauty from the other night at Grimm's," Rosalie announced, gently rocking Charity in her arms. "She was a real sweetheart."

"Oh?" Miss Ethel encouraged.

"She was a looker, I'll give you that," Jayden added. Turning to him, he said, "Are you sure you don't want to do a switch like we used to in high school?"

"No!" he barked, before realizing what the vehement opposition would say about his feelings toward Morgan. Giving his head a shake, he just said, "We're beyond those juvenile pranks."

"Are you turning over a new leaf, *Mr. Don't-let-the-door-hit-you-in-the-ass-on-the-way-out*?" Rafe asked, his voice full of incredulity.

Shooting a glare Rafe's way, he grumbled, "I wasn't that bad."

He was grateful when Miss Ethel intervened before anyone else could weigh in an opinion concerning his player ways. "Keep the table conversation civil, boys." Turning to him, she said, "I'd like to hear more about this young woman."

Shrugging, he said, "There's not much to tell. She's a great woman, but I found out today she's an Olympic swimming hopeful."

That announcement brought surprise and a fast round of questions from everyone.

"An Olympic swimmer? I thought she said she was a grad student?" Rosalie asked, her brow knit.

"She never mentioned swimming?" Zander added, taking Charity from Rosalie and bouncing her a little to soothe her.

"Why did she keep that a secret?" Jayden asked, his attention riveted on him.

Swallowing his bite before he choked, he said, "Whoa. One at a time. Yes, she's a grad student, but also a swimmer. I have no idea what events. Um…she just qualified for the next Olympic trials. I went by the sports complex the other day to return an earring she had left at my place…" His words faltered as he offered Miss Ethel a sheepish look.

She waved her hand dismissively, saying, "Goodness, boy, go on with your story."

"Well, I went by the gym, actually, the swimming arena over on Lafayette. And she was just finishing a race. I got to congratulate her and give her the earring back."

"And?" Eleanor prompted, leaning forward, her expression hopeful as Rafe wrapped his arm across her shoulders.

Shrugging, he said, "Uh…that's it. I met her, we clicked, and now she has her life…I guess."

"That's it?" Regina asked.

The men chuckled and he recognized that they were used to Miss Ethel being the only inquisitive female and now, with Rosalie, Eleanor, and Regina in their fold, it was much harder to get past a dinner conversation without someone digging for details.

"Yes, that's it. She'll be leaving soon, and I got a glimpse of her dad, who I think is also her coach." Shaking his head, he said, "He'd never allow her to do much more than prepare for the Olympics. Driven is one way to describe him."

"She seemed lighthearted and funny the other night," Jayden said.

"Yeah, she is. Well, was. I really liked being with her. But, then, when I saw her at the pool, she was an amazing athlete, but once out of the water, seemed caught between wanting to see me and keeping an eye out for her dad."

"Sounds like he's a slave driver to me," Zander said, a scowl on his face.

"So, are you going to see her again?" Miss Ethel asked.

"I'd love to." Looking at the grins coming from the others, he chuckled. "I know. Me, the perpetual bachelor who didn't want to settle with just one woman. But, man, she was something." His mirth ended, and his smile slid from his face. "It's not meant to be. I've got a job here and she's leaving town to compete and train before the Olympics. It's like we exist in two different worlds."

The conversation turned to other topics and Rosalie jumped up to assist Miss Ethel bringing in the dessert. As the gathering began to break up, he found himself hanging back with Jayden, saying goodbye to the others. Rosalie and Zander, with baby Charity, Eleanor and Rafe, Regina and Cael, Asher, and Zeke all left, heading to their cars.

Jayden stayed and he knew it was because his twin understood his hesitation. Miss Ethel smiled at the two of them and invited them into the living room.

The room was just the same as it had always been, comfortably furnished with a dark green sofa with colorful throw pillows against the back, wooden end tables covered in white, crocheted lace, and a thick rug covering the center of the wooden floor. Two, deep cushioned chairs sat facing the sofa, Miss Ethel settling in one, her knitting bag at her feet. The walls on either side of the fireplace held bookshelves, filled with children's books.

He and Jayden moved to the sofa, the familiar feel and scent of the room bringing back two decades of memories. No one spoke for a few minutes, the clicking of knitting needles the only sound in the room.

Finally, Miss Ethel started, "I still remember the day that each of my boys came to me. When it was the two of you, my goodness, it was so exciting to get twins."

"You weren't scared of getting two at once?" Jayden asked.

"Well, it was certainly different, but it was a lot of fun as well. I already had Zander and Rafe. Then you two came to live with me and, soon after, we gained Cael. Of course, Asher was next."

Shaking his head, he said, "I know we were a handful." Chuckling, he added, "We tried to switch our names on you, but somehow you knew us right away."

"Our aunt always got us mixed up and her fiancé never tried to figure us out."

She nodded, her smile leaving her face. "I often wondered about your aunt. She tried to care for you for several years, but having never been a mother herself, it must have been overwhelming. And then, not getting the support of the man she was going to marry? Well, I'm glad she did the right thing and allowed you to be placed here."

"Best place we could have landed," Jayden agreed.

Quiet settled over them once again, before Miss Ethel said, "I'm proud of you boys. I don't know if I've told you that lately. All of my boys joined the military out of high school and when you two joined up, I was proud as punch."

Easing back into the sofa cushions, he breathed a little easier. Being in Miss Ethel's comforting presence had always been calming.

"A rescue worker and mechanic. So impressive. My George was a mechanic and I was surprised that you both did not go in for the same thing to stay together."

"We almost did," he admitted, nodding toward Jayden. "I really wanted to work on the trucks, but when I was presented with the possibility of running the emergency medical response ambulance, it just struck me as something I wanted to do."

"I think you have always sold yourself short," she said. "You two were so much alike as children, but it was clear you considered your role to be more of the jokester of the two of you. I knew from your early days here with me, that while Jayden had a more serious outlook, you were hiding a wonderful heart behind your laughter."

Allowing her words to flow through him, he remained quiet, pondering her point. He never talked about it, but Jayden understood. He could not take things too seriously, because that opened the door for getting hurt. He loved Miss Ethel, was thankful every day that they had ended up with her, but losing so many people that were meant to protect him—his mother, his grandmother, and then his aunt—all by the time he was six, had left its mark. The truth was, he did not want to be left again. Maybe, when he met the right woman, she would be worth taking that risk.

Morgan's face popped into his head and his breath got caught in his throat. He hadn't been concerned at all with her, had he? One smile from her had chased away all his concerns, all his fear. *Damn, I've got it worse than I thought.*

Miss Ethel continued, pulling him from his thoughts, "You have a healing spirit, Jaxon. Whether with shared laughter or with your medical knowledge. You, my dear, are a healer."

He grinned, his lips curving in a sly smile. Wanting to move on to lighter subjects, he teased, "Come on, Miss Ethel, tell us how difficult we were."

"Oh, is this story time?" she quipped, her smile broadening as she lifted her eyes from her knitting to peer at each of them. "Well, let's see. I remember getting a call from the principal of your middle school one time. It seems that your artwork, Jaxon, was about to win a prize and when I looked at it, I knew it had been done by you." She glanced Jayden's way. "When I questioned you two, it became clear that my dear Jaxon was trying to impress a girl in his art class and so he had Jayden paint the winning painting."

Barking out a laugh, Jayden said, "Oh, my God, I forgot that. You really liked MaryLou Battles and were always trying to impress her in seventh grade."

"How on earth do you remember her name?" he asked, his brows lowered in stunned surprise.

"Just 'cause you can't remember the names of the girls you've been interested in. Though, it's not surprising since none of them last more than a...uh... short time," Jayden stammered, covering his almost slip up, "I, on the other hand, have a fabulous memory."

Miss Ethel laughed and said, "Well, it seems that Jaxon can remember the name of the beautiful swimmer."

"Oh, yeah. Morgan McAlister."

Miss Ethel's gaze lifted again before returning to her needles. "McAlister...interesting. And you're sure there's nothing there?"

"I spent less than twenty-four hours with her and, yet, that's a lot longer than most women I meet. I know that's nothing to be proud of, but yeah, there was something there. If she wasn't who she was, I'd be asking for a second date but, as it is, her life's path is completely different."

"Well, you never know if your paths will cross again."

12

"You want him to have more responsibility?"

Jaxon was talking to his Captain, Ted Burke, at their meeting concerning the trainees.

Ted nodded, saying, "According to you, Bob's ready. I've also talked to Mary and she agrees. To begin with, let him have more driving responsibilities. I want him to get used to being in the driver's seat alone, with you still in the front of the ambulance for now. It'll still give you a chance to monitor his decisions."

"You got it, Captain."

Walking out, Jaxon gave Bob the good news. Meeting up with Mary, the three hustled out as the next call came in. Bob drove, with him giving pointers where needed.

"Slow down at the intersection…proceed with caution…make eye contact with the other drivers…you got it."

The call took them to a house fire, but as they stayed for assistance, the fire department extinguished the fire and it was discovered there was nobody at home. Pulling out of the driveway, they headed back to the station.

Within a moment, another call came in, 24-D-3.

"What does that mean?" he quizzed Bob.

"Pregnancy, imminent delivery."

"Good. Husband on the side of the road. He was driving to the hospital when wife began pushing. Siren on," he said. "If she's pushing, then we need to get there fast and if they're on the side of the road, we need assistance." Calling it in, he reported. "On route. ETA three minutes."

As they neared, Bob expertly pulled in behind the car, angled so that it would be protected from traffic.

Hopping out, he and Mary ran to the open, back passenger door, gently moving to the pale, crying man holding a newborn that appeared to have just emerged. Bob opened the other door, climbing in to support the shaking, and also crying, mother.

"You're fine, you're fine," assured Mary, smiling at the woman. Bob inserted an IV line as Jaxon took the baby and cut the cord, while Mary worked on extracting the afterbirth.

Sirens approaching indicated the fire truck had arrived and the police moved in as well, to direct traffic safely past their vehicles.

"Hey, little man," he cooed to the tiny baby, wrapping it in blankets after suctioning the mouth. The baby gave a lusty cry and the woman's arms instinctively reached out for him. "We're going to transfer you to the ambulance, and as soon as you're inside, you'll have your baby," he promised.

Within a moment, they had her comfortably settled on the gurney with her baby wrapped tightly in her arms. The husband was in no condition to drive so one of the policewomen drove his car behind the ambulance to ensure he arrived safely.

Receiving heartfelt thanks from the new parents, he, Bob, and Mary headed out. Once more, Bob handled the ambulance like a pro as they headed to lunch. They had no sooner eaten than another call came in.

"Siren on and proceed with caution," he said, sure that his words were unnecessary, but feeling the need to say them anyway. He spoke to Mary, who assured him that she was ready, which was also unnecessary considering she was always prepared.

Morgan sat in the parking lot of the sports arena, her mind in turmoil. The elation from her recent win and guaranteed placement in the next Olympic trials had dwindled as the loneliness of her life weighed heavily on her. She had friends, just not close ones. She was friendly with other swimmers, but there was always underlying competitiveness that kept them from becoming close. She thought back to the bar, where she had met Jaxon and had spent time with his friends. She envied the camaraderie, the ease with which they talked and joked, the obvious affection among them.

And, if the picture in his apartment was any indication, there were others in his group—his band of brothers, as he called them, that she wished she could meet.

Pulling out into traffic, she shook those thoughts from her mind. *Maybe someday. But now, as Dad constantly says, I gotta keep my eyes on the prize.* She just wished she could convince her heart of that.

Hearing a siren, she slowed down, seeing the flashing lights coming in the opposite direction. Her light was green, but she hesitated at the intersection, watching carefully to see if the ambulance needed to turn in front of her. Moving to the side, she pulled forward a bit and then stopped, waiting for it to pass.

Bob accelerated gently, switching lanes as he anticipated the traffic patterns ahead, mumbling thanks as several cars moved out of their way. An intersection was at the end of the block and he slowed, honking the horn in addition to the siren. The light was green as he approached, but he decelerated even more, entering at a crawl.

"Jaxon?" Mary called from the back.

"Yeah?" he turned to look behind him.

"Fuck!" Bob yelled, hitting the brakes, bringing Jaxon's head swinging back around just as a fast-moving pickup truck slammed into the side of a car on the opposite side of the street that had stopped to allow the ambulance to pass. The horrific sound of crunching metal, squealing tires, and shattering glass filled the air, cutting through the sound of the siren. The truck was traveling at such speed that its impact pushed the car directly in front of the ambulance before coming to a halt.

"Goddammit," he yelled, his foot hitting the imaginary brake on the passenger side as Bob stopped the ambulance quickly. He called in the accident on the radio. "Category Two, multiple vehicles. The intersection of West Main and Petersburg. We're on scene. Transfer other call. Need police, fire assistance." Throwing his arm out, he pointed to the side, directing Bob to park close to the wreckage.

Flinging himself from the ambulance, he ran toward the closest vehicle and peered inside at the driver of the pickup truck. His airbag had deployed, but he was immediately responsive and mobile. Ignoring the cursing driver, he shouted for Bob to take care of the man as he and Mary ran to the car.

The small, older model, silver Toyota was completely crushed on the driver's side. With the truck still buried into the car's metal, he hurried to the passenger door, peering inside. The only occupant was the female driver, whose face was turned away, head hanging down, but he could see her left arm appeared trapped in the crushed door. He was unable to see her left foot, but prayed it was not trapped as well.

Shouting instructions to Mary, he waved away a few Good Samaritans, begging them to not stand in the road and to move along unless they had witnessed the accident. Sirens filled the air and he threw up a word of thanks that the police would soon have the traffic under control.

Mark and Ben, two firemen he recognized, ran over, and he immediately stepped back to give them a chance to assess the vehicles, while saying, "We've got to get her out through her door if possible." The front of the pickup truck was severely dented but not crushed, even though it was still embedded into the car's door.

With the driver of the truck now sitting on the side of the road and being seen to by Bob, the firemen managed to roll the truck back to give them room to inspect the driver's door of the car.

Mark shouted, "We're gonna have to cut it off. Stabilize her and we'll get ready."

He threw open the passenger door and crawled onto the seat, leaning over the console. The lack of movement from the female victim had him swallowing hard but as he placed his hand on her right wrist, the pulse underneath his fingertips brought a sense of relief.

She groaned and he shifted closer to get his head in front of hers. Ignoring the firemen, now at the driver's door, he supported her chin as her eyes blinked open. Unfocused. Unseeing. And absolutely sky blue. *Morgan!*

"Shit, Morgan. Morgan. Can you hear me?"

Another groan of pain was the only sound she managed to make, and he twisted his head to shout at Mary. Attempting to keep his shaky voice calm, he called out what he needed. Mary then turned to call out to the other rescue squads now appearing. Bob, handing off the care of the truck driver to the others, moved in behind him, leaning over his shoulder, passing him the neck brace.

He wrapped it around her neck, fastening it as

gently as he could. Speaking softly, he kept up a continuous dialog. "Morgan, it's Jaxon. Hey, girl. We're gonna get you out of here as fast as we can. Got men working on the door right now. Can you tell me your name, sweetheart?"

"Mo..ga," she cried, as tears streamed down her face.

"Good job. I've got your neck stabilized and I'm gonna crawl over to see what we've got on the other side, okay?"

She made no motion, so he shoved his body further over the steering wheel, observing multiple cuts on her face and neck, due to the shattered glass. They all looked superficial and he reported back to Bob. Her left arm was not as trapped as he first assumed, but it hung against the crushed door, broken and bleeding with a piece of embedded metal above her elbow.

Looking through the broken window at Ben, he reported, "Need to get the door off to get her out, if possible, but her arm is not trapped in the door. If you can't get her out safely, I think we can extricate her from here."

"We can get it loose with the Halligan bar and bolt cutters," Ben replied. "Shouldn't take too long."

With a curt nod, he felt Bob hand him the IV equipment. His hands shook, but he efficiently inserted the IV into a vein in her right hand.

Mary climbed into the back seat and leaned forward to assist. Her eyes searched his and from her cocked eyebrow, he knew she was questioning his ravaged face. Mouthing, *I know her, well*, he continued to speak softly.

"Hey Morgan, the noise you hear is the firemen

getting your door open. It'll take just another minute or two and we'll be able to get you out and into the ambulance. You're doing well. Can you tell me what day it is?"

Her pain filled eyes, with tears spilling down her pale cheeks, held his, breaking his heart. The sounds of traffic being directed all around them hummed in the background, but he only had ears for her.

"Okay, sweetheart. Hang on."

Looking out the window, he wondered what was taking so long, but just as he was about to bark out the question, Ben leaned in and said, "Got it loose." He pulled off his fire hat and stuck his head through the window, his movements careful of broken glass. Looking down, Ben then lifted his gaze to Morgan and offered a smile. "All right, Miss, we'll have you out soon." Looking back up to him, he said, "Assessment? Can we take the door away?"

"Yes, I've got her arm tucked against her body, but am reticent to move it too much." The unspoken words of the extent of her injuries swirled between them.

Mary stayed in the back seat, holding the IV line, and he slid out of the car. His boots pounded the pavement as he raced around the hood to the other side, while Bob took his place. Ben gave a curt nod, and with the creak and groan of metal scraping metal, the firemen shifted the door away and stepped back.

As soon as the door was off the car and out of the way, he bent over, immediately bracing her mangled arm while Bob supported her body from behind. Now that he had an unobstructed view of the injured appendage, he shuddered. Securing her left arm to avoid more movement, he nodded to the other paramedic. With assistance, he shifted her body out of the open doorway and onto the gurney placed at his side. Another EMT appeared, taking the IV from Mary and she hustled to them as well.

One of the policemen leaned in and picked up her purse that had landed on the floorboard. "I'll look for ID—"

"Morgan McAlister," he barked, his heart pounding as he worked on stabilizing her arm. "Richmond's Olympic swimming hopeful."

The *"shits"* and *"fucks"* abounded from the various rescue, fire, and police personnel around. Ignoring them, he looked up at Mary and gave the command. They rolled her into the back of the ambulance, Mary going into action while he put his foot on the back step to climb in. A hand at his arm stopped him.

Twisting, he bit out, "What?" causing Bob to wince.

"Jax...I'd be driving in the front...alone. I mean, this...I was driving when this happened—"

"Don't go there. This wasn't on you. But you gotta do this. You gotta man the fuck up and do this."

With a resolute nod, Bob hastened to the front as the doors closed. Turning to Mary, his voice broke, as he pleaded, "Please…"

"I'll take care of my end. You do what you can." He looked down at Morgan, his heart constricting, but Mary interrupted his thoughts. "Jax, Richmond General has the best orthopedic surgeons. We'll get her there."

He nodded, but his stomach churned. He had seen her arm. Saving it would be a priority, but his gut told him that her Olympic dreams had just been as crushed as her arm.

Her eyes were closed and as he settled at her head, he brushed the strands of her hair away from her face, noting the numerous cuts, some with small shards of glass still embedded. With shaky hands he took her blood pressure, barely listening as Mary called in the vitals to the hospital's ER. Knowing she was alerting them to the necessity of an orthopedic team, he also heard her give the patient's identity.

"Hey, Morgan," he said, softly, his hand automatically doing what was necessary for his job, but his heart firmly latched onto the woman and not just the patient. "Hey beautiful," he continued, as her eyes blinked open. "Can you tell me what happened?"

Tears continued to fall as she moaned, grimacing in pain.

"Okay, Morgan. We're almost to the hospital and you're going to be fine. You have some minor cuts from the glass and the other injuries will be looked at as well."

"Arm…"

Swallowing deeply, he said, "Yes, you have some injuries to your arm. The doctors will take a look and decide the best way to fix things." He forced his eyes to look at the piece of metal embedded deeply into her upper arm and knew that there was the possibility that it would need to be amputated. His entire body shuddered as though ice water ran through his veins.

Her eyes blinked closed again and he did not have the heart to try to get her to speak. Leaning down, he put his mouth close to her ear and whispered, "Morgan, babe, I'm here. Jaxon's here. I'm gonna see this through with you, I promise."

Her breathing relaxed as the pain medicine eased through her system and he shot a grateful glance up to Mary.

It was a rare treat for Morgan to float on a pool lounger in her parents' outdoor pool. She loved to float on her back, face up toward the sun with the buoyancy of the water supporting the float as she drifted over the pool. She spent so much time at the sports arena that when she had the opportunity to swim in her parents' outdoor pool, she often just floated her cares away, not spending the time practicing. She felt her body rocking slightly as the water moved her from side to side. Peaceful...so blissfully peaceful. No cares, no worries. The sun drifted behind the clouds as the sky grew darker. She tried to open her eyes when the sun was no longer on her, but her eyelids were too heavy. Hoping she had used sunscreen, she settled into the rhythmic rocking of the water, letting sleep take over. Her watery world was peaceful and she breathed deeply.

Jaxon looked out the back window, seeing they had arrived at the ER. The back doors were thrown open wide and he and Mary jumped down, pulling the stretcher along, racing inside with Morgan as they moved into an open ER bay. Mary reported to the nurse in charge as he listened to the doctor bark out orders.

Hands on his hips, he watched as Morgan's left arm was unwrapped and the orthopedic surgeon stalked into the room with a confident swagger. The doctor immediately began shouting orders to his team and within a few minutes, she was rolled out of the ER, heading to surgery.

All he could do was stand there and watch her pass by, his heart being rolled away at the same time. He stared at her blood covered arm, her russet hair surrounding her pale and cut face, and her closed eyes, hiding the blue from his gaze.

He felt, rather than saw, Mary standing by his side, guiding him out of the area. Keeping her voice low, she said, "I've talked to the Captain. He understands she's a personal friend of yours. He's clocked you off and says you can stay here. The hospital will call the family. Bob and I'll head back to the station."

Bob walked up to them, his face pale as he shook his head. "I had the siren on. I was entering the intersection slowly—"

"This is not your fault," he said, turning his attention to his partner.

"I keep thinking that if I had stopped, the truck might have stopped as well—"

"The police will want a report and the traffic cam will show what happened. Her accident was on the truck driver, not you."

Bob nodded and clapped him on the shoulder before

walking back down the hall. Mary held his gaze and finally said, "I'm sorry, Jax. Real sorry."

He watched the two of them exit the ER and looked down at his shirt, smeared with Morgan's blood. Racing to catch up to them before they left, he reached into the back of the ambulance, grabbing a small bag where he kept a second shirt. With a final pat on the doors, signaling they could pull out of the lane, he watched them drive away. Hustling back in, he headed to a staff shower, quickly washing off. He stood in the changing room for a moment, his bloody shirt in his hand. Covered in blood. Her blood. Wadding it up, he placed it in a bag before pulling on a clean RES shirt.

With his phone in his hand, he took the elevator to the surgical waiting room, texting Jayden as he went. Reaching the room, staring at the chairs filling the area, he gave his information to the waiting room reception-ist. Then, sitting down, he sucked in a huge breath. Swiping his hand over his face, he leaned back, settling in for the long wait, no longer wondering why his heart was pounding and his stomach was twisting in knots. The pull to Morgan was strong, something he had never felt toward another woman. Right or wrong, good timing or bad, it was there.

13

The elevator doors opened and Jaxon heard footsteps enter the room, but did not look up until a hand landed on his shoulders. Jerking his head upward, he heaved a sigh as Jayden sat next to him.

"What happened?"

Swallowing hard, he said, "Routine call out. Bob was driving, and I was coaching him through the intersection. Pickup truck speeded by, not heeding the siren or stopped cars and slammed into Morgan's car."

"Fuck, man. I'm sorry."

Nodding slowly, he said, "It's bad." Hearing Jayden's swift intake of breath, he shook his head. "Her arm, I mean. Her left arm was broken in several places and a piece of metal was embedded just above the elbow."

"But, she'll live?"

He lifted his gaze to his twin and said, "Yeah, but—"

"That's what you've gotta focus on, Jax," Jayden reminded, his gaze penetrating.

"I know that, but her career? Her life? Her whole

world is tied up in the pool and she's so close to the Olympics."

Nodding, Jayden held his gaze. "I get that, man, but right now, that's secondary to her being able to live a life, even if it's out of the water arena."

He swallowed deeply, hearing his twin's words and believing them, but wondering how Morgan would react when she realized what had happened. "I was right there. It happened right in front of me and there was nothing I could do about it. God, Jay, if I'd lost her?"

"Oh, Jesus, Jax. I'm sorry. When did you know it was her?"

"Not until I got into her car. But thinking about it now? Fuck, if I had known it was her car when she was struck, I don't know that I could have moved. As it was, once I saw her, I had to go into autopilot or my brain would have shut down."

"Naw, man. You've always pulled through when any of us needed you."

He tossed a grateful nod toward his brother but looked up as the elevator doors opened again.

"Where the hell is my daughter?"

The booming shout came from the man he recognized from the swimming arena. Morgan's father. Tall, barrel-chested, reddish hair, now with a little white mixed in. Dressed in a navy polo and khaki shorts, his cheeks were ruddy on a square head. A tall woman rushed in next to him, and with one look, he was sure she was Morgan's mother. Her hair, cut at chin level, was still mostly blonde. Athletic and slender body. Her face, with high cheekbones, blue eyes, and a delicate nose gave evidence that Morgan's beauty came from her.

Morgan's father continued to demand loudly for someone to tell him what was going on. The receptionist at the surgery waiting room desk attempted to quiet him but had little success.

"Sam!" Morgan's mother hissed, gaining his attention. Lowering her voice, she said, "Stop yelling. This poor woman doesn't know."

Seeing beyond the bluster, he recognized panic and concern etched in Morgan's father's face. Standing, he walked over. Already knowing the answer, he asked, "Are you here for Morgan McAlister?"

"Yes," her mother answered, her voice betraying her fear and, at the same time, her father barked, "Who the hell are you?"

"I'm Pamela McAlister, her mother," the woman rushed on. "This is Sam, her father. I see you work here—"

"No, ma'am. I'm with the RES...Richmond Emergency Services. I was the EMT who was at the accident scene with your daughter."

"Oh, thank God," Pamela breathed, grabbing her husband's arm for support.

"I know you...I saw you at the arena with Morgan," Sam said, his eyes narrowed on him. "What the hell were you doing with her?" Sam jolted as Pamela jerked on his arm. "What?" he asked, staring down at his wife.

"Will you, for once in your life, shut up and listen?" Pamela begged, her words clipped as her blue eyes sparked.

"Yes, sir," he interjected, bringing their eyes back to his face. "I have met your daughter. But today, I was on a call when your daughter was involved in an automobile accident. We were first on the scene and worked with the fire department to extricate her from her car, stabilizing her—"

"Oh, Jesus, sweet Jesus," Pamela breathed, her face paling.

"Ma'am, let's get you a chair." He waved his hand outward to indicate a few empty chairs nearby. She nodded and allowed him to lead, Sam following, still mumbling under his breath.

Once everyone was settled, he continued, "The impact on her car was on the driver's side, so the fire department had to cut the door off. I was able to be on the inside with her, as well as two of my co-workers.

"How bad was she injured?" Sam asked, interrupting his wife who asked at the same time, "Was she in pain?"

Keeping his eyes on Pamela, he nodded. "Yes, ma'am, at first. But we were able to get an IV in and give pain medication. Her vital signs were elevated, but we wanted to get her here so that she would be able to have surgery as quickly as possible."

"Surgery on what?" Sam asked, his ruddy cheeks becoming redder, his eyes wide with fear.

Lifting his gaze to her father, he replied, "Her arm. Her left arm."

"Fucking hell," Sam cursed, leaning heavily back in his chair, his eyes squinting closed as though in pain. "I'll sue the pants off whoever caused this to happen."

"Just her arm?" Pamela asked, ignoring Sam as her

eyes pinned onto his, hope burning bright. "Nothing else?"

"I'm not a doctor, so I can't answer that. But to the best that we could see, the airbag protected her body. She had minor lacerations on her face from the glass shattering, but her arm sustained the most injury."

"Oh, thank God," Pamela gushed. Leaning forward, she grabbed his arm, clutching it tightly. "Thank you so much for what you did for her."

"It's my job, ma'am," he said, not giving any indication to his real feelings.

She turned to her husband, and said, "Sam, isn't this good news?"

"Good?" Sam all but yelled.

Before he had a chance to say more, the receptionist called out, "Family of Morgan McAlister?"

Sam and Pamela jumped up from their seats and bolted forward. The receptionist led them to a door at the end of the room and they moved through it to speak to the surgeon, leaving him standing alone, staring after them.

He felt a hand on his shoulder and without turning, knew Jayden was there, giving him support. Blowing out a long, slow breath, he said, "Wish I could have done more."

"Jax, you did your job by giving aid and comfort to an injured woman, and one you care for at that. You came here and were able to give her parents some information to give them peace."

"Peace?" he bit out. "Don't think her dad has any peace right now."

Sighing, Jayden agreed. "Yeah, Mr. Warm and Fuzzy, he's not."

He scrubbed his hand over his face, tired to his bones and knowing he would not get a chance to see her until the next day. Twisting his head, he looked at Jayden and said, "Let's get outta here. I'll come to see her tomorrow."

Walking out into the sunshine, he piled into Jayden's SUV and leaned his head back against the headrest, exhaustion pulling at his body. As they drove out of the parking lot, his eyes drifted back to the hospital and he wondered how she was doing.

Inside Captain Burke's office the next day, Jaxon sat next to Bob. His sleepless night made his eyes bleary, but he focused on the meeting, knowing the importance of what was being discussed. Mary was included in the meeting as well, but since she had been in the back of the ambulance, she was unable to add to their report of what occurred at the intersection prior to the crash.

"So," Ted stated, "You slowed, had the siren and lights on, determined traffic had stopped and proceeded?"

Bob, clearly nervous, bobbed his head, glancing sideways toward him. "Yes. The intersection cleared, and I proceeded forward. The light was still green when I entered, and all traffic had stopped. A car to the left...uh...it was Ms. McAlister's vehicle, had pulled slightly into the intersection but stopped when she saw me. Then, from the right, a pickup truck moving at high speed, ran the red light and slammed into her driver's side."

Ted continued to take notes and said, "We will, of course, look at the traffic cam, but from the report you have given, it appears the fault lies with the driver of the truck. The police will be interviewing you as well, but I wanted to make sure we had our ducks in a row before the media circus becomes too extreme."

"Media?" Bob asked, his eyes wide.

"This would have been a blip on the evening news, but with the victim being someone famous, what with her Olympic trials coming up, the media will swarm us. I have the city's PR person involved, but I do not want any of my people talking to the media."

Ted pinned them with a hard stare, but it was unnecessary. The last thing he wanted to deal with was a media shit storm. His attention was snagged by Bob's heavy sigh. Glancing to the side, he watched as Bob's chin dropped to his chest.

"Damn," Bob said, "I keep playing it over and over in my mind, thinking of what I could have done differently."

"And what would that have been?" Ted asked, leaning back in his creaky seat, his penetrating gaze heavy on the younger man.

Bob's head shook side to side as he replied, "I don't know. Just waited…not entered the intersection at all. I mean, she had slowed down for me and the guy hit her car. If I had stopped, then she would have proceeded at normal speed and he—"

"He wouldda hit someone else, possibly killing them," he interjected, frustration spearing his fatigue. "He ran a red light at high speed. You can't know what wouldda happened."

"Jaxon's right," Ted said. "The driver of the truck was going to hit someone, driving recklessly like he was. You all were right there and because of that, Ms. McAlister's arm, and possibly life, was saved."

Dismissed, they walked out, Mary clapping him on the back, words not necessary between the two of them. She stopped Bob with a hand on his shoulder and said, "You wouldn't be a good man or a good EMT if this didn't bother you. Think about it, then put it to rest. Stay sharp for the next time."

Bob nodded, offering them a small smile before walking down the hall. All three were on leave for a day, Ted not taking a chance that his team was not in the best shape. Mary headed to the locker room as he jogged to the parking lot, hoping to see Morgan.

14

When underwater, the sounds from the world above were always muffled. Thankful for the peace, Morgan allowed herself to remain where the world was a little quieter. Words no louder than a whisper. No whistles. No coaches yelling. No questions from reporters. Just the muted sound of indistinct words.

Her body was blissfully weightless. Finally ready to emerge from her safe haven, when she attempted to kick her legs to rise to the surface, she simply continued to sink deeper.

"Morgan? Morgan, honey, can you hear me?"

She wondered why her mother was at the pool calling for her instead of her dad. The world was black, and she lifted her right hand in an attempt to straighten her goggles, but the only thing she accomplished was to drop her fingers to her face, no goggles found.

"Morgan!"

Unable to speak underwater, she drifted, letting the current take her far away. Down to the depths but, instead of a concrete pool bottom, she felt her feet drag along a sandy bottom. Suddenly a light shone down and she moved her body slightly, swimming along, the peace lulling her back to sleep.

Jaxon, with his hospital visitor's ID label stuck to his shirt, made his way down the hall to the nurses' station. Only one nurse was at the desk and she was on the phone. She lifted her hand to indicate for him to wait and he nodded. Leaning back against the counter, he heard voices coming from a nearby doorway labeled Family Consultation. He recognized Morgan's parents talking to a woman, but he was unsure if she were the surgeon or another of her doctors. Intending to wait for just a moment, he unashamedly eavesdropped.

"She is incredibly lucky," the doctor said. "The arm laceration did not sever the nerves completely, although there was significant muscle involvement. Her bones have been screwed back together with plates and—"

"You call this lucky?" Sam questioned.

"Sam," Pamela hissed. "Will you let her finish?"

"What I meant, is that as severe as the accident was, she could have died or had internal injuries that would have had more life impacting relevance. I know she is a swimmer—"

"A swimmer? A swimmer?" Sam bit out. "My daughter is scheduled for the final Olympic trials in a week. A week. Do you think she'll make that?" he asked, the facetious words dripping with anger.

"No, Mr. McAlister, I don't. I can't pretend to know how this feels for you and when she awakes, how she will feel. But, I do know that she is very lucky to be alive. Very lucky the paramedics arrived when they did. And, one day, hopefully, she'll be as strong as before and back in the water."

"Back in the—"

"Thank you," Pamela interrupted her husband.

Jaxon watched as a woman in a white doctor's coat walk out of the room, her face composed, and he wondered if she heard arguments like Morgan's dad offered all the time. Turning his back to the door, he heard her parents' footsteps as they left and her mother suggested they return later in the day after they had a chance to eat lunch. Her father continued to grumble, so he breathed a sigh of relief when the elevator door closed.

Finding out Morgan's room number from the nurse, he walked down the hall, stepping inside the dimly-lit room. Her face, pale against the pillow, captured his attention immediately. He was not thrown by the various machines and IVs attached, nor the way her left arm, swollen and propped on a pillow at her side, was covered in a mass of stitches and external pins. His medical training made it easy to separate the patient from the woman. The patient was in good hands. But the woman lying in the bed took his breath away.

He had never responded to a call for someone he knew. And he knew her. Intimately. In the short time they had been involved, he knew her laugh. Her smile. The way her eyes twinkled when they danced and the way they widened, the blue darkening, when she climaxed.

Blowing out his breath, he walked toward her, moving to her less injured side. His gaze shot to the monitors, noting her stable heart rate, oxygen rate, breathing. Her hospital gown was open on her left side, covering her breast but allowing her shoulder and arm full exposure.

He stared at her left arm, knowing the radius and ulna had multiple fractures. The surgery incision started at her wrist and made its way to her elbow, staples embedded in the red and angry skin. He knew that metal plates and screws would have been used to hold the pieces of bone together. In order to provide more stability, she had also been given an external fixture, pins protruding from her arm and screwed together with an external plate.

Another group of staples were above her elbow, sutured where the metal shard had been removed. Lacerations covered her shoulder and upper arm from the shattered glass, but none needed stitching.

The left side of her face and neck was also covered in tiny cuts, coated in antiseptic cream. He knew they would sting but heal quickly. Dropping his gaze back over her arm, his breath left his lungs slowly. He knew that was where the life-changing injury lie.

The image of her powerful strokes in the water hit him, knowing it would take months of healing and physical therapy to regain the strength in her arm. And, there was the very real possibility that she might not swim at Olympic competitions again.

A shift under the covers jolted his gaze back to her face and he startled to see blue eyes staring back at him. As she blinked several times, her face held no recognition.

Bending closer, he greeted, "Hey, Morgan. I'm Jaxon. I don't know if you remember me, but I—"

She licked her lips before opening her mouth. Only a croak emerged, and he reached to the table next to her bed and picked up a cup with a bent straw in it. Holding it to her lips, he encouraged, "Here's some water. Take a sip to help with your dry throat."

She obliged and sucked on the straw several times, swallowing gratefully. "Of course I know you," she breathed, her voice still a whisper, but with more strength. "Why are you..."

Instead of answering her question right away, he asked, "Do you know where you are?"

Her head barely moved but her eyes darted from side to side. "Hospital."

"Yeah, that's right. I wanted to come to see how you were doing. Do you remember anything?"

Again, she licked her lips and he could see her mind working behind her eyes as she attempted to process her surroundings. Her brow furrowed and she gave a slight shake of her head.

"You were in a car accident."

Her eyes gave no indication that she remembered what he was talking about.

"I was in the ambulance with you, so I knew you were here."

Her eyes widened slightly, and she whispered, "Accident?"

He watched as her gaze drifted down her body, landing on her arm propped on the pillow.

She gasped, croaking, "I can't feel my arm. I can't feel anything there."

"Morgan, babe," he called to gain her eyes back on him. "I'm going to call for the nurse, but they've got you on some pretty powerful painkillers." He pushed the call button and, in a moment, a pleasant-faced nurse walked in, her smile wide.

"Good to see you awake, Morgan. My name's Connie and I'm your primary nurse."

"I can't feel my arm," she said, her voice sounding stronger and more panicked.

"That's good, dearie," Connie said, moving over to check her injuries. "Right now, you're still on a morphine drip. The doctor will be in this afternoon and will determine when we go to the PCA pump so you can control the pain medication yourself."

"My arm..."

Connie shared a quick glance with him before saying, "Your arm was broken in several places, as well as needing surgery to repair the damage from a foreign object that had become embedded in the muscle. The doctor will go over the various surgical procedures, but they were able to save your arm."

"Save?"

Connie bent over, her voice soft and caring. "It was a pretty severe injury, Morgan. But thanks to the work of the paramedics and getting you here so soon, the surgeons were able to save your arm when you got to surgery."

He watched Morgan closely, knowing the pain medicine was making her fuzzy and unable to process the nurse's words quickly. Connie patted her arm and said, "Call me if you need me," before walking out.

He moved back to her side and sat in the chair, leaning over so she was able to see his face easily. "You understand what she was saying?"

She shifted her gaze from her arm to his face, her brow lowered in confusion. Shaking her head slightly, she closed her eyes.

He realized the morphine was pulling her under and knew that rest was the best thing for her at the moment. Bending over he placed a kiss on her forehead before heading back out the door. Just as he turned the corner, he noticed her parents appeared to be arguing by the nurses' station. Wanting to avoid her father's negativity, he ducked out of the way, waiting until they had left before he headed to the elevator.

Jaxon lay in bed that night, his arm thrown behind his head as he stared at the ceiling fan slowly turning. The media had not gotten hold of the story yet, but he knew it was only a matter of time. Snorting ruefully, he wondered how her dad would manage the frenzy when it hit. Rolling over to his side, his heart felt heavy at the thought of how Morgan would handle the storm.

He had spent several hours at his computer,

137

watching old video clips on YouTube of Morgan as she rose through the ranks of the swimming world. He viewed her as a child prodigy swimmer. Observed her through her awkward, early adolescent years—a time when her gawkiness disappeared as soon as she entered the water. Then he watched several of her college meets, admiring her strong body gliding through the water, smashing college times before moving to the national level of competition.

How the hell can I be consumed by a woman I barely know? The answer to that question did not come to him as he lay for hours, unable to sleep. He had two more days off and planned on going back to the hospital tomorrow. *Maybe I just feel sorry for her and, once she is better, I'll be able to move on.*

Rolling over to his other side, he heaved a sigh, knowing that whatever he felt for Morgan was not going to disappear quickly. And that thought, surprisingly, did not scare him...not even a little.

15

Stopping at the nurses' station, Jaxon asked, "Are Morgan McAlister's parents here? I thought I would visit when she had no other visitors."

"No, they came this morning and will probably be back later."

Nodding his appreciation, he walked down the hall and peered into the room. This time, Morgan was lying in bed with her head raised in an elevated position, her eyes pinned on the wall. Her left arm was still propped on a pillow to assist in reducing the swelling. He knew the doctors had her pumped full of antibiotics in an effort to reduce the risk of infection.

He stepped into the room and heard the sound of the TV in the corner. She never looked at him, keeping her eyes fastened to the newscast.

"Richmond's Olympic swimming hopeful, Morgan McAlister, was involved in a near fatal automobile accident two days ago, shattering not only her arm, but possibly her chances to swim competitively again. Her father and coach, Sam McAlister, stated that she is doing well, spirits are good, and she should be released in a day or so from the hospital. He assures us that she'll be back in the pool as soon as she is able and fully expects her to be right back at the Olympic trials in four years, stronger than ever. We certainly wish her the best with her recovery. And now for the weather—"

Channel flip.

"In national sporting news, powerful swimmer, Morgan McAlister, the American hopeful for the upcoming Olympic games, will not be able to compete due to a tragic car accident that left her fighting for her life. Her coach assures us she will be back, quoting her as saying, 'Swimming is my life'. This now opens the field for other swimmers, with her out of the competition until she recuperates and returns to the field of honor—"

Channel flip.

"Today, the swimming world was shocked to learn that Morgan McAlister—"

Walking over, he gently took the remote from her hand and clicked the TV off. Her eyes jumped to his and she scowled.

"Morgan. Don't. Don't watch the news."

She spoke, her voice soft, yet gravelly. *"Fighting for my life? I'll be back?"*

He winced at the guttural sound. "I think that the news just wants to make the story a headliner—"

"A headliner?" she said, her eyes shining with unshed tears.

He stepped closer, "Babe, please take it easy. This isn't good for you—"

A harsh chuckle came from deep inside her chest. "Good for me?" Shaking her head, she sucked in a ragged breath, her chin quivering.

As she continued to repeat what he said, he knew she was still in shock mentally, unable to understand all that had happened. "You need time to heal and then you can start physical therapy. It'll take a while, but you're in top physical condition—"

"Everything's gone."

He stood perfectly still, unsure how to respond.

She continued, blinking back tears. "All my life...all my work...everything. Gone."

"You can come back from this," he began.

She interrupted him again, nodding slightly as she fought to compose her face. "I know. I know." Looking at her swollen arm, with stitches crisscrossing from her wrist to almost her shoulder, she said, "I...I'll swim again. Time...it'll just take some time."

Morgan's gaze moved back to his, but he saw nothing in the blue eyes but shock and disbelief. He did not know what to say, so he chose to remain quiet, slipping into the chair next to her bed instead. He reached over and placed his hand on her right one, hoping to offer her strength through his touch.

For a second, he thought she was going to pull her hand away, but after a flinch, she let it stay in his hand. He watched as she swallowed several times and he wanted to tell her to go ahead and cry, but hesitated.

After a few minutes, she turned her head away from

him and closed her eyes. Whether she was sleeping or faking sleep, he was not sure. When it was apparent that she was not up for more talking, he stood, bent over and kissed her forehead. "I'll be back, Morgan," he whispered. "We'll get through this. I promise."

As the door closed behind him, Morgan allowed her tears to escape. Ever since she had woken up to this nightmare in the hospital, she had tried so hard not to cry. The narcotics had kept the pain at bay but as the fog in her brain had cleared and her eyes had focused, she'd stared at her swollen arm. The Frankenstein appearance of metal pins jutting from wounds and stitches holding it all together had been overwhelming.

The surgeon had explained the internal and external fixators, the metal rods and plates holding her bones together until they could heal.

Swiping at her face, she let out a shuddering breath and stared at the blank screen of the TV. Grateful Jaxon had turned it off, she winced at how she had clicked from one news station to the next, repeatedly hearing how her life had altered in an instant.

Hearing a noise at the door, she looked up as her mother walked into the room, a smile plastered on her worried face.

"Hey, darling, it's good to see you awake."

"Mom," she acknowledged, her gaze glancing over her mother's shoulder to watch for her dad's entrance.

"He's not with me right now," her mom explained.

"He's dealing with…uh, some things, and I thought I'd take the opportunity to visit alone. How are you feeling today?"

"I don't feel much," she admitted, refusing to look back at her arm. "The pain medicine still has me numb."

"Good, good, sweetheart. That's best for now."

Her foggy mind slid back to what her mother said about her father. "You said Dad was dealing with things?" she asked, tilting her head slightly.

Her mother's face contorted slightly as she sat in the chair recently occupied by Jaxon. Letting out a sigh, she replied, "Honey, he's giving some interviews to ease the way for you."

"Ease what way? I had the news on earlier. Why did he tell them I had a life-threatening accident? I don't understand."

"Oh, Morgan, he's just trying to feed the media to keep it from becoming a frenzy. Keep it at bay for now. At first, all we knew was that you were in an accident. We had no idea how bad it was, and frankly," her mom dropped her eyes to her arm, shuttering, "this isn't good."

A tear slid down her cheek, plopping on the ugly blue hospital gown as she dropped her eyes once more to her arm. "Not good," she repeated numbly.

A nurse bustled into the room and her mom took the opportunity to jump up, seemingly glad to have a chance to escape the heavy emotions. "Yes, yes. I'll let the nurse take a look at you and come back later with your father. By then, we can talk to the orthopedist again."

She watched as her mother walked out of the room and let out her held breath slowly. Too tired to think, she pressed the PCA button, allowing the pain medicine to course through her body, easing her way back to sleep. The last conscious thought she had was that it was going to be a long time before she was part of the swimming world again. And it was the only world she knew.

"I had no idea what to say to her."

Jaxon sat on Miss Ethel's sofa, scrubbing his hand over his face, his shoulders hunched as he unburdened himself. The familiar room with its corresponding scent of roses gave him more peace than he had had since the accident. Sucking in a deep breath, he added, "I'm just not good at this."

Her sharp, grey eyes pinned him as she asked, "Good at what?"

He shook his head, self-recrimination pouring from him. "Knowing what to say to make someone feel better. I know the medical stuff, how to take care of someone until we get them to the hospital, but afterward, I'm never around them. Not like a nurse or doctor who knows what to do. Hell, not like my brothers."

She lay her knitting needles in her lap and tilted her head to the side. Pinning him with her grey eyes, still sharp behind her wire-framed glasses, she said, "Jaxon, I can usually read all my boys, but you just jumped from not being like nurses to not being like your brothers. Son, I need you to give me a little more to go on."

Leaning forward, he rested his forearms on his knees, clasping his hands together. Dropping his head, he sighed. "When Rosalie was in the hospital, Zander read to her. Gave her a lifeline until she was conscious again. Rafe was always connected with Eleanor, giving her what she needed when she doubted herself. And Cael? Jesus, when his niece, and then Regina, went through their cancer treatments, he was there, giving them comfort all through the procedures."

Nodding slightly, she leaned back in her chair. "Ah. And you think you don't have that ability."

"I know I don't," he bit out. "She's losing everything that's important to her, and I just sat there, not saying anything, like some bump on a log, completely useless."

They sat quietly, the sound of knitting needles clacking once again filling the room.

After a few minutes, Miss Ethel said, "Do you remember when Asher fell on the sidewalk while running and skinned both legs?"

Looking up, he watched as her fingers never faulted, even though her eyes were on him. Nodding, he said, "Yes, ma'am."

"You jumped in and took your shirt off, made Cael take his off as well, and quickly tied them around his bleeding legs. Your action was what was needed at the moment. Later, that evening, Zander read to him, taking his mind off his injuries, but it was you that got the immediate help to him."

He sat quietly, unsure what she wanted him to take from his.

"You wrote a letter to me when you were in the Army and had been out on a medical mission. You talked of having to take cover when the rescue you were on took a turn for the worse and it was touch and go as you drove the ambulance back to the base."

"Miss Ethel," he began.

"You're a man of action, Jaxon," she said, halting his words. "You were there when Morgan needed a man of action and you probably saved her arm."

Nodding, he said, "I get that, but what about now?"

"Just be what she needs."

"How do I know what that is?" he asked, his heart heavy.

"She'll let you know what she needs with each stage."

"Stage?"

"Of grief," she replied easily, lifting her gaze to his. "Jaxon, grief is the emotion we have when we lose something dear, not just to death. We grieve the loss of relationships, employment, our health. Shock, denial, anger, bargaining, depression, and finally acceptance."

"So, she'll go through each of those in order?"

"Oh, no, my dear. Our grief journey is never that easy. She may skip one to return to it at a later time. She may stay in one stage for a long time and then hardly spend any time in another stage." Holding his gaze, she asked, "What emotion did you see with her today?"

"Shock and some anger coming through," he admitted. "I know a lot of that is from the pain meds, but it was as though she could not quite believe she was injured." Looking down, he nodded. "Shock…that's the first stage, isn't it?"

"You recognize shock as a medical term, but it is very much a reaction to emotional upheaval. Right now, her mind cannot process the accident, much less the repercussions."

He leaned back, cracking his knuckles, a grin slipping out as she winced at the noise. "Sorry."

She shook her head, saying, "You and Jayden were my only two boys who cracked knuckles. You, to relieve stress. Always drove me crazy." Sobering, she said, "Give yourself a break, Jaxon, when it comes to Morgan. Just realize that she will have a lot of ups and downs as she deals with the aftermath of the accident. Be supportive. Don't patronize. Don't let her give into depression, while understanding that she will need to have days where she feels depressed."

Snorting, he quipped, "That's all?"

Setting her needles down once more, she stood, and he immediately jumped up to assist. She patted his arm and said, "You'll be fine. Just keep being you, Jaxon."

She walked him to the door and added, "Don't let her push you away. Her father has practically had her living in the water her whole life. Now, she needs to figure out what to do on her own."

He bent to kiss her cheek before he headed out to his motorcycle. Roaring down the street, he thought of her words. *Don't let her push you away.*

16

―――――――――

"Morgan, at this time, we don't know what all you'll be able to do, but we're going to start as soon as you're able and work on occupational therapy as well as physical therapy."

Morgan stared at the young woman standing next to her bed, hearing the words but unable to process them quickly. "Occupational therapy?"

Theresa, the physical therapist, nodded. "She'll start with simple things like making sure you can hold a spoon, fork, and knife. It's good that you're right handed so that writing will not be impacted. Being able to button a blouse, pull on socks and pants, things like this are what the occupational therapist will want to work on first."

"Socks." Her voice was soft, her mouth hanging open in stunned silence after the one word was uttered.

Theresa's smile slipped, and she stepped closer. "Morgan, I know who you are and what this accident has cost you. I won't pretend to understand what you must be feeling right now to have your Olympic hopes dashed at this time."

"But she'll be swimming again just as soon as she's cleared to get back into the pool, right?"

Their heads swiveled in unison, seeing her father walking through the door, her mother right behind. Before either of them could speak, he continued.

"I've talked to her surgeon, who admits that he doesn't know what she will be able to do, but I know my daughter. We want an aggressive regiment of PT to strengthen the muscles once the bones are healed and then she can continue with PT in the water. I'm lining up the best sports medical evaluation for when she's ready."

"Sir, I understand your desire, but it'll be a long road and we need to focus on one thing at a time. With the nerve damage—"

He drew himself up, announcing, "Missy, I'll take the word of the orthopedist over a hospital physical therapist any day."

"Dad...please stop."

Three pairs of eyes landed on her and she shifted uncomfortably, wincing at the pain. "I don't want to hear arguing now. I can't take it."

Theresa smiled and patted her shoulder. "We'll talk later when your doctor is here." With a nod toward Sam and Pamela, she walked out of the room.

Before she had a chance to speak, her father said, "I'm not having negativity around you, Morgan. This is a setback, but one that can be overcome. The Olympics this year are shot to hell, but with the right spin on this and a lot of work, you can be billed as the comeback queen."

His words landed like a punch to her gut and she grimaced. She looked down at her useless arm and for the first time, tried to move her fingers. Nothing. She felt nothing. *No...no...this can't be right. It's the pain meds. They're keeping me from being able to move.*

Panic slithered through her, snaking from her gut to her heart. Her breath caught in her throat, but she let it out slowly, using the breathing techniques learned from years in the pool.

"Morgan," her mother said softly, and she shifted her eyes to her.

"We don't know anything yet, honey, and there's no reason to think you won't be back to one hundred percent."

Nodding, her head moving in a jerky motion, she agreed. "I know. It'll take time."

"Time and hard work," her father interjected.

"I'm not ready for hard work," she whispered, the panic returning.

"Morgan—"

"Sam, hush," her mother said, placing her hand on his arm. "Let's let her rest some more and come back later when the surgeon is here." Turning back to her, she added, "When you get discharged, I'll have clean sheets on your bed and will make sure you're comfortable."

It took a few seconds for her mother's words to penetrate. Jerking, she responded, "Why? I've got my apartment."

"No need to pay for your apartment when you need someone to look after you," her mother assured.

Before she had a chance to respond, her father butted in with, "That way I can monitor your progress and can make sure the therapists are on the right track."

Sucking in a quick breath through her nose, she said nothing, but her heart sank at the thought of spending even one night in her parents' house and under her father's thumb. "We'll see. Right now, I just want to get back to my apartment."

She watched as her father pursed his lips, wanting to argue but holding back. He patted her leg before turning and walking out as her mother bent to kiss her cheek, sending her a sad smile. "Baby, it'll be fine." Turning, her mother followed her father out.

The room was quiet, the monitors now unhooked, the PCA pump no longer in place as the nurses were giving her pain medicine by mouth and no longer intravenously. She blew out a long breath again, her mind exhausted from all the information slamming into her.

She had no idea how much time passed as she stared into space. A noise at the door caused her to look up and, seeing Jaxon standing there, she was unable to keep her lips from curving.

"Hi," she said softly. Too exhausted to care about her dirty hair, horrid hospital gown that today was a pea-green, and the fact that she must look like an alley cat that had been in a fight, she offered a smile.

He smiled in return and walked into her room, stopping at the bed. "How's it going today?"

Shrugging, she said, "Okay." Seeing his lifted

eyebrow, her heart plunged, and she amended, "Well… maybe not so good."

He sat in the seat next to her bed and reached for her right hand. Rubbing his thumb over her hand, he gently ordered, "Tell me."

She hesitated, but he was patient and she finally blurted, "I have no idea what's going to happen." He remained silent and she continued to unburden. "A physical therapist was just here and told me that once the bones heal I will start therapy. And that includes learning how to hold eating utensils and put on my clothes." She watched his face for signs of shock and disbelief, but his gaze remained steady. Swallowing hard, she added, "But my father has plans for me to become the Olympic comeback queen."

That got her a blink and as she continued to stare at him, she saw a flash of anger in his eyes, but his hand continued to offer her steady comfort.

"The accident was days ago, and they'll release me soon. My parents want me to go to their house, but I can't live there." Her voice broke and she swallowed several more times to gain control over her emotions. "I've got a little apartment and my roommate is getting married and has already moved out."

"What do *you* want?" he asked, his voice soothing and gentle.

"To be unbroken and heading to the Olympics," she answered honestly.

"I know you do," he agreed. It was clear from his voice his heart was aching for her. Visibly strengthening, he clarified, "But I meant, what do you want to do after you're discharged."

Shaking her head, she thought for a moment. "I just know I don't want to be at my parents' place. My mother will hover and be watchful of my every movement, wondering what my father's reaction will be. My dad will be on me to get in the pool every second I can. He means well, but he's just...*too* focused, you know?" She felt tears prick her eyes and she whispered, "I just can't do that. I can't handle that right now. Every second will be an in-my-face reminder."

"Then, I think the answer is obvious. You need to go back to your place."

She stared at him but observed only sincerity in his eyes. "That simple?"

"Well, I think the *answer* is that simple. I think the execution of it will take some planning."

She cocked her head at him, her brow knit in question.

He chuckled, his thumb still moving circles over her hand. "What I mean is that you'll need some help with things for a while. Cleaning, grocery shopping, cooking, etc. For a bit, you'll be one-handed, but you'll get the hang of doing what you need to do."

"I'll be fine, Jaxon," she said, hoping her voice was as sure as her words as she stared at her arm. "I think I'll be better out of the hospital. This place makes me feel weak."

"Babe," he said, and her eyes jumped to his. She liked that he called her babe. It could be such a throwaway word and, yet, when said the way he said it, she felt warm inside. And that was something she had not felt in days.

"You are anything but weak. But, you're not strong yet. You gotta take care of yourself and listen to those who have your best interest at heart."

Staring dumbly at him, not understanding what he meant, she waited for him to explain. Instead, he stood and leaned over her, both hands planted on the mattress next to her.

Leaning closer, he said, "Your doctor wants your arm to heal. Your therapists want you to get strong again and be able to have a full life. I know your dad wants you to swim competitively again, but his wishes need to take a back seat to the doctor and therapists. They'll push you at the appropriate times."

She knew he was right but secretly wondered if it was possible. Looking up at him, she blurted, "Why are you here? With me?" She watched as his brow lowered, and she rushed on. "I'm nobody now."

Anger flashed in his eyes before being replaced by frustration. "Morgan, when I was with you I had no idea you were anyone other than a grad student. My desire to be with you had nothing to do with your swimming."

Her face fell as she mumbled, "Sorry. I guess I just feel…adrift."

He leaned down a few inches and rested his lips on her forehead, the skin underneath his cool. He kissed her softly and said, "Rest some more, babe. I'll be back because I want to be back. What you do means nothing to me. It's who you are on the inside that captured me."

She watched as he walked out the door and

wondered what he saw on the inside of her, because right now, all she felt was a mess.

Connie assisted Morgan back into the bed after making a trip to the bathroom. Faced with trying to pull her panties down just to sit on the toilet, Morgan now understood what Theresa was alluding to. Her left-hand's fingers would not cooperate and her arm, with the metal pins and plate sticking out, was difficult to maneuver. *How am I ever going to manage in my apartment alone?*

With a sheen of sweat covering her face, she settled back into the bed, pondering her future, uncertainty now mixing with anger. A noise at the door had her looking up in surprise.

"Nonnie!" The first genuine smile lit her face as she watched her grandmother being rolled into her room by another elderly woman.

Her arm still hurt like a bitch, but she raised her bed up to a sitting position and swung her legs around to stand.

"My gracious, Morgan, get back into bed."

She continued to maneuver out of bed without wobbling too much and bent to give Nonnie a right-handed hug, holding her left arm away from them. Standing, she blinked the tears in her eyes away as the comforting, rose-scented perfume filled her nostrils. Her grandmother's face had a touch of powder and her cheeks were pinkened with a blush. Her white hair was coiffed, and she exuded her casual elegance. Closing her eyes, it was easy to pretend she was at Nonnie's nursing home, well and whole, visiting as usual.

Smiling as she glanced to the woman behind her, her smile faltered as she tried to place the familiarity of her face. Her white hair was pulled back in a bun and she had wire-rimmed glasses that did nothing to hide the grey-blue eyes smiling at her.

"This is my friend, Ms. Wiseman," Nonnie said. "She and I met many years ago and she still comes to visit me."

"It's nice to meet you, Ms. Wiseman," she greeted, now remembering having passed her in the hall the last time she visited Nonnie in the nursing home. "Please have a seat," she offered before sitting back on her bed.

Focusing on Nonnie again, she said, "I still can't believe you've come." Her grandmother's gaze dropped to her arm and she heaved a sigh. "I know. It looks horrible."

"I'd say it looks painful," Nonnie said, the creases deepening in her face.

"Yeah..." agreed said, not knowing what else to say.

"When will they let you go home?" Ms. Wiseman asked.

"I'll probably stay two more days and then I'll be discharged. The surgeon had to not only piece the bones back together with screws and metal, but there was some nerve involvement as well."

"My precious girl, you're alive," Nonnie exclaimed. "That was all I could think about when your mother called me."

Nodding, she forced her lips into a smile. Nonnie stared hard at her and she dropped her gaze, unable to bear the scrutiny.

Lowering her voice, Nonnie said, "I know you're hurting, little mermaid."

A sob erupted from deep within her chest and she pressed her right hand over her mouth to still her quivering lips.

"But, you have to know that you are more than just a swimmer. You're a daughter and a granddaughter, and we know you are so much more than just what the news calls you. You're alive and that's all that matters."

Nodding, silent tears slipping down her cheeks, she looked up in surprise as Ms. Wiseman handed her a box of tissues. Offering her a watery smile of thanks, she wiped her eyes and blew her nose. "I know, Nonnie. I'm just a little lost right now."

"Of course you are, Morgan. But you must take care of you and don't worry about the future."

"Dad says—"

"Fiddle-sticks on your father," Nonnie bit out, eliciting a chuckle-snort from Morgan. "He's grieving over the loss of the dream too, but he needs to take a back seat to your healing."

Wiping her nose again, she nodded. "I know." Lifting her gaze to Ms. Wiseman, she said, "I'm sorry for us meeting this way."

"Oh, my dear, don't apologize. I wanted to bring your grandmother here as soon as I knew you could enjoy her visit." Stepping closer, she lifted her thin hand to her cheek and said, "Ernest Hemingway said in A

Farewell to Arms, 'The world breaks everyone, and afterward, many are strong at the broken places.' You, my dear, will become stronger in the places you feel the most broken."

She stared in dumbfounded curiosity at her grandmother's friend for a moment, unable to discern how she could feel strong while so broken, but a strange peace slid through her at the words. Nodding slightly, she bent to kiss Nonnie's cheek and watched the two women leave her room.

Alone once more, she wondered how she would ever feel strong again.

17

Morgan sat on the edge of the bed, her small bag packed, waiting for her parents to come for her discharge. Hearing heavy steps coming into the room, she looked up, surprised to see Jaxon. His thick, dark hair was pulled back into a ponytail and he was wearing his navy pants and Richmond Emergency Services polo, his biceps straining at the arms. A flash of memory hit her, of his face leaning over hers as he powered into her body the night they spent at his place. That memory was quickly replaced by the one of his face leaning over her's as she sat in her car. She did not remember the pain or fear…just his face near hers.

"What are you doing here?" she asked, unable to keep a small smile from her face.

"I knew you were being discharged today and wanted to see you again."

"You can come by to visit me at home, you know," she blurted, hope attempting to blossom in her chest.

Grinning, he walked over to her and sat on her right

side, careful of her arm. "I'm glad. I wasn't sure if…well, if you wanted to keep seeing me."

She reached out and touched his arm, the skin feeling warm underneath her cold fingers. "I don't want you to feel obligated." She jerked her hand back, her gaze landing in her lap. "I mean, it's been nice for you to check on me, but you don't—"

"Morgan," he said, his voice soft. He reached over and lifted her chin with his knuckles, turning it gently so that her eyes landed on his. "I want to see you. This isn't pity. This is me wanting to get to know you better. Wanting to spend time with you. If that's okay?"

She licked her lips, the desire to lean in for a kiss overwhelming. She nodded, uncertain of so much in her life except for wanting to see him again. "I'd like that. I…uh…have no idea what things will be like for a while, but…uh…well, I'd like to—"

"Ready to go, Morgan?" Her nurse walked into the room, her hands full of discharge papers. "Your parents are bringing around their car and I need you to sign these, then we can roll you out."

She winced, mouthing *sorry*, and he chuckled.

"I've got to get to work anyway. I'll see you soon. Take it easy today, okay?" He bent over as he always did when leaving but, this time, instead of kissing her forehead, he lightly touched his lips to hers.

"It's the only way I can take it," she joked, her heart lighter than the previous days. She watched him wink before he walked out.

"You're fine, Bob. Stop agonizing." Jaxon had been back in the driver's seat of the ambulance for the past several days, but insisted that Bob take over as a driver once again. He knew the best way for Bob to get over his fear after the accident, was to get back into the action. But, then, he also knew that at each intersection, he found his fingers twitching, replaying Morgan's accident over in his head.

Bob wiped the sweat from his face and handled the ambulance perfectly. They pulled up outside the home and met the screaming mother as she came running around the house from the back yard.

"He's here, he's here! Oh, God, help him!"

Grabbing their equipment, they raced to the back yard and his gaze landed on a trampoline with part of the safety net crushed in on one side. A young boy, lying prone and unmoving on the ground, was next to the trampoline.

"Goddamn death trap," he muttered under his breath, hearing Mary cursing as well. They dropped to the ground, immediately securing the child's neck in a brace.

As they went to work, Mary called into the hospital, explaining the child's condition. He was glad to see the boy's eyes blinking open, but was terrified at his lack of movement from any extremities. Knowing a broken neck was a possibility, they followed protocol, with help from the arriving fire department, and moved him to a gurney.

A policewoman had taken the mother to the side of

the yard, attempting to calm her while finding out what happened.

"He was just jumping," the mother cried. "Then the whole side fell over and he screamed. I got out here and saw him like this." She began screaming again, falling to her knees.

Moving the child quickly, they lifted him into the ambulance. Turning to the policewoman, he said, "Bring the mom. We need room to work in here." That was his way of letting her know a hysterical mother would hinder more than help.

Bob did not question about the driving, immediately jumping behind the wheel, and he shot up a prayer of thanks. Minutes later they pulled into the ER ambulance lane and were met with the hospital services. As they whisked the boy off, he noted the policewoman escorting the mother inside and blew out a huff.

Looking up as he finished his report, he watched one of the nurses smile and walk over. "Hey, Shauna."

"Trampoline?" she asked, her head jerking in the direction the mother was heading.

"Yeah," he sighed. "They come with warnings, but I wonder how many parents would buy the damn things if they really knew the risks."

"I made a bunch of my friends watch a video compilation of backyard trampoline accidents and every one of them declared them off limits for their kids."

Mary walked over and added, "But what about those indoor trampoline parks or playgrounds? My grandkids were pissed when I wouldn't let them go to a birthday party at one of those. Kids crashing into each other left and right. Jesus, it's an ER nightmare."

He finished the report, handed the tablet to Shauna, and followed Mary back out to the ambulance. Looking at the clock, he wondered how Morgan was doing at home and hoped the afternoon passed quickly, so he could check on her.

Morgan sat in the back seat of her father's SUV, her left arm resting on a pillow in her lap to keep from bumping it on the car. She was dressed in sweatpants and an old, large t-shirt that had the left arm cut out of it. She made sure to take extra pain medication before leaving the hospital and, while it was not a narcotic, she was glad for any relief from the pain.

Her father was grumbling as he drove, still discontent that she was not going home with them. Her mother kept twisting around to check on her and her facial muscles were tired of attempting a smile.

Twenty minutes later, they arrived and she carefully exited the vehicle while her parents carried her small bag into her first floor, tiny, two-bedroom apartment. Now that her roommate had moved out, she thought the space would feel bigger, but the reality was that all the rooms were little. Her bedroom held a bed and a dresser. The bathroom at the end of the short hall was just a tub, toilet, and single sink. The living room held a sofa, an end table with a lamp, and one chair, all facing the TV on the wall. The kitchen was a small U-shaped room, with counters on each side and a breakfast bar where their stools were.

Glancing down at her almost immobile arm, she wondered how she would be able to maneuver without slamming it into a wall or furniture. Pushing those thoughts aside, she sank gratefully onto her sofa, keeping the pillow in her lap.

Her mother sat on the sofa, close but not too close, and said, "Honey, I've filled your freezer with some pre-made meals, but I don't want you to feel alone. We'll be back to check on you daily and are just a phone call away."

Her father sat on the edge of the chair, his hands clasped together. Clearing his throat, he said, "Morgan, I know this has all been a shock and disappointment... for all of us."

She looked up at him, seeing uncertainty etched into the lines on his face. Lines she had not noticed until the last few days.

"Your mother keeps telling me not to push too hard, but I don't want this to be your defining moment."

Unsure how to respond, she remained quiet, her gaze pinned on him.

"I know you have to heal before you can start rigorous training, but as soon as you're able, the therapists can work with you. I just don't want you to give up. You've had a dream, a goal, for so long. This is a setback, but not the end."

Swallowing deeply, she forced her words to sound more upbeat than she felt. "Sure, Dad."

Her simple words seemed to be what he was looking

for and he smiled, heaving a sigh of relief. "Well, good, good. I wish you'd come back home, but just know that if this is too much for you to handle, then we're just a phone call away." He stood, seemingly proud of her for not falling apart.

Her mother stood with him but leaned over to kiss the top of her head. "I can't believe that you're insisting on staying here alone."

"Mom, there's little I can do now but rest. I've got my own bed, my own pillow, and I'll be fine. I'll talk to you tomorrow."

With a final one-sided hug, she watched as they walked out the door. Throwing the latch, she leaned her back to the door and sucked in a huge breath. *Alone.* For the first time since the accident, she was completely alone. Sick of the hospital and the constant people coming in and out of her room, this was what she wanted. *Isn't it?*

Blowing out the breath she had been holding, she moved into her kitchen and pulled down a glass, filling it with water. *One-handed. I can do this.* Taking a long drink, she moved back to the sofa. Hating the absolute quiet, she reached for the remote and turned on the TV. Her face was on the news, so she quickly skipped over that channel. Not wanting to watch any sports, she left it on the cooking channel, the sound low. Leaning back on the sofa, she tried to find a comfortable position to rest her arm. Unable to find one, she settled in, hoping the pain medicine would last until the evening.

An hour later, she felt the walls closing in. Unable to go outside her apartment for fear of bumping her arm, she sat. The evening sky darkened and the illumination from the TV became the only light in the room as night descended. She had not moved from her place on the sofa and as perky chefs darted around the TV kitchen, whipping up culinary delights, her mind did not focus on anything but the cold that began slithering around her.

She tried to not look at her arm but with it propped on the pillow in her lap, it was hard not to see the still-reddened skin puckered around the metal frame holding it together.

The days in the hospital had run together and she could no longer remember what day it was. She reached for her phone, checking the date. Sucking in a quick breath, she realized the next swim trials had been yesterday. Surprised her father had not mentioned the events, she flipped the channel over to ESPN. It only took a few minutes before the results were on the screen. The TV filled with the large swimming pool and the splash of water as the swimmers dove in. Skipping to the results, she watched as her competitors finished, all swimming over to congratulate the winners, now the official Olympic team.

She recognized all of them since she swam with them for years in various meets. She heard the cheers. She could even swear she smelled the chlorine. She should have been there. That should have been her, excited to be one step closer to her dream. Maybe if she had given it more, given it everything, like her dad, this would not have happened. If only she had a second chance. She would be completely dedicated, never second guessing a thing. Never wondering about the friends she did not have or the love life she was giving up.

Jaxon's face came to mind and a sob caught in her throat. His warmth, his strength, his heart. Would she really trade him for a second chance?

Her phone pinged an incoming text. Looking down, she saw it was from him. Laughing without mirth, her eyes watering, she read,

Do you feel like company or are you resting?

Her finger instinctively hovered over the *yes* reply, but she halted, her throat burning with unshed tears. Turning her phone to silent, she tossed it to the side.

Sitting in the dark, with the flickering light from the TV showcasing the loss of her dreams, she felt more alone than she ever had in her life. The death of a dream crept along her spine and for the first time, she realized life was never going to be the same, regardless of what her father wanted.

And the tears came.

Jaxon sat on his motorcycle parked on the street outside Morgan's apartment, waiting to see if she would answer his text. He could see the mostly dark interior, lit only by the flickering lights of what, he assumed, was her TV. *Maybe she's asleep. She probably took a pain pill. Hopefully, she's resting.*

He knew he should head home but hated to leave. *Her world's turned upside down.* It was as though he could feel her anguish through the walls. Walking to her front door, he placed his hands on the wood, his fingers hesitating at the doorbell. Hearing a slight noise from the inside, he glanced behind him to assure himself that he was alone, and placed his ear against the door.

The sound of a sob hit him and he closed his eyes. Knocking softly, he was not surprised when she did not answer. Turning his back to the door, he slid down, resting his hands on his bent knees.

Pulling out his phone, he began to type, a quote from author Jon Katz coming to mind.

Please Morgan, know that I care. "Friends are part of the glue that holds life and faith together. Powerful stuff."

After a moment, he heard a slight shuffling on the other side of the door. He jumped to his feet so that she could see him if she peeked through the peephole.

"Jaxon?"

He heard her soft voice and closed his eyes for a second. "Yeah, I'm right here."

"I don't really feel like seeing anyone right now. I'm…uh…getting ready for bed."

"Sure, that makes sense. I just wanted you to know that I was here. I'll come back tomorrow."

"Jaxon, I don't know that I'm ready for…I…don't know…I…"

He listened as her voice drifted off and said, "Morgan, you don't have to be ready for anything. But, I'm not going anywhere. I'll be back tomorrow, and the day after that, and the day after that, until you're ready for company. So, take care and sleep well."

He held up his hand to the door and waited, unsure for what, but just knowing he wanted to touch something that was hers even if it was not her.

On the inside, Morgan watched through the security hole and lifted her right hand, placing it flat on the door as well. Closing her eyes, she could swear she felt his palm against hers. Breathing deeply, she watched as he turned and walked to his motorcycle. She continued to watch as he tossed his hand up in a wave before roaring down the road.

And the tears came anew.

18

Morgan shot her mother a text and asked her parents not to visit today, saying that she was resting well and would see them another day.

The reality was she had barely slept. She had been sure that leaving the hospital would allow her to finally rest but, unable to find a comfortable position last night, she had given up on her bed and moved back to her sofa where at least the drone of the TV kept her company.

Standing, she walked into her kitchen and stared at the bottle of pain reliever. Having forgotten to ask her mother to open them before she left the day before, she fiddled with the bottle, unable to unsnap the child-proof cap. Blinking back tears, she moved into her bedroom and pulled out clean clothes. Carrying them with her right hand, she walked into her bathroom.

Staring at the shower, she flipped on the water, hoping she would be able to at least wash away the hospital smell from her hair. Exhausted after wrestling one-handed with her clothes to get them removed, she moved into the shower. Just as she turned around to keep her arm from getting wet, she bumped it on the shower door.

Pain sliced through her and she dropped to her knees, the water hitting her in the face. Barely able to reach up to turn off the water, she crawled onto the soft bath mat and curled into a ball, tears of pain and anguish flowing freely.

Her phone buzzed and she now hoped her mother was calling to say she was coming over anyway. Answering without looking at the caller ID, she cried, "I can't do it. I can't do it alone in this tiny space. I need help."

"Morgan?"

She heard Jaxon's voice and cringed. "Oh," she sniffed, wiping at her tears, but unable to stop them. The nerves in her arm felt on fire and another sob slipped out.

"Baby, I'm outside. Can you let me in?" Her breath hitched and he said, "I can jimmy your lock. Do you give me permission? Morgan, please."

Still curled up on the bathmat, pain and frustration overtaking her mind, she mumbled, "Mhh hmm."

Within a minute she heard footsteps approaching and before she had time to process what was happening, he was there, his face filled with concern.

"Oh, sweetheart," he said softly, throwing a large, soft towel over her shoulders, covering her now shivering naked body. Kneeling, he gently assisted her to her feet, wiping her tears with his thumbs.

Maneuvering her carefully down the hall, he had her sit on the edge of her bed. Quickly arranging the pillows behind her and on her left side where her arm could rest, he pulled the covers up over her.

Looking up at him with watery eyes, she whispered, "I couldn't get the Ibuprofen bottle open."

Without a word, he turned and hurried to the kitchen, returning with several pills and a glass of water. She took them, swallowing the pills gratefully.

Setting the glass on the nightstand, Jaxon sat next to her on the bed. Leaning forward, he brushed a long strand of hair behind her ear. Her eyes were dull, the color of a stormy sea, with dark circles underneath. Her hair, limp and tangled. Her face, pale and tear-stained.

"Talk to me, Morgan. Tell me what you need," he coaxed.

She sucked in a shuddering breath and shrugged her shoulders slightly. "I'm lost," she said, her voice whisper soft. "So fucking lost."

He shifted around to the other side, careful to not jostle her arm. Thinking of what Miss Ethel said, it was obvious that Morgan had slid from denial to sadness, but he was not sure where anger or bargaining was. *Miss Ethel said no one goes through the stages of grief the same way. Just be what she needs at each stage.*

Deciding to let her draw comfort from his body, he pulled her gently over so that her head rested on his chest. Wrapping his arms around her, his hand moved slowly up and down her back. "Just talk, babe. Anything that needs to come out, let it out."

Morgan said nothing for a few minutes, the only

sound in the room her ragged breathing. Soon, the gentle touch of his hand on her back began to penetrate the cold and she said, "Nothing's the same. A week ago, I was on top of the world. Now...I'm nowhere."

He said nothing, so she continued. "At first, all I felt was numb. My arm was numb, and my mind was numb. Now, all I feel is pain." Her breath shuddered again. "I can't find a position to sleep. I can't take a shower. If I bump my arm at all, the pain is so intense."

"What about staying with your parents...at least for a little while?"

Snorting, she took the proffered tissue and wiped her nose. "I'm so tempted. Just to go and let my mom smother me, do everything for me, but then there's my dad. He's relentless on my getting better as soon as possible so that I can start intense training again. It's always in my face now what a disappointment I am. He doesn't mean it like that, but that's how it feels."

His hand stopped rubbing for a few seconds, then he asked, "I don't want to bring up an unpleasant subject, but you can't participate in this year's Olympics, so the next one is four years away. Why is he so impatient?"

Letting out a long, slow breath, she explained, "People who did not get chosen for this Olympics are already in training for the next one. They'll work hard for four years to be ready. Every month I'm not in peak physical condition, there's someone out there who is gaining on me."

A sob ripped from deep in her chest again and she said, "I can't think about it. I don't want the constant reminder from Dad that I'm losing ground every single day. But I may have to. I've been home less than twenty-four hours and I'm a mess. I can't do anything on my own." Another sob hitched her voice as she added, "I'm so tired. So fucking tired. I'm trapped between worlds and don't know which way to turn."

"Oh, babe," he said, holding her tight. "You have so much more healing to do and you're not giving yourself time to do it."

"But, I don't know that I can do it here," she said, defeat oozing from her soul.

"Then let's go somewhere where you can."

Lifting her head, she twisted around to stare at his blurry face with her watery eyes. "Huh?"

"My place," he suggested, sure and definite.

Wiping her nose again, she sniffed, her brow lowered in confusion. "Your place?"

"Yeah. Think of it, Morgan. This place is too tiny. You need a larger place to move around with your arm full of hardware that shouldn't be bumped. You've seen my bathroom with its big, walk-in shower and double sinks. My kitchen is larger than yours and is open to the living area, which is an open, warehouse plan. I always thought it was just utilitarian, but now that I think of it, it's perfect for you right now."

"But—"

"No, really, consider it. Look, my place is bigger and easier for you to get around. I'll be there to help, but you'll still have your privacy because of my work shifts." He cupped her face with his palm and held her gaze. "It'll be a perfect place for you to land back on your feet."

"This is nuts—"

"Why?"

"Because, we barely know each other...and that's a big commitment on your part...and you only have one bedroom...and...uh..."

He chuckled and nodded. "Okay, good points. We are new friends, but when you moved in with your first college roommate, did you know her very well?"

"No. We were just picked by the university to be dormmates."

"So, you at least know me. With my job, the commitment on my part will be to help with your injury and taking care of stuff like cooking while you're recuperating. That takes those headaches away from you, so you can just relax more and concentrate on healing."

"Okay..." she said, her eyes never leaving his, not able to believe she was considering his proposal. "What about the one bedroom?"

"Do you trust me?"

Blinking, she jerked. "Trust you? Well, yes...uh... yeah. I do."

"I have a king-sized bed, as you know. I may be big, but I don't need to take up more than half. And I may be a guy but, Morgan, I can control my baser instincts. I promise, you'll be safe with me."

He wiped the remaining tears from her cheeks and smiled as she stared open-mouthed at him. Bending forward, he placed a kiss on the corner of her mouth, and whispered, "Please, come live in my world for as long as you need. Let me take care of you."

Nodding slowly, she sucked in her lips, the feel

of his mouth near hers sending tingles throughout her body. "I may be crazy, but yes...I'll come with you."

He laughed and slid from the bed, careful to not jostle her arm. Stalking to her closet, he threw it open and found a suitcase on the top shelf. "Just tell me what you need, and I'll pack it."

"The Ibuprofen is working so I can help," she said, standing to move closer. Supervising his packing, she watched as he threw her comfy clothes and toiletries into the case before snapping it shut. "My mom stocked my freezer, but it will be fine to leave here for when I return."

"You can let her know where you are later, once you're settled in. It's a good thing I drove my Jeep over. We'll be at my place in no time and can have breakfast there."

She smiled, glad to not be heading to her parents' house nor staying in her tiny apartment. A strange sense of freedom moved over her as she looked around. She slid her feet into slippers and followed him out the door.

As he settled her carefully into the passenger side and buckled her in, she looked at his face, so close to hers. "Why are you doing this for me?" she asked, her gaze pinning him in place.

His face was mere inches from hers as he opened and closed his mouth several times. Finally, he said, "Each friend represents a world in us, a world possibly not born until they arrive, and it is only by this meeting that a new world is born."

Her breath left her lungs in a rush. "Where did that come from?"

"Anaïs Nin. From her diary. It meant something to me and I guess I just memorized it."

She had no words to say so she leaned forward and placed her lips on his in a soft, subtle kiss. Leaning back against her seat, she murmured, "Thank you," with a smile.

19

Jaxon did not give himself time to think about his offer but was glad that Morgan had accepted. This time, as he escorted her inside, he noted a sigh of relief escaped her lips. He watched her enter, protective of her arm, but once inside his large, open apartment, she seemed to breathe easier.

"You okay?" he asked.

Nodding, she said, "Yeah. When I was here before, I thought your place was nice, but now that I'm injured, I see it in such a different light. You're right, the kitchen is open to the rest of the room, so there is less of a chance for me to hit my arm. The space is wide and with few, but comfortable, furnishings. I can move around easily."

"Good. Now, I need to get you settled so I can fix breakfast."

Her gaze jumped to his and her eyes widened. "Oh, my gosh, what about your work?"

Grinning, he said, "I'm off today, so I've got all day to see to you and make sure you have what you need here."

He watched as she wobbled slightly and he dropped her bag. "Okay, first things first. We need to get some food in you and then we'll work on the shower."

Not giving her time to think about the shower assistance, he moved her to the sofa and helped her sit down, making sure her feet were up and she had a pillow for her arm. Heading to the kitchen, he chattered as he fried bacon slices, scrambled eggs, and popped bread slices into the toaster. After a few minutes, he noted she was no longer responding and he glanced over. Her head was leaned back against the sofa at an angle that looked uncomfortable, but she was sound asleep.

He turned off the stove and walked to her, standing over her, his hands on his hips. Her dark red hair was pushed back from her pale face. The smattering of freckles over her cheeks captured his attention and he smiled. Then, his gaze dropped to her arm, resting on the pillow. The skin around the stitches was only pink now, and not angry red. The skin around the pins protruding from her arm was also healing well. *Jesus, babe. What I would give to take this from you.*

For an instant, he realized if it was not for the accident, she would not be in his apartment or in his life right now. Pushing that thought away, he squatted in front of her and placed his hand on her good one.

His heart ached as he remembered seeing her slumped in her bathroom, crying her heart out at all she had lost. "You're not going to be lonely anymore," he vowed softly.

Gently shaking her, he said, "Hey, Morgan? Wake up, sweetheart. I want to feed you, help you shower, and then tuck you into bed where you can rest without breaking your neck."

Her eyes opened and she blinked several times. "Oh, I'm sorry."

"Don't be. You're exhausted." Moving her arm pillow to the side, he handed her a plate and placed the fork in her right hand. "Eat, babe."

She looked at the food with wide eyes, sniffing appreciatively. "What about you?"

Chuckling, he said, "No worries, I made plenty." He stood and headed to the kitchen counter, where he picked up another plate before returning to sit next to her. "Eat up," he ordered gently, smiling as she dug into the food.

Morgan, her stomach filled with delicious comfort food, now stood in the bathroom of Jaxon's apartment and wondered what she was doing there. He had removed her tank top, careful of her arm, and had slid her yoga pants and panties down her leg, making sure to keep his eyes on hers. She was not wearing a bra, but he had been such a gentleman, she felt sure he had not even peeked. *Jesus, it's not like he's never seen me naked before*. Glancing down at her arm, she shuddered. *Yeah, that was when I was pretty. This thing is a cock-block for sure.*

"You doin' okay in there?" he called out from the other side of the door.

Standing from the toilet after finishing her business, she flushed before calling him back in. He stepped into the room, holding a towel in front of him, which he wrapped around her body before turning on the water.

"Okay," he began. "I know it'll feel weird, but once the water is warm, we'll get into the shower together. The shower head is also on a hose, so I can use it to help wash you off without the stream of water hitting your arm. I can also use it to wash your hair."

"Oh," she breathed, her gaze finding his. "That actually sounds lovely." She glanced down at the towel wrapped around her and said, "Um…how should we do this?"

She watched as he hesitated for a moment before taking matters into her own hands and throwing caution to the wind. "Listen, Jaxon, it's fine. I get it. I look nothing like the girl you brought here a couple of weeks ago. So, I'll just get naked and you do what you need to do."

His eyes opened wide as he blurted, "You look nothing like you used to? What does that mean?"

Blushing, she said, "It means that I can get naked and know that you're not interested—"

"You must have had a worse concussion than I thought," he muttered. "Believe me, you're a beautiful woman, no matter the accident. And it'll definitely take my self-control to be with you wet and naked. But," he placed his hands on her shoulders, "this is about comfort, not sex." Winking, he added, "Just don't confuse me taking care of you with not being interested."

"Oh," she said, her face still blushing. Looking at the shower, she sucked in a deep breath. "Okay, I'm ready."

Dropping the towel, she stepped into the stall, holding her left arm away from the water. "They said it would be fine for it to get wet, but I'm just kind of afraid right now."

"That's understandable," he said, nervously working the shower hose to make sure it did not hit her arm and that the water stream was on her and not too hot.

She held out her right hand and he squirted shower gel into her palm, which she slathered over her front as he soaped her back. His hands were strong and sure, digging in slightly, like a watery massage. "Oh, my God, that feels amazing."

Using the shower hose carefully, he rinsed her off before having her tilt her head back so he could get her hair wet. Her scalp tingled as he coated her hair in shampoo, his fingers working the suds through the strands while delivering a massage. She felt her shoulder muscles ease in relaxation, and tears of relief stung her eyes. He followed up with conditioner and she groaned again at the pure ecstasy of having her hair washed.

Jaxon's hands were buried in Morgan's hair and he seriously doubted his sanity at the moment. Her naked body was on display and as much as he promised her this was not about sex, the message was not relayed to his cock. Gritting his teeth, he focused on his fingers soothing through her strands of silken hair, forcing his wandering mind to the task at hand. Once he was sure the conditioner had been sufficiently rinsed, he flipped off the water and stepped out.

"Give me a second to get your towel and I'll help you out," he said, while her back was still to him. Grabbing the first one he could, he wrapped it around his waist, hoping to hide his erection while, at the same time, reciting medical terminology over and over in an effort to control his eager cock.

Scooping up another thick towel, he wrapped it around her back and held her hand tightly as she stepped from the wet tile of the shower onto the bathmat.

His gaze caught on her face, freshly scrubbed and smiling widely. Unable to hold back a responding grin, he cupped her cheek. "Feel better?"

"Oh, Jaxon, you have no idea. This is the first time in a week that I feel completely clean. And relaxed. Thank you so much," she enthused.

"My pleasure," he mumbled, hoping her eyes stayed above his waist.

"I know this is a complete interruption of your life," she said, her shoulders drooping. "I can't believe you offered all of this. But, I promise that, as soon as I can, I'll be out of your hair."

He stepped closer, his thumb caressing her cheek. "Hey, where did that come from?"

She lifted her left arm and said, "I know what you said earlier, but I also know this is gross."

"Babe," he said, his voice low. "In my profession, I see everything and, believe me, this is not gross." She tilted her head to the side, her brows lowered. "Honestly," he insisted. "Your arm is not gross to me. It's injured, sure, and I know it's painful and uncomfortable. But," he leaned closer, "not gross."

Still unconvinced, she bit her lip and her gaze dropped. Shaking his head, he warned, "If you don't want proof of how un-gross it is, your eyes had better stay above my waist."

She sucked in a quick intake of breath as she naturally dropped her gaze to his towel, still barely concealing his erection. Jerking her gaze back to his face, she opened her mouth, but a strangled, "Oh," was all that came out.

Laughing, he grabbed another towel and began drying her off, all the while maintaining her modesty with the first one, keeping it draped around her. Once finished, he stood behind her and towel-dried her hair before running her comb through the thick tresses.

"How should I help you dress?" he asked.

"Um, since I'm not going anywhere today, will it make you uncomfortable if I go braless?"

"No, ma'am," he said, eliciting a giggle from her.

"Then, I have an old sweatshirt jacket that might work, if we cut off the left arm. I earned it at one of my college races…I really love it, actually. But I don't want to ruin too many clothes, cutting them up, and that one makes me feel so cozy." Biting her lip for a second, she let out a sigh and shrugged her right shoulder, looking resigned.

"Hang on," he said, leaving the bathroom.

After a moment, he returned dressed in jeans and had a large t-shirt and one of her tanks in his hand. Maneuvering the tank top over her head and weaving it carefully around her left arm, he settled it around her waist. Then, he held up the large t-shirt of his and worked it over her arms as well.

With the oversized shirt, Morgan felt warm and covered, her arm free to move without any material to irritate it. Jaxon bent and, as she balanced with her right hand on his shoulder, he assisted her into her panties and yoga pants. Standing, he beamed at her and said, "How's that?"

"Oh, Jaxon," she began, her chin beginning to quiver. "You have no idea how good I feel right now. I'm clean and warm and comfortable. For the first time since the accident, I feel a little more like myself."

He cupped her face once again and leaned forward to kiss her forehead. "I know you're exhausted, so let's get you in bed and see if you can take a nap."

She had fought off the exhaustion during breakfast and the shower, but now felt it in every bone in her body. Nodding, she agreed and followed him into the bedroom. "I appreciate this, but I doubt that I'll be able to get comfortable."

"Well, let's see what we can do."

Looking over his shoulder, he asked, "Which side do you prefer to sleep on?"

"My right, but I can't do it with my left arm in shackles," she quipped, watching in fascination as he pulled down the covers to his king-sized bed and began moving pillows.

"Come over here," he called, and she walked to him on the left side of the bed. "Okay, first sit down and lay on your back."

Once she followed his directions and placed her head on a soft pillow, he placed another pillow longways on her right side.

Supporting her left arm, he said, "Now roll to your right side and place your left arm on this pillow."

Once she had rolled, he gently assisted her left arm to be supported next to her. His mattress was comfortable and his pillows were soft. Her body immediately settled into the familiar position and her eyes felt heavy.

"I usually work day shifts, but because I occasionally work a night shift, these curtains are light-blockers. I don't want you to sleep all day because I want you to sleep tonight, but your body is crying for rest. So sleep a couple of hours and then I'll get you up and we'll have lunch."

She heard his words and barely grunted her response as sleep carried her away.

20

Jaxon puttered around the house, making sure to be quiet while Morgan slept. He checked on her every fifteen minutes but, so far, she had not moved and, with her left arm still propped on the supporting pillow, she appeared to be comfortably sleeping.

Hearing the sound of boots on the walkway outside his apartment, he jumped up from the sofa and hurried to the front door before anyone could knock.

Throwing open the door, he greeted his brothers with a "Shhh," as he moved back to let them in.

Jayden's eyes narrowed as he stepped through the threshold, but before anyone could ask, he said, "Morgan's asleep in my bedroom."

Noticing eyebrow lifts on the others, he ushered them into his living room with another order of, "Stay quiet."

As Rafe, Asher, Cael, Zeke, and Zander followed Jayden in, he walked to the kitchen to grab bottles of beer before joining them in the living room.

With his voice lowered, he explained, "She was having a tough time at her apartment and didn't want to go to her parents' house. Her apartment is tiny and everywhere she moved, she was bumping her arm. She couldn't sleep and couldn't take care of herself and couldn't get the top off the pain medicine—"

"Whoa, man," Cael said. "We get it."

He let out a breath. If anyone understood what he was talking about it was Cael, who had plenty of experience helping when his young niece was being treated for cancer and then when his fiancée was also undergoing cancer treatments.

"She's got a shit place and you can take care of her here. It makes sense," Cael assured.

Shooting him a look of gratitude, he breathed a sigh of relief. "I don't know how her parents will see it."

Jayden said, "From what you say, her dad isn't going to want anyone else to get in the way of her rehabilitation."

"I don't plan on getting in the way," he defended himself. "All I offered her was a larger place to recuperate and someone here to help with her needs until she can gain some strength and take care of them herself."

"You care for her," Zander stated, leaning back against the sofa cushions.

Nodding, he dropped his head, staring at his hands as he rested his forearms on his knees. "Yeah, I do. It was supposed to be a hookup." Lifting his head to stare at Cael, he added, "Kind of felt like you did." Cael had also engaged in what was originally supposed to be a one-night hookup, with Regina, but he ended up not wanting to lose the woman he quickly became infatuated with. Guess they were two for two in shared experiences.

"It happens, man," Cael admitted.

"The difference was that we had no choice with where her swimming was going to take her. She was leaving town and not going to be coming back for months. Her world was swimming, competitions, endorsements, travel. Hell, everything that goes along with being an Olympic contender. Me being part of that world was not going to happen."

"And now?" Asher asked.

"It's weird, I'll admit. I know that once she gets back to peak strength, she'll go back to that world, but for now, it's nice to get to know her better."

"Does she know?" Rafe asked, his gaze intense. "About the accident?"

Sighing, he shook his head. "She doesn't remember much about it."

"And are you going to tell her that you were there?" he prodded. "I mean, the reason she slowed down in the first place." Lifting his hands, palms out, he said, "Not that it was your driver's fault, but just that you were there."

Scrubbing his hand over his stubbled jaw, he said, "I hadn't planned on it. I mean, Bob was not the cause of the accident and our being there probably saved her arm."

"Agreed, but Rafe's right. I know, first hand, that keeping things secret can really come back to haunt you," Zander said.

"I know you do," he nodded, understanding, "but, her dad's hell-bent on going after the truck driver and I just figured there was no reason to muddy the waters. So, I haven't said anything."

"You might want to reconsider," Jayden said. "It'd be better coming from you than from someone else."

He nodded but was uncertain of how Morgan would take him having anything to do with the accident at all —the accident that had changed her life and stolen her dreams. Noncommittal, he turned and flipped on the TV, keeping the sound down low so they could all watch the ballgame.

Morgan's eyes blinked open and it took her a moment to discern where she was. *Jaxon's apartment. Jaxon's bed.* She stretched and felt an ache in her arm, but other than that, she felt better than she had since the accident. She remembered he had had the light-blocking curtains pulled over the windows, but he must have come in sometime while she was sleeping and opened them slightly, so the light could wake her gently from her nap.

She carefully sat up and let the fuzziness in her brain settle. Swinging her legs over the side of the bed, she rose and moved into the bathroom. She managed to pull her pants and panties down so that she could use the toilet before struggling to lift them over her hips again.

Washing her hand, she looked into the mirror and was stunned at the state of her hair. It was completely unruly since it had dried while she was sleeping. She found her comb, which Jaxon had placed on the counter along with her other toiletries, and attempted to drag it through the tangled tresses, to no avail.

Smelling the scent of pizza, her mouth watered and she gave up on the brush. Walking down the short hall, she stepped into the living room, calling out, "Please tell me that's pizza!" Seeing the room filled with men—gorgeous men—she stumbled and skidded to a stop.

Her gaze landed first on Jayden and Zander, both of whom she had met at Grimm's weeks ago. "Oh…uh…oh," she stammered, her right hand coming up to her head, knowing she looked frightful with bedhead and a Frankenstein arm.

"Morgan," Jaxon called, walking from the kitchen, plates in his hands, setting them down next to the pizza boxes. His eyes landed warmly on hers. "How'd you sleep?"

She turned her wide eyes toward him, aware of the men in the living room all standing in greeting. "Uh…good…good."

He came to her, standing right in her space, and lifted her chin with his knuckles so he could peer into her face. "Really? Really good?"

She focused on him, seeing the concern in his eyes and a soft smile curved her lips. "Yeah, really good. Thank you."

"No need to thank me. I'm just glad you finally got some rest."

"I think the combination of being out of the hospital, the Ibuprofen, the warm shower, breakfast, and a big bed that allowed me to sleep on my right side all combined to make sure I was sleeping like the dead."

"Good," he said, bending to kiss her forehead.

She did not have time to think before he took her by the shoulders and gently led her toward the sofa. "Hope you don't mind, but it was my turn to host our football day."

"Jaxon," she blushed, "please don't worry about me. I'm the one who's taking up your time and place."

"Nonsense. You're here because I want you here. You remember my brother, Jayden," he began.

"Yes, of course," she smiled, looking at his twin, now seeing subtle differences between them. "It's lovely to meet you again. I'm sorry I look such a fright—"

"Don't even think that," Jayden said, his smile warm as he bent to kiss her cheek. "You look amazing. I'm so sorry about the accident, but am glad you're doing as well as you are."

Surprised his words did not slash through her, she accepted his condolences, saying, "Thank you. That's very kind."

"And you met Zander," Jaxon continued.

Zander lifted his hand, taking her right one in his, giving it a gentle squeeze. "Rosalie would love to see you again, whenever you'd like some company."

Eyes wide, she nodded. "Please tell her I'd love to see her again, as well."

Zeke stepped forward as he greeted her. "I'm Zeke."

"I remember you brought out the delicious wings that night at Grimm's."

Zeke smile widened. "I'm glad you enjoyed them."

Jaxon continued, "These are my other brothers, Rafe…"

She smiled at the dark-haired, gorgeous man and could have sworn she had seen him in a calendar a former roommate had hanging in their room. *He's certainly model-worthy, but still, he has nothing on Jaxon.* He shook her hand and said, "My Eleanor would love to meet you as well. She's also a nurse. Just, you know, in case you need anything."

"Thank you," she said, her smile growing wider.

Introduced to Cael next, she tilted her head way back to meet his eyes. He was at least three inches taller than the others and his reddish-blonde hair had him standing out in a way that made her think of a Viking on the bow of a ship.

"My Regina will not miss the opportunity to meet you also," he said. "Maybe all three can come over sometime to get to know you."

The last to meet was a tall, quiet man, whose eyes held warmth. "Asher," he said, as he took her hand. "Sorry for what you've gone through."

While he was quieter, she felt the care exuding from him. Offering a smile, she stepped back, and said, "Well, I'll grab a piece of pizza and leave you to your game."

"Do you need to lie down?" Jaxon asked, moving to stand in front of her, holding her gaze.

Shaking her head, she answered, "No, but I can entertain myself—"

"Then, you'll stay with us," he declared, taking her hand and leading her over to the counter.

She soon found herself surrounded as everyone began filling their plates. Nervous at first, she quickly realized they gave her left arm a wide berth, no one coming close to jostling her. As large as they all were, she wondered how they managed to accomplish that feat.

Jaxon soon settled her on the sofa, next to him, with her left arm resting on the cushions as the game resumed after half-time. She ate the pizza and watched the game, not worried about calories, carbs, or a lazy day, and had a good time with Jaxon's friends. Resting her head on his shoulder, she relaxed and enjoyed herself, watching the football game and getting to know Jaxon's brothers.

Wishing she had that kind of camaraderie in her life, she looked forward to when their women might come to visit.

Jaxon looked over at Morgan, curled up on the sofa, the guys long gone and the evening sky sending shadows across the room. Her arm was propped up on a pillow and her eyes were droopy. He had fed her a dinner of store-bought lasagna, declaring that he could cook simple meals, but for anything too complicated, he just bought ready-made. He had toasted garlic bread and put together a salad to go with the lasagna.

He knew she was exhausted, but both of them

wanted her to try to stay awake until nighttime so that she would be on a normal schedule. She had an appointment with a physical therapist the next morning and with his afternoon shift, he would be able to take her.

"I like your brothers," she said, her gaze lifting to his.

He smiled as he twisted on the sofa to face her, sitting closely. "I'm glad, sweetheart."

He watched as her eyes drifted to the photograph on the wall, the one in which they were little boys, Miss Ethel standing behind them, arms spread wide to accommodate them all. Seeing the questions, as well as the hesitation, in her eyes, he said, "You can ask me anything."

Her head turned, her eyes jumping to his. Sucking in her lips, she said, "I just wondered about your brothers. Were you adopted?"

"Not exactly," he explained, leaning his head into his hand, elbow propped on the back of the sofa. "Jayden and I were in foster care."

Hearing her soft, rapid intake of air, he shook his head and said, "Don't feel sorry for us. We came from rough but landed soft."

She opened her mouth, but shut it quickly, allowing him to continue.

"Our mom was a teenager and an addict. She died giving birth to us, so we don't remember her, but from all accounts she was neglectful during her pregnancy and we were lucky to have been born without any problems."

He looked down as her right hand darted out to take

his, squeezing his fingers while tears filled her eyes. "That was the rough, babe, but we were young. Our grandma took us in for two years, but then she passed, so our aunt took us in and raised us for the next four years after that."

"You lost your grandma too? I'm so sorry."

"Thanks, babe," he said softly, feeling her compassion for him. "To be honest, we don't really remember her either. Our aunt is really the only relative we have significant memories about."

"Was she good to you?"

"Yeah…in her own way. She was overwhelmed with two little boys, but we were warm, dry, fed, and clothed. She was dating a man who was not a fan of his woman having two little boys around. Plus, and I don't think she wanted us to know this but kids hear more than adults think, he didn't want the kids of a drug addict hanging around. So, one day, she packed us up and took us to a house. We were greeted by a woman and two other little boys, Zander and Rafe. Best place in the world, Miss Ethel's house."

Morgan smiled, her gaze straying from his face to the photograph on the wall. Filled with the desire to know all about him, she pleaded, "Tell me about her."

"She had a big house in a nice, older neighborhood. She was a widow and had never had children. So, she began taking in foster boys. Zander was first, then Rafe. Jayden and I came next. Cael came after us and then Asher. Another brother, Zeke, came after that. There were others, but we were the original gang."

"How did she manage with all those boys?" she asked, eyes wide in astonishment.

"She was fair, calm, steady. Things some of us lacked before arriving at her doorstep. She worked hard to make sure we considered each other to be brothers. We all stayed until we graduated from high school and then we each joined the military."

"I had no idea you were in the military!"

"Army. I drove ambulances…Afghanistan."

Shaking her head, she breathed, "What a life you've lived."

"Never knew any different. Gotta tell you though, since I've been an adult, I've come to learn that a lot of people had shit childhoods. Mine may have started rough but, like I said, I landed in a soft place. No better mother in the world than Miss Ethel. She took a rag-tag group of boys and, with love and perseverance, turned us into a family. She understood each of us, encouraged us to become whatever we wanted."

"Is she still living?"

"We see her all the time. I suspect she'll be wanting to meet you real soon," he said with a wink.

Her mouth fell open and she wanted to ask 'Why', but snapped her mouth closed instead. He was watching her closely and she got the feeling he knew what she was thinking.

"I talked about you…before. I felt something after we first met, Morgan, but knew you and I were in totally different places." He winced a little at the unspoken meaning in that statement.

Her face fell and her shoulders slumped. "Yeah. I

know." They sat silent for a moment before she said, "I don't want to think about what I've lost right now, and I didn't have the kind of childhood that you had. Thank you for sharing that with me. It breaks my heart to think of you and your brother in that situation." She smiled softly, apologetically. "So," she straightened her spine a little, "tell me more about Miss Ethel."

Jaxon walked out of the bathroom, flipping off the light. Bare-chested and wearing lightweight drawstring pants, he stared at Morgan, leaning back against several pillows, her eyes on him.

They had spent another hour on the sofa where he shared light-hearted stories from his childhood. She was going through a lot and he could understand the need for levity. He often fell back on smiles and a good laugh when feeling overwhelmed, so he was a pretty much a pro. When he described Miss Ethel always knowing when her boys were up to something she nearly fell over, giggling and holding her stomach.

Now, with his help, she was in another one of his large t-shirts, teeth brushed, and face washed. He had also taken a brush and tamed her long locks, the deep russet color shining. She smiled as he walked to the bed and slid under the covers.

"You gonna be okay with me here?" he asked.

She twisted her head and looked at him. "Yeah," she

said softly. Staring at her lap for a moment, she smoothed the comforter with her right hand. "Jaxon?"

"Right here," he replied, a smile on his lips.

"Thank you, for everything."

"Morgan, you don't have to—"

"No, please, let me finish," she begged, turning her face back to his. "When we first met, I knew what I wanted and where I was going. Or, last least, I thought I did. Then, a week ago, my world was turned upside down and everything I thought was going to happen changed. I was stunned and couldn't believe that my Olympic dream had been taken away. I...I haven't really accepted that yet, even though I know it's true."

She blew out a deep breath as he scooted closer to her, wrapping his arm around her shoulders, pulling her close. "I know that I probably should have moved in with my parents, at least until I was able to do more things by myself but, I just couldn't. My dad...well, he's driven. I know he loves me, but he's my coach and expects the best and accepts nothing less."

"And right now, that's not what you can focus on," he said, his fingers trailing lightly on her shoulders.

Nodding her head sadly, she agreed. "I have no idea what tomorrow holds...or the next day...or the next week, next year. And I'm not sure Dad is ready for...I don't know...for whatever comes."

"It's too soon for you to be planning that far in advance, anyway," he said. "At least that's my opinion, for whatever it's worth."

"No, no, I agree. I mean, my arm will heal. And I'll

get into PT and begin swimming again. And I'm sure I'll train again..." her voice trailed off.

"Listen, right now, all you need to think about is that you need to slide down in bed, get your arm settled and go to sleep. Tomorrow's another day and we'll face that day when it comes."

She breathed easier and said, "I like that."

He leaned over and made sure she was comfortable with her left arm propped on a pillow and her back to him as she lay on her right side. He turned off the nightstand lamp and rolled toward her. He wanted to touch her but did not want her to feel uncomfortable.

After a moment, she whispered, "Will you hold me?"

"Oh, yeah, babe," he said, immediately curving his body into hers, spooning her from behind. With his arm over her waist, he heard her let out a sigh.

"Go to sleep, Morgan," he said, his breath washing by her ear.

Just as she was drifting off, she heard him say, "'When you come out of the storm, you won't be the same person who walked in. That's what this storm's all about.'"

"Who said that?"

"Another writer. Haruki Murakami."

"How do you know so many perfect quotes?" she asked, barely awake.

He grinned into her soft hair and said, "Miss Ethel. Always Miss Ethel."

Sitting in Jaxon's jeep the next morning, driving to the physical therapist office, Morgan felt her heart pounding, her nerves stretched tight as a bow. He reached across the console and held the fingers of her left hand.

"You're gonna be fine, sweetheart," he assured. "They'll just do a review of your medical condition and a general evaluation."

"I know," she said, trying to calm her nerves as he parked outside. "I've spent untold hours in PT, training, injury recovery. Although, that was for things like a pulled muscle or tendonitis. Nothing like this." She glanced down at her now-common attire of yoga pants, tank top, and a large t-shirt. She loved wearing his t-shirts, feeling comforted when in them. Looking to the side, she noted the way his jeans fit over his thighs and was reminded of waking up with one of his thighs pressing tightly to hers. He was drool-worthy and he was there for *her*. At that thought, she was unable to keep the smile from her face.

With a silent nod, she indicated she was ready. Waiting for him to come around, she whispered to herself, "You've got this. You can do this."

Once inside, he assisted with the paperwork and when the physical therapist called her back, she turned and said, "Please, Jaxon. Come with me." He readily agreed and, together, they followed the PT into the examining room.

Theresa smiled at them and said, "It's nice to see you again, Morgan. You look good today."

Meeting her smile, she agreed, "I'm nervous but I do feel better getting out of the hospital."

"Are you at your parents' house or on your own?"

"Neither," she admitted. "Jaxon has me staying with him. He has a much larger place and can help with some things I need until I can do them on my own."

Theresa's smile widened. "Wonderful. I cannot tell you how important it is that you have this kind of support after an injury like this. Jaxon, it's nice to meet Morgan's significant other."

She opened her mouth to refute the title, but he jumped in. "I just want to be as supportive as I can," he said, reaching over to hold her hand. Her eyes moved to his and she was unable to keep the smile from her face. She knew in her heart that he was not her *significant other*, like a boyfriend, but to her, right now, he was her most significant other. She just hoped he did not mind the moniker.

"Okay, I'll do an exam first and then we can talk about the exercises you need to do at home and the timeframe in which you can expect to move through the therapy. I know you want to get back into the pool as soon as possible, but we need to allow the bones to reconnect and give the muscles and ligaments a chance to heal as well. I know there was some nerve damage with the severe laceration, so only time will tell exactly when you need to proceed with your training."

She nodded, listening to each word, aware that Theresa was not assuring her she would be an Olympic contender again. Swallowing deeply, she jolted when she felt Jaxon's thumb rubbing circles on her hand.

He leaned over, asking, "You okay with this?"

Nodding, she forced a smile. "Yes." Looking at

Theresa, she added, "I don't have much of a choice right now. I have to take it slow…work at my ability and gain strength."

"Absolutely," Theresa said.

She opened her mouth to ask the sixty-million-dollar question but closed it quickly, uncertainty clawing up her throat.

Theresa, observing her closely, leaned forward and placed her hand on her knee. "Morgan, I know you want to know what you'll be able to do. But, after an open reduction internal fixation surgery, your body has a lot of healing to do. Right now, there's no one who can give you that answer. But I promise you that our staff has worked with many similar patients and athletes."

"My father…"

"Yes, I know about your father," Theresa said, "and remember him from the hospital. I know he's your coach, also. That's why I gave him the wrong time for your appointment today."

Both she and Jaxon looked at each other before turning their attention back to Theresa, surprise written on their faces.

Theresa grinned. "He called yesterday and wanted to be here. I simply told him it was later than this, so that we would have a chance to speak first. I'm also having you do your work in this smaller, private room instead of our larger PT area. I figured that you would prefer the privacy and this will keep others, including the media, out of your therapy as well."

"Oh, thank you," she gushed. "I love my dad and I

know he wants the best for me. It's just that, right now, I can only handle so much."

"Then let's start on what you can handle." With that, Theresa began.

Thirty minutes later, with a sheen of sweat covering her body, Morgan sat on the table, blowing out a long breath. Her arm hurt and she felt disheartened. And that was just from the examination! Theresa gave her simple instructions for the next week and a list of gentle movements she could begin working on. She forced a smile onto her face and slid off the table with Jaxon's assistance.

"Where's Morgan McAlister?"

She and Jaxon looked at each other just as her father walked into the room, a harried receptionist trailing behind, her eyes shooting daggers at him.

Before he could begin to bluster, she called out, "Dad, don't start. I've just had a good examination and have some exercises I can work on. What I don't need is you coming in here taking over."

Her mother stepped from behind her father, her eyes taking her in, as though to assure herself she was alright, before sliding to Jaxon, widening slightly.

"I want a report on everything that is happening," her father said to Theresa.

Holding up her hand, Theresa said, "That will only be with Morgan's permission. She is the patient and according to HIPPA—"

"Don't give me that crap," her dad blustered. "I'm her coach and—"

"That does not matter," Theresa began.

Before her dad had a chance to threaten further, she interrupted. "Dad, stop. Right now, I'm doing all I can to hang on to my sanity. Don't make this worse!"

Theresa slipped out the door, saying, "I'll give you some privacy."

Her mom placed her hand on her husband's arm and the slight action seemed to calm him. "Morgan, we can talk at home. I know you didn't want company yesterday, but I need to see that you're all right. Your apartment is so small and—"

"It's covered, Mom. I've moved in with Jaxon."

His hand still held hers and he gave a little squeeze, standing closer, his other hand resting lightly on her waist. Her heart skipped a beat at his show of strength and solidarity. For a few seconds she allowed herself to believe they were a couple. A real couple. One that could face adversity and come out stronger. Her breath ragged, she knew he was only being a good friend, but the idea of being with him gave her courage.

"Jaxon," her father said, incredulity dripping from his words. His eyes moved from her to the man standing next to her. "You…you're the paramedic, the one who was at the hospital." Staring, he bit out, "You save a famous person and now you decide to become part of her world?"

Not rising to the bait, Jaxon held her father's gaze, steady and without rancor. "I'm content to let Morgan decide who she wants to be with."

"Morgan?" her mother called out, her brow crinkled in confusion. "I didn't even know you were seeing someone."

"We're friends, Mom. I couldn't handle my small apartment on my own and he offered to help."

"You could have come home," her mom began.

"You *should* have come home," her father blustered, his face set in anger.

"Dad," she said, softly. "I need space. I need time to figure out my life—"

"Your life? Your life is getting back in the pool."

"And I will as soon as I'm cleared to do so," she countered.

"Jaxon?" Her mother's focus was on now on the man standing beside her. "Uh...I'd like to bring some food... or something..."

"Mrs. McAlister, I've got her covered, but I'm sure she'll be glad for your company when she's up for it. She can send you the address and you'll be welcome at her invitation."

Her mom's short nod indicated she understood his response, and she realized Jaxon was saying he would open his home to them when she deemed it to be the right time. She looked at him, shocked at the level of generosity he was showing her family when he barely even knew *her* yet.

As if reading her mind, her father growled, his hands on his hips, "I don't even know you."

"Dad," she brought his eyes back to her. "I need rest. I need to follow the physical therapist's recommendations and continue to heal. If we push this too hard there will be no chance for recovery, you know that." Throwing her hand out, she added, "I know you've got some athletic trainers itching to get at me. As soon as I can, I'll be back in the pool." Sliding away from Jaxon, she walked toward her dad and placed her hand on his arm. "I'm not giving up. This matters to me too, it really does. But, Dad, I *need* this. We can't wish it away. This is how it is." She pleaded with her eyes for him to understand.

His mouth worked but he did not argue. Sighing, he said, "I'm worried about how all this is messing with your head. I want you to see a sports psychologist—"

"Sam," her mom said, softly.

He pinched his lips together and said, "I'd like you to see one."

Nodding, she said, "I think that might be a good idea."

Her father's shoulders relaxed for a second, before he shifted his to Jaxon. "I still don't agree with you living with a complete stranger."

"We're not strangers," she said, a smile curving her lips. "We had already met before the accident. It just so happened that he was there to help when the accident occurred."

Her father remained quiet, but she could see he was not happy.

"We've got to go but, Mom, I'll come by to visit you and Dad in a couple of days."

Her mother nodded, and she smiled as she kissed her cheek. Looking at Jaxon, she said, "Nice to meet you."

"Likewise," he replied, his voice warm as he slipped his hand around her waist once more.

Her parents left, leaving her slumping against Jaxon, allowing him to take her weight. He looked down at her, his eyes assessing.

"Let's go," he said. "You're fuckin' exhausted. Wish they hadn't shown up at a time when you're vulnerable and tired."

"It had to happen sometime."

"Yeah, well, your dad's timing sucks."

A giggle slipped out as she agreed. "You're right about that."

He led her to his Jeep and assisted her up into the seat, strapping the seat belt around her. "I've got an afternoon shift, so I'll get you home and get you settled."

She reached up to cup his jaw and smiled. "Sounds good." As he started to close her door, she said, "Jaxon." Once his eyes were back on hers, she added, "Thank you…for everything."

He stared for a second before leaning in and placing a soft, barely-there kiss on her lips. "My pleasure, Morgan."

As he closed the door, she leaned back in her seat, a smile curving her lips.

22

Before Jaxon left, he prepared Morgan a lunch and gave her strict instructions to take it easy. When it was time for him to leave, she stood at the door, watching him walk away, resplendent in his simple uniform of navy pants and RES polo—which did little to hide the muscles underneath.

Turning, a smile on her face, she walked into the kitchen and opened the refrigerator. Looking at the contents, she wished she could cook for him. She loved to cook, although, during intense training, she stuck to chicken and fish and veggies. Sighing, she closed the door, inwardly vowing to cook for him as soon as she had more control over her left arm.

On her way back to the living room, she stopped as a knock came at the front door. Scrunching her face in confusion, she wondered who would be visiting, since it appeared Jaxon's brothers knew his work schedule. Sucking in a sharp breath, she hoped it was not her parents. She had texted the address to her mother, but also told her to give her a few more days before visiting.

Peeking out the security hole, she saw several women standing there. Opening the door, she was struck by the individual beauty of each woman. Eyes wide, she latched onto Rosalie's face and relaxed her stance.

"Morgan!" Rosalie called out in greeting. "I hope it's okay we came by?"

Stepping backward, she swung out her right hand and enthused, "Yes, yes! Please come in."

Rosalie entered and, turning, introduced, "This is Eleanor, Rafe's wife."

She greeted the dark-haired woman, noting the side of her face and neck were covered in burn scars. However, her smile was so wide and genuine it immediately stole her attention away and she was immediately filled with the desire to know her better.

"And this is Regina, Cael's fiancé."

She laughed as she viewed the beauty with the chin-length, reddish-blonde hair and joked, "Another ginger like me!"

Regina gave her a hug and cried, "Ginger sisters!"

Turning, she saw another woman stepping up to the door and her jaw dropped. "Ms. Wiseman! How?"

Taking her hand, the older woman leaned over to kiss her cheek. "My dear, forgive me for intruding, but when the girls asked me to come, I just had to. I'm just sorry I did not bring your grandmother with me."

Still astonished, she led the group over to Jaxon's

large living room and they were soon settled, but not before Eleanor made sure her arm was propped up.

"I should explain," Rosalie interjected. "Miss Ethel told us that she had met you at the hospital when she brought your grandmother. So, I insisted she come today, so she could see for herself how you're doing."

"You're, you're Miss Ethel?" Her gaze jumped to the photograph on the wall and now she could clearly see that she was indeed the woman with her arms around the young boys. "Jaxon's spoken so highly of you. It's such an honor to meet you."

"Oh, posh," Miss Ethel said, her face beaming in spite of her words.

"So, how *are* you doing?" Eleanor asked.

"Fine. I'm fine, as you can see. I went to physical therapy today and should be able to get back into shape very soon." She hoped her words carried more certainty than she felt, but years of giving the press what she and her father wanted to hear, made her an expert in speaking to the crowd.

"No," Eleanor said, leaning closer. "How are you *really* doing?"

Eleanor's eyes penetrated the fog surrounding her and before she could think, she blurted, "I have no idea." A sharp intake of breath resembling a sob overtook her and she blinked furiously to keep from crying. Unable to understand what was happening, she looked down quickly, focusing on the edge of the t-shirt caught in her fingers.

Regina was sitting next to her and reached over to

place her hand on hers. "I think we understand, Morgan. At least a little bit."

She jerked her head up, torn between wanting to rail that they could not possibly understand and hoping against hope that they had a clue to her pain. Swallowing, she said, "Jaxon told me a little about each of you."

Nodding, Regina said, "I was a childhood leukemia patient who had a relapse a year ago. Jaxon and the others donated stem cells and I was treated successfully, but it's been a hellacious couple of years. His little niece battled cancer successfully at the same time."

"Oh, I'm so sorry," she said, realizing that Regina had fought a fatal disease whereas, for her, only her arm was broken. "How selfish of me—"

"No, no, not at all," Regina assured. "Each of us has to take our own walk with pain, illness or injury, and grief at what might have been. Yours is just as real and since you are going through it in the shadows of the Olympics, more significant right now."

She was unable to keep her gaze from drifting to Eleanor's face, no longer focusing on the scars but on her kind eyes.

Nodding, Eleanor said, "My burns came from when I was a nurse in Afghanistan. After recuperating, I learned my family had been killed in an accident and so I shut myself away for several years."

Slumping back against the cushions, she said, "Oh, my God, Eleanor. How horrible."

Eleanor shrugged and smiled softly. "I probably would still be a recluse if it wasn't for Rafe. He pulled me out of hiding and I began to find myself again. Redefined...but still me."

"Redefined..." she said, the word sounding curious as she thought of her situation.

"And then, there's me," Rosalie said, with a shrug. "I was attacked and left for dead. Zander found me and stayed with me in the hospital. I had no memory and, together, we worked on finding the pieces until it all came back. So, I got my memory and got the man."

"I'm...I'm...well, I have no idea what to say."

"How about just letting us know how you really are doing, my dear," Miss Ethel said.

She turned her gaze to the elderly woman, sitting erect in Jaxon's comfy chair, her white hair pulled back into a bun and her wire-rimmed glasses surrounding her clear, grey eyes. She exuded warmth, so similar to Nonnie.

Nodding, she opened her mouth and the emotions began to flow. "All I know is swimming. And for a week, all I've known is pain. The physical pain has been agonizing, but at least there's pain medication that keeps it at bay. But, it's my head, what's going on in my head that has me so unbalanced. I still can't believe that the Olympic final trials have occurred and I'm not there. Not standing on the podium. It's like a nightmare, but I'm not waking from it."

"May I tell you what I said to Jaxon, when he told me he wanted to be with you?" Miss Ethel asked.

Turning to her, she nodded. "Yes, please."

"Grief is the emotion we feel when we lose something. Not just losing a person to death, but losing anything that means something to us. We each grieve differently, but we each grieve. You, my dear, have lost something precious. No matter what happens in the future, you have lost the Olympic chance for this year."

"Yes," she breathed. "My dad, who's my coach, wants me back in shape as quickly as possible to be able to go the distance next time, but all I can think about is now."

"And now is what you should be thinking about," Miss Ethel advised. "Taking care of you. Healing."

"What about Jaxon?"

At the sudden change in topic, her gaze shot to Rosalie.

Rosalie blushed and, lifting her hands, said, "I know that sounded so rude. But, to be honest, I've never seen Jaxon like this. Caring so much—"

"Fiddle-sticks," Miss Ethel interjected, pursing her lips at Rosalie. "He's always caring."

"Well, he certainly saved me, that's for sure," Morgan admitted.

Miss Ethel held her gaze for a moment as a slow smile crossed her face. "I think, my dear, that you once saved him as well."

Not understanding her words, Morgan cocked her head to the side. Before she could ask her meaning, Miss Ethel continued.

"He may joke, but never mistake that for not caring. For him, it was a way of coping."

"He told me of his upbringing," Morgan rushed to say, gaining the attention of the other women. "I was awed…and humbled."

"I'm sorry," Rosalie said. "It's just that to see him so

taken with you and, well, I just don't want to see him hurt."

"It's fine," she said, realizing her emotion was as honest as her words. "We got together for a short time before I was to leave town. We both knew it couldn't be anything more. But now? I can't give you a definitive answer. I really like him, but I can't expect him to take on all my baggage. I have no idea what's going to happen with me." Sighing heavily, she added, "But I'm uncomfortable talking about this with you and not him. As soon as he and I figure out what we are and what we mean to each other, I'll let you know."

Rosalie's smile brightened her face and she winked. "Perfect answer, Morgan."

The group lightened their conversation and laughed as they listened to Miss Ethel's stories of all the boys. Her admiration for the foster mother who became a mother grew as the afternoon progressed.

As they left, each hugged her and gained her promise to see them again soon. Miss Ethel reached for her, pulling her into an embrace, and whispered, "Helen Keller once said, 'I wonder what becomes of lost opportunities? Perhaps our guardian angel gathers them up as we drop them and will give them back to us in the beautiful sometime when we have grown wiser, and learned how to use them rightly.' You must focus on getting well, my dear, and you will find how to deal with lost opportunities at the right time."

Her heart was in her throat as she watched the women leave, she shut the door before leaning her back against it. Emotionally drained, she also realized she felt lighter than she had in a long time.

"You're not wearing a wedding ring."

Jaxon turned to the side, sighing as he observed Susie standing at the nurses' desk, her face a mixture of pissed and pouting. Her hand was on her cocked hip and her foot tapped out a staccato, illustrating her irritation.

He, Bob, and Mary had just brought in a man in his late forties who'd had a massive heart attack in his front yard. Unfortunately, he died in the ambulance. They tried to revive him and knew the ER had done everything they could, but to no avail. On top of that, he could still hear the wails of the wife as she pleaded for them to save her husband. Dropping his head for a few seconds, he tried to compartmentalize his thoughts to keep from lashing out at Susie.

Arms hanging at his sides, he lifted his head and looked her straight in the eye. "Susie, I'm not married. I lied and, for that, I'm sorry. But the truth of the matter is, when you and I spent a few hours together, that was all it was. I made that clear and you appeared to be on board with that situation. I've got no desire to spend more time with you and I'm not trying to be an asshole about it. I hope that you can forgive my lie and move on to find someone in your life you really want to be with."

He watched the play of emotions cross her face and

prayed she was not going to create a scene. She swallowed hard and looked down at her clasped hands.

He continued, "I'm now involved with someone and, while I have no idea where it will go, I plan on giving her everything I can."

Finally, she nodded and sighed heavily. Her mouth opened and closed several times as she held his gaze. "Thank you, Jaxon. I'm sorry. You're right. You made things clear the night we were together, and I thought that we could, well, I just thought I could change your mind. I...well, I wish you well."

With that, she turned and hustled down the hall and he suddenly felt very tired.

"You handled that nicely," Mary said, coming up beside him, her hand on his shoulder.

"It's hard to face the fact that I've been a jerk."

"I don't think you've been a jerk, Jaxon. You're young, not settled down, have enjoyed being single. As you say, you never led anyone on, so if they wanted more, that's on them."

He turned and looked at her, a smile playing about his lips and one eyebrow lifted in surprise.

"What? You think just 'cause I'm an old married woman I don't remember what it was like to be young, free, and enjoying life? I wouldn't trade my Hank for anything or anyone, but before we met, we both dated a lot of other people. I never thought you acted like a jerk just because you enjoyed the ladies."

Chuckling, he said, "I appreciate that. No, I don't regret looking for fun where I could find it. I just regret lying to Susie to get her to leave me alone. Hell, even

Morgan lied to cover for me when we saw Susie out somewhere."

"Speaking of Morgan, how are things with you two?"

As he and Mary walked out of the ER toward the ambulance, he smiled. "She's staying with me as she recuperates, but we're just friends."

"Just friends?"

He nodded. "Yeah. I'd like to be more, but she needs time to cope with everything on her mind. Not feel pressured by me to take it to another level."

Mary's face broke into a huge smile and she clapped him on the back. "You're a good man, Jaxon. Don't ever doubt that."

Climbing into the driver's seat to give Bob a break, his heart felt lighter. Calling in their location, they headed back to the station.

23

Jaxon was anxious to get home, looking forward to seeing Morgan when he stepped through his front door. He had received a text from Zander warning him that the women had visited her earlier that day and had taken Miss Ethel with them. Hoping she had not been overwhelmed, he jogged down the hall.

Entering, he immediately observed her sitting on the sofa, her eyes closed, and her arm propped on a pillow. He tiptoed over and knelt by her, lifting his hand to brush a lock of hair from her face. Her thick eyelashes formed crescents on her cheeks and her pink mouth was open slightly, the deep breaths rising from her chest giving proof to her slumber.

Something stirred deep inside him. Something that had been growing since he first danced with her at Grimm's. Something that had never been present with any other woman. Something that made him want to find out everything about her.

He began to stand when she moved slightly, her eyes

fluttering open. Her blue eyes stared in confusion for a few seconds before her lips curved and she breathed, "Jaxon."

He sat on the coffee table and placed his hand on her knee, giving a little squeeze. "Hey. How are you?"

"I'm fine," she replied and, with his assistance, pushed up to a seated position. Swiping her hair back from her face, she added, "I must have been really tired to fall asleep so easily."

"This morning was rough on you and I heard you had some visitors this afternoon."

Eyes wide, she smiled. "How did you hear?"

"Zander let me know you were invaded by the women and Miss Ethel. Was it too much?"

"Oh, no," she assured. "I loved meeting them. And would you believe that I had already met Miss Ethel."

"No way! Where?"

"She's an old friend of my Nonnie. She brought her to the hospital to visit me last week."

Shaking his head, he was stunned. "Small world."

"I really liked her," she admitted, leaning back against the sofa cushion. "After hearing about your upbringing last night, I loved meeting the woman who helped you become who you are."

"I know she was glad to meet you. I would have taken you to her, but wanted you to feel more up to visiting first. I should have known the women wanted to meet the person I had invited into my house."

"So, I'm not just your run-of-the-mill charity case?"

His gaze held hers and he grinned, recognizing she was fishing. Leaning forward, he cupped her cheek and said, "You are not a charity case, Morgan." His heart pounded in his chest as he confessed, "I wanted to see more of you after our first night together. When I brought the mermaid earring to you, I planned on asking you out again. If you had not been leaving town, I would have made sure you knew just how much I wanted you around."

Morgan stared, his words flowing into her heart and, yet, pulling at her mind at the same time. *How can the end of one dream be the beginning of another?* "I wanted you too. I just had no idea if you would wait for me. I mean, that would have been stupid to ask, for you to wait after only one night together."

"Do you believe in destiny?" he asked, his thumb still caressing her cheek.

"I don't know," she confessed. "I believed in hard work. I believed in setting a goal and doing all in my power to meet that goal. But now? I have no idea what to believe."

"I don't want you to think that I'm glad you were hurt," he said. "I'm not. Honest to God, I'd take your pain if I could. But, I'd be a liar if I said that now that you're in my house, I hope you stay. At least, as long as you can."

"I have no idea what the future holds," she reminded.

"I know. And I'll help you achieve whatever goals you want to achieve. I won't hold you back. And if you need to leave to chase your dreams, I'll still be here, cheering you on."

A sob erupted from deep in her chest and she grabbed his shirt with her right hand and pulled him toward her. Her lips landed on his and he felt the rush straight to his cock. After a moment, he pulled back, hating the break in contact.

"What?" she moaned, her eyes jumping to his, her brow lowered.

"I want what's best for you, Morgan," he said, his voice tortured.

Grinning, she pulled him back in and mumbled against his lips, "I think I know what's best for me."

"I'm trying to be noble."

"To hell with noble. Please…"

"Morgan—"

Giving his shoulders a little shove, she huffed, "I know my arm looks disgusting, but can't you just pretend it's not a problem?"

He jolted, stunned. "Disgusting? I told you I understand injuries, Morgan. It's not disgusting. And secondly, it's not that it's a 'problem', it's just something we have to consider. I don't want to injure you further."

"This," she bit out, holding up her arm with the stitches and metal bars protruding, "is taking over my life." Sighing, she shook her head. "Look, I know my Frankenstein arm is a cockblocker, but I just thought—"

"Babe," he said, lightly smoothing out her brow with his forefinger. "Ever since I first saw you, I've wanted you. Sure, it was sexual at first, but by the end of our night together, I wanted *you*. All of you. So, I'm trying to be the man you deserve, and to my way of thinking, that'd be one who doesn't jump you when you're still healing."

"Oh," she said, sucking in her lips, eyes wide. "You

promise it's not because of the way it looks? And I know what you said," she rushed to add. "It's just, I think it's disgusting, so why wouldn't you?"

He leaned in and placed a sweet kiss on her lips, before pulling back. "I promise. You can trust me, Morgan."

She nodded, then, after a moment, tentatively asked, "Um…what if I don't want you to do the right thing…I mean, what if the right thing isn't the right thing you're thinking of?"

Blinking several times, he chuckled as he watched her blush. "Sorry? I'm not following."

She reached over and grabbed his hand, holding it tightly. "Ever since the accident I haven't felt like me. I don't even know who *me* is anymore. But, with you, I at least feel *right*. Like I'm in the right place at the right time with the right person."

His breath left his lungs in a rush, knowing her words were heartfelt. And, they were exactly what he needed to hear. "What do you need? I don't want to hurt you."

She leaned forward and, with her lips only a whisper away from his, said, "This. And don't stop, as long as you can be creative."

He angled his mouth to accommodate her lips fully and mumbled in return, "Oh, baby. I can get creative."

Kissing her, he moved his lips over hers, feeling her softly yielding as she melted into him. Wanting her comfortable, he slid his hands underneath her armpits and gently lifted her as he stood. She reached up to hold onto his arms, and winced, dropping her left arm immediately.

"Oh, Morgan," he said, doubt flowing throughout him.

"No, no," she rushed. "I just have to be careful, but please don't stop!"

"I won't stop, but let's do this right. Come on." He took her hand and led her to the bedroom, stopping at the bed. He eyed her arm and pulled her t-shirt over her right side and then bunched the material together to draw it over her left arm.

Wearing only a camisole underneath, he gently pulled the straps down, careful of her arm once again. With her luscious top exposed, he bent and took one nipple in his mouth, pulling deeply. Her moan shot straight to his cock, already straining against his zipper.

He lavished attention on each breast before dropping to his knees, kissing along her tummy until she giggled.

"I'm ticklish," she explained, unnecessarily. Her hand clutched his shoulder before sliding through his hair.

He hooked his fingers in the waistband of her yoga pants and slid them, along with her panties, down her legs, making sure she was steady as she stepped out of them. First kissing her knees, he then placed more kisses along her thighs, loving the sound of her continued moans.

Standing, he glanced to the bed and said, "You okay with easy vanilla, babe? I'll do all the work and promise to take care of you."

Biting her lips, Morgan nodded, thinking that vanilla with Jaxon would be perfect.

"Okay, let's get you settled."

She pouted, complaining, "I'm forcing the spontaneity out of this."

"Don't think of it that way," he admonished. "I had no idea we would be doing this ever again, much less so soon, so to me, this is a treat that I want to savor."

Her lips curving, she breathed a sigh of relief. Following his instructions, she sat on the bed and scooted to the middle. Lying on her back, with her head on a pillow and another one under her left arm out to the side, she nodded when he asked if she was comfortable.

"But, I'll be more comfortable when you're as naked as I am!"

He threw his head back in laughter and climbed from the bed. Grabbing his polo, he pulled it over his head and it landed on the floor. Unbuckling his pants, he kicked them off after toeing off his shoes.

Her gaze never strayed from his body as he stripped, and she could not keep the grin from her face. From his thick, curly hair to his incredibly muscular upper body, he was perfect to her. Watching as he fisted his cock, she licked her lips, letting her knees fall to the side, opening herself for his view. She ignored the self-conscious hesitations, determined to make it as easy for him as possible.

"Jesus, Morgan," he groaned, his gaze dropping from her face to her sex. Grabbing a condom from his wallet, he crawled over her, careful to not jiggle the bed excessively.

"You won't break me," she said, wanting him to hurry. She lifted her right hand and wiggled her fingers in a *come to me* gesture.

"Patience, babe." He settled on the bed, his knees near her ankles, reaching for her thighs. Dropping his head, he tongued her folds before latching onto her clit.

"Oh, God," she moaned, the feel of his lips on her electrifying.

He licked and then blew a puff of air over her swollen nub, sending shivers over her entire body. Reaching between her legs, she clasped his hair with her fingers, grabbing to hold him close.

Drowning in the taste, scent, and feel of her against his lips, Jaxon inhaled deeply. It was every bit as intoxicating as he remembered. Latching onto her clit once more, he inserted a finger into her core, the motion causing her hips to jerk upward.

With his other hand splayed over her tummy, he pressed her back down to the mattress. He felt her inner muscles begin to tighten and he crooked his finger before adding another. Scissoring them deep inside, he sucked hard once more and heard her scream his name as he felt her orgasm wash over him.

She clutched the sheets, grunting in pain and he quickly lifted his head, seeing her left hand rising slightly above the pillow.

"Babe," he admonished. "You're supposed to just lay there."

"Mmmm," Morgan moaned, lifting her head to see

him staring at her, his beard moist with her juices. "God, you're gorgeous."

"That's my line, beautiful."

Sated, she plopped her head back on the pillow as he kissed his way back up her body.

Stopping to pay homage to each breast again, Jaxon reveled in the feel of her. Continuing his trail of kisses, he latched onto her lips, his tongue thrusting into each crevice. Her taste was heady and he could not get enough of it.

Her tongue slid against his and his cock swelled even more, if that was possible. Groaning as he dragged his lips away, he sat back on his knees and grabbed the condom he tossed to the mattress. Ripping it open, he rolled it on under the watchful gaze of her eyes, the blue shining directly at him.

Positioning himself between her spread legs, his eyes darted to the side before he warned, "I'm gonna go nice and slow, but you gotta keep your arm protected on the pillow."

"Sure thing, bossman," she quipped.

He narrowed his eyes and, placing the tip of his cock at her entrance, he halted. "You want this?"

"Oh, you know I do," she mewed.

"Then protect your arm," he warned, sliding his nose along hers before nuzzling her ear. "Or I'll show you bossman."

Giggling, her mirth ended in a long moan as he edged his cock into her sex, inch by glorious inch. "Jaxon, you can boss me anytime you want," Morgan breathed, just before all thoughts, other than what her body was crying for, left her mind.

The feel of her tight sex squeezing his cock made Jaxon want to lose control and thrust uncontrollably, but he knew he had to hang on, making sure she was not only enjoying herself, but was not hurting.

He kept his weight off her chest with his arms on either side of her head, cognizant of her arm. Without realizing it, his thrusts slowed down and he startled when she grabbed his face with her right hand and pulled his attention back to her.

"Okay, bossman, listen up. You don't worry about my arm. That's for me to keep outta your way. You just think about your cock in my hoo-ha and taking us both where we want to go."

"Hoo-ha?"

"Jesus, Jaxon. That's all you got outta that?"

"No, but let's just say I've never been propositioned like that before."

Glaring, she narrowed her eyes. "You want me to get up and leave right now, you mention any other propositions that may have come your way in the past."

Grinning, he slid his tongue along her collarbone and around her neck. "I promise, there's no one and nothing on my mind but you, me, my cock, and your hoo-ha."

With that, he began to move, his dick swelling more with each thrust. His world narrowed to the feel of his body joining with hers. Nothing had ever felt more right in his life. Kissing her once again, he continued to focus on her, wanting her pleasure before his own.

Her head leaned back against the pillow and she

wrapped her strong legs around his waist, her heels digging into his taut ass.

"Come on, baby, are you close?" he asked, bending to suck on her pulse point while tweaking her nipple.

Suddenly, her inner core tightened and he felt his cock squeezed, taking him over the edge along with her. Both groaned, her with her fingers clutching his shoulder and he, with his neck extended, the corded muscles standing out as he emptied himself.

His arms shook with exertion as he forced his body to remain off her chest. Finally, he slid out, lifting back on his knees as he removed the condom. Grabbing a tissue from the nightstand, he wrapped up the used condom and tossed it to the side. With her carefully laying on her right side, he snuggled up as close to her as he could.

Tucking his head on the pillow next to her, he slid his arm underneath her breasts and whispered, "You okay?"

Sated, she whispered, "Yes, you can stop worrying."

"I'll always worry about you," he vowed.

She twisted her head to look into his eyes. "Always?"

He lifted his hand to tuck her hair behind her ear. "Yeah…always." He had never had pillow talk with a woman before Morgan but, suddenly, he wanted to make sure she understood what he was feeling. "In my life, I have Jayden…Miss Ethel…my brothers. And I thought that was enough. Now, you've fallen into my life as well, in a way that I know is life-changing."

She opened her mouth, but he cut her off, leaning over her so that she did not have to twist her neck to focus on him. "You don't have to say anything, Morgan. I know your life is rearranged right now and involves a lot more than me. I just wanted you to know that I'm here for you, in whatever way I can be."

Reaching her hand up, Morgan cupped his jaw, the feel of his beard underneath her fingertips now familiar. "You once said that landing at Miss Ethel's was a soft place to land."

He held her gaze, unsure where she was going with this.

She sucked in her lips before continuing. "Jaxon, you've become my soft place to land. In the middle of my entire world being altered, you are the one thing that makes sense. I want you in my life...not just as a place to land, but as a place to be."

His breath left his lungs in a rush as he watched a tear slide from the corner of her eye. Bending forward, he kissed the salty trail, then moved to place a soft kiss on her lips.

Shifting to the side once more, he kept her wrapped tight as their bodies, relaxed and sated, fell into slumber.

24

Several days later, Jaxon stood in the kitchen shoving a bagel covered with cream cheese into his mouth and washing it down with coffee. His eyes stayed on Morgan as she rounded the counter, her hair still sleep-tousled and her eyes lazy as they met his.

"Babe," he said, swallowing the bite, "I can't believe I can't take you to the doctor today. When my supervisor called to say that two team members had the flu and I was needed—"

"Sweetheart, it's okay. I have to see my parents today anyway." She sighed and scrubbed her hand through her hair.

"I just wish I could be there. I know your parents aren't glad about you staying here, but hopefully they'll be supportive at the doctor's office."

Her eyes held his and she shrugged. "Mom will be okay. Dad will be…well, Dad. If the doctor gives me good news, then he'll be itching to get me to a sports orthopedist. If not..." dropping her head, she sighed again.

He wrapped his arms around her shoulders, tucking her face to his chest, right over his heartbeat. "I'll be worried. Will you promise to call me? Even if I can't pick up right then, I'll want to hear. Good or not so good."

Morgan nodded, the feel of his soft polo against her cheek soothing as she breathed in his comforting scent. Determined to take his strength with her to the appointment, she leaned back and accepted his kiss, reveling in the simple things in life that she had wanted for so long, and had never had.

"The site of the external pins and plate look excellent," Dr. Roberts said, examining her arm carefully. "You're doing a great job of taking care of it and keeping it clean and free from infection."

She smiled while, at the same time, inwardly grimacing at the slight pain of his examination. "Thank you. I've made it a priority to do what I need to, plus my boyfriend is an EMT and he makes sure it's well cared for also."

At the word *boyfriend*, her father made a growling sound deep in his throat, but she tried to ignore him. "I've been very careful about propping it up as often as I can and have been pleased as the swelling has gone down. I've followed all the instructions I was given at discharge but confess that I'll be glad when I can get it wet."

"Yes, when can she do that?" her father asked.

She shot him a pointed look but turned back to the doctor and corrected, "I was referring to making things easier in the shower."

"At this time, you can certainly get it wet in a shower. I would not take a bath, where it would be submerged in the water for any length of time, but a shower would be fine."

She smiled, thrilled at the thought of being able to move more comfortably, while secretly thinking of how much more creative she and Jaxon could be in the shower without her having to hold her arm out of the water.

Dr. Roberts continued to have her move her fingers and wrist, watching the motions she was able to perform. "I'm most concerned with your elbow movement, but that will come in time as the bones continue to heal."

"How long before the external plates come off?" her mother asked. "I know it makes it hard for her to dress, and she constantly has to worry about snagging them on something."

"I'd say she's got another four weeks with the external fixation plate and then, as long as the bones are healing well, we can do the surgery to take it off."

"Four weeks," her father mumbled under his breath.

Dr. Roberts held her gaze for a moment before shifting his focus to her father. "Mr. McAlister, with the severity of her injuries, you have to realize that, once the external fixation plate and pins come out, she will still have a long recovery time. I know you want her in the pool, and she can certainly get in the water for leg exercises, but no swimming. She should not use her arms for any water resistance. My best estimate is that she will not be able to do anything strenuous for several months."

As much as the news surprised her, her eyes immediately jumped to her dad, seeing his eyes bugging out of his head and his ruddy cheeks growing redder.

"Months? She can't begin practice for months?"

"She can get in the water, move around, exercise her legs—but not her arm. I want the bone splinters to heal completely without any stress on them."

"You know who she is. What she's already lost. My daughter's gone from being an Olympian to nothing because of a freak accident. To be ready for the next one, we've got to give it everything we have. She was at peak. In four more years, she'll be competing against younger athletes."

His words washed over her and ugly speared directly into her gut. *Nothing...I've gone to nothing.*

"Sam, please," her mother begged. "We've talked about this." Turning to her, her mom said, "We'll just take it one day at a time."

"Well, I think we can kiss my competitive swimming career goodbye," she threw out. "In spite of Dad's earlier, optimistic predictions."

"You will swim again, honey. You just have to

believe. It'll take time and hard work, but your Olympic dreams will come true."

She stared at her mother for a long time, words not coming, before allowing her gaze to slide to her father, noting his averted eyes and his jaw ticking in anger. How could she say what was in her heart right now? *My dream is gone. Dad's dream is gone. I have no idea what I will do tomorrow, much less in four years.* Swallowing hard, she tightened her jaw to keep her chin from wobbling.

Finally, conquering the desire to cry once again, she nodded toward Dr. Roberts. "Thank you. I'll make sure to follow all your instructions."

He appeared to want to say something else, but simply nodded instead. Turning, he stepped outside the door and the nurse assisted her down from the table.

Walking outside, the sun was bright, but she barely felt it with the cold that emanated from deep inside.

She had waited outside Jaxon's apartment building when they picked her up and she wanted them to drop her off the same way, but her mother insisted they come in with her. Opening the door, she walked in and they followed.

"Oh, wow, his place is nice and open," her mother said, looking around.

Her father grumbled, "You're staying with someone and we've barely even met him?"

Fatigue moved through her, stealing not only her energy, but leaving her emotionally drained as well. "Dad, you've rarely met the men I've dated since I've become an adult." Inwardly, she knew she had never dated anyone seriously but, at the moment, did not want to get into that with him.

"He's not in the business, I know that," he shot back.

Eyes wide, she shook her head. "Business? You make this sound like the swimming mafia! Jesus, Dad, he's a good man, an EMT, and I really like him. Maybe the silver lining in all this is that I finally get to have a life of my own for a while."

"A life of your own? What the hell do you think your mother and I've sacrificed all these years for? It was so you could have your dreams."

"Sam," her mother said, placing her hand on his arm, calming him slightly.

She looked at them, realizing for the first time how they interacted when it came to her. He lost his temper, demanding more, and her mother held him back, acting as a mediator. Blowing out a breath, she said, "I'm really tired."

"Yes, let her rest for now," her mother said, pulling gently on her father's arm.

"I'll see you later," he said, moving out the door.

Her mother turned to her and kissed her cheek. "Honey, be patient with him. He's really upset at the loss of your dreams." Holding her hand up quickly, she added, "Yes, and it was his dream too. He's having a hard time adjusting."

"Mom, so am I. But at least I choose to surround myself with someone who is supportive of me. Not disappointed."

Her mother smiled as she pulled her purse strap upon her shoulder. "I'm glad, Morgan. I really am. And,

I promise your dad will come around to whatever happens."

Doubt filled her, but she nodded. Watching her mother leave, she moved to the sofa, sinking into the cushions and propping her arm up automatically. Her cell phone buzzed in her purse, but she left it on the coffee table.

The words of the doctor and her dad washed over her, sinking deeply into every pore. *Months before you can swim. Months before you can practice. She'll be competing against younger swimmers.*

She realized she had been telling herself there would be another Olympics. But four years was a long time. *I'll be twenty-eight. Competing against eighteen-year-olds.* A harsh, cold reality slid into her heart. *It's over. I'll never be an Olympian. Ever.*

And with that reality, the next thought came. *So what now? Who am I without that goal?*

Jaxon pulled his motorcycle into the parking spot next to his Jeep and jogged up the stairs. He had been calling Morgan all day, wanting to know about her doctor's appointment and visit with her parents. His heart pounded in fear, since she had not replied with either a text or a call. *What if the news was bad? What if her parents convinced her to move back with them? What if...?*

Unlocking the door, he stepped in, his nerves taut. The room was unlit, but the evening sun came through the windows, illuminating the area with a gentle light.

His gaze swept the room, but seeing no movement, he hustled toward the hall. A slight noise from the side halted his steps and he whirled around.

Morgan was sitting on the sofa, her arm propped, but she was not moving. Unsure if she was asleep, he softly walked over, kneeling in front of her.

Red-rimmed eyes met his, but they appeared to be unseeing, similar to when she was first in the hospital. He reached out and clutched her cold hand. "Morgan? Babe? Sweetheart, talk to me."

She blinked several times, her eyes slowly focusing, as though waking from a long sleep. Shifting, she winced.

"Is it your arm?"

She shook her head and said, "No. I'm just stiff. I must have been sitting here a long time." Looking at the fading light from the windows, she added, "Oh, is it evening already?"

"Have you been here since your doctor's appointment?"

She nodded and attempted to stand. Wobbling, she accepted his assistance. "Yeah, I guess so."

"Babe, you're scaring me. Can you tell me what happened?"

"I need to go to the bathroom first." She wobbled again and lifted her hand to her forehead. "I'm a little woozy."

"Have you eaten today?"

"Uh..." she rubbed her forehead. "I don't think so."

He wanted to hear all about the appointment but knew her needs had to be met first. Escorting her into the bathroom, he gave her privacy, but immediately assisted her as soon as she was finished. Leading her back to the living room, he settled her onto the sofa again, saying, "I'm going to fix something for you to eat and then we'll talk." Gaining her nod, he hustled into the kitchen and pulled out a homemade chicken and rice casserole that Rosalie had brought over. Popping it into the microwave, it only took a few minutes for it to be steaming hot. Plating it, he brought a tray over to her and set it on her lap.

"Eat up," he ordered gently.

She acquiesced and began spooning the delicious food into her mouth. Finishing, she nodded slightly as he took the tray.

Sitting on the coffee table so he could face her, he spread his knees to encompass hers and leaned forward to hold her hand. "Okay, give it to me. Give it all to me." He watched as she blew out a long breath, her face etched in sadness.

Shrugging, she said, "Not much to tell. Dr. Roberts said the pin sites look good. Said I can now get it wet in the shower. Even said I could get in the pool if I wanted."

He stared, cautious, because her words were positive but her mood was not. "Okay...and...?" he prodded.

Her eyes dropped to her lap and she lifted her shoulders. "I don't know."

"What exactly did he say, baby?"

"Um...he said I can get in the pool but can't exercise my arm. I can walk or kick my legs but can't use any water resistance on my arm. Considering that if my arm is in the water, I'd be using it in some capacity, I guess that means that I'd need to hold it above the surface."

"Okay," he prodded again.

She lifted her gaze to his and said, "It's over, Jaxon."

His heart seized as his eyes widened. "Over? What's over?" he choked out.

"My career."

Licking his lips, Jaxon said nothing for a moment, trying to decide what to say. At first, he thought she was talking about them when she said it was over and his heart nearly stopped. But realizing she meant her goals, he felt guilty for immediately thinking of himself. *Jesus, I told Miss Ethel I was no good at this!* Forcing his thoughts to calm, he remembered her words. *This is depression... and I need to be whatever she needs with each step.*

"Talk to me about it, sweetheart. Tell me what you're thinking." He was afraid he would sound patronizing, but breathed a sigh of relief when Morgan began to speak.

"It's all I know. My dad had me in the swimming pool when I was a baby. He'd been a collegiate swimmer but missed making the Olympic team. He always lamented that his parents had not started him sooner or supported his dream. I think he was determined to be what they were not. Swimming, physical training, orthopedists to help with sports injuries, other coaches, and hours daily in the pool. It's all I know."

She lifted her eyes back to his and her voice shuddered. "It's all gone, and I don't know anything else."

"Did the doctor say your career was over?"

She gave a barely perceptible shake of her head. "No. But it'll be months before the bones will heal completely and that's *if* they heal completely. It'll be another month before the surgery to remove the external fixation plate and screws. Then, more physical therapy to regain some strength. He said it might be a year before I have complete functionality again."

He continued to rub her cold hand, taking her fingers and gently massaging them to get the blood flowing once more. Looking down at her unmoving left arm, he reached over and felt her icy fingers. Rubbing them, as well, he hoped she could feel his concern.

Morgan sucked in a quick breath, the touch on the fingers of her left hand strange and wonderful all at the same time. After a moment, she continued, "I'm twenty-four years old, Jaxon. In four years, at the age of twenty-eight, I would be getting too old for the Olympics. Not impossible, if I were in peak condition, but with almost a year or more out of the competition...well, let's just say that the reality is, I'll never be what I was."

Jaxon, scared to say the wrong thing, instinctively knew she did not need platitudes. So, speaking from his heart, he leaned forward, touching his forehead with hers and simply said, "I'm so sorry, Morgan. So very sorry."

They stayed that way for a few minutes before he

finally he heard her suck in a deep breath, noting it was not shuddering anymore. He leaned back and took in her moist eyes, paired with a slight curving of her lips.

"Thank you for not trying to either tell me I'll be fine or guilt me by saying I'm lucky to be alive."

He grinned, cupping her face. "I just want to be here for you. Whatever you need."

She remained quiet for another moment before lifting her eyes to his. Biting her lips, she asked, "You want to watch some TV? How about some old, scary movies?"

He smiled wider and, cocking his head, asked, "Popcorn?"

"Yes, absolutely, popcorn," she nodded.

"You got it, babe," he said, moving to the kitchen.

Morgan watched him come back a few minutes later with a huge bowl of popcorn in his hands, which he gave to her before turning to the TV to select a movie.

He grinned over his shoulder and called out, "Bela Lugosi? The Devil's Bat from 1946?"

Unable to keep the smile from her face, she nodded. "Perfect." As he put the movie in, she realized that word described not only the movie, but Jaxon. *No bullshit. No platitudes. No expectations for her to be anything other than just her. Just honesty. I could fall in love with him.*

The last thought slammed into her and her heart jolted. He turned around and settled onto the sofa, pulling her into his body and she fought to still her pounding heart. Still not knowing what her life path held, she knew, in that moment, she wanted to be with him when she finally figured it out.

The tang of chlorine hit her nostrils and Morgan sucked in the sharp scent. Looking down at her swimsuit, she was glad she had managed to shave her legs, bikini area and, with some difficulty, under her arms. With a towel wrapped around her, she walked from the locker room to the pool.

In the local YMCA, she noted the small pool size when compared to the massive Olympic sized pool she had been using at the arena. Hearing her name, she looked over, seeing Jaxon walking toward her.

His hair was pulled back from his face and she blinked at the sight of his body. Dressed in low-slung swim trunks, his muscular body was on display in all its glory. Thick, corded muscles defined his chest and abs. His arms and legs were equally as magnificent. Desire settled in her core and she considered telling him she wanted to disappear into the locker room with him, hoping they would not be caught as she devoured his body.

"You ready?"

Blinking again, she stared at him, wondering for a second what he was referring to.

"Getting into the pool?" he chuckled, a chesire grin spread across his face.

Busted! "Oh, yes," she blurted, her cheeks burning with a deep blush. "Sure."

He assisted her to the steps and she walked into the water. The cool rushed over her and she longed to plunge into the familiar world where she lived under the water. He moved into the pool behind her, but as she stopped at the bottom of the steps, he waded a little further out.

Looking toward him, she said, "You don't have to stay right with me. Go on and swim some. I'll be fine just walking in the shallow end for a while and can keep my arm above the water."

"No, no," he insisted. "I'll walk with you."

Grateful the pool was almost empty, they walked side by side for a few short laps, keeping to the area that did not have lane ropes. While the water felt refreshing, she was stunned by how quickly she became exhausted. "I can't believe how out of shape I've become in only a few weeks away from any exercise."

"Want to get out now?"

She debated for a moment and then said, "I think I'll sit on the steps so I can keep exercising my legs for a bit. You go ahead and swim."

She watched as his eyes shifted to the side, staring at the long lap lanes. "Is everything all right?"

He brought his gaze back to hers and admitted, "I'm not much into swimming."

"You do know how to swim don't you?"

"Sure," he answered a bit too quick. A rare blush stained his cheeks and he said, "Well, I know the fundamentals. Miss Ethel made sure we all had lessons, so I can freestyle down a lane, but that's about all."

"Oh, Jaxon," she said. "I wish I could teach you. The water is so freeing and such good exercise."

"You can teach me, you know. I mean, not right now, but later. When you're back in the water and able to swim some."

She grinned and said, "Of course, I'll teach you. It'll be fun." He looked back toward the deep end and, even though he was well over six feet tall, an expression of doubt crossed his face. She reached out and placed her hand on his arm. "I promise, it'll be fun."

He held her gaze, a small smile curving his lips as well. "Okay, I'll trust you to not let me drown." His breath caught in his throat as he confessed, "You once saved me from going under…many years ago."

Her forehead crinkled as she stared in confusion. He continued, "I was ten years old and in a pool for the first time. The other boys were swimming all around and I was nervous. My feet slid out from under me and a little, six-year-old, red-headed mermaid came to bring me back to the surface."

Her eyes widened, their blueness piercing right through him as her mouth opened wide. "I remember. I was envious of all your brothers playing when I had to do laps. But…how did you know it was me?"

"Your dad called out your name a bunch of times."

Rolling her eyes, she nodded. "Of course, if you were around me in the pool, you would have heard dad yelling 'Morgan'." They stared at each other for a moment, each lost to their own memories. Finally, she said, "I'm glad I was able to help you."

He stepped closer and said, "Maybe we were destined to be together." He looked around at the pool and added, "Perhaps I will learn to swim better so that I'll be able to join you in the pool more often."

Her smile warmed his heart and she moved around in the water, still protecting her arm. "I did some teaching a few years ago. I worked for a pool and taught classes for little kids, and then some water exercises for some elderly as well. I really liked it."

"Why'd you give it up?"

"Oh, Dad had me on a regiment of serious training and I didn't have the time."

He moved closer to her until he was standing right in front of her, his gaze warm upon her face. "Maybe this isn't the right time to say this, and who knows what the future holds but, maybe sometime, you can teach again." Shrugging, he admitted, "I know it's not like the Olympics, but…"

She tried to ignore the pain that shot through her heart, knowing his words were meant to be positive, but the idea of such a life change was still so foreign to her. Nodding her head in a jerky fashion, she simply said, "Sure."

He settled next to her and, as they kicked their legs together, she eventually relaxed once again. It wasn't full emersion but, she had to admit, the water felt wonderful.

"I need to know the specifics of the accident," Sam said, talking into his phone while Pamela walked around him in their kitchen, fixing lunch. "The automobile insurance company wants the police report so that her claim can be attended to. My daughter's car was totaled and, while we have the driver of the truck's insurance information, they need the police report to make sure it wasn't her fault."

His words were biting and he grimaced as he ran into one obstacle after another. "Yes, yes. Here's my email to send it electronically." He rattled off the email address before disconnecting.

Looking at his wife, he shook his head. "I swear, trying to get anything done is like ramming my head into a brick wall."

She walked over and wrapped her arms around his waist. "I know you're frustrated, Sam. This is an untenable situation for all of us, but you've got to let go of your anger when you're around Morgan. She doesn't need your emotions on top of hers."

"I know...you keep reminding me." He heaved a sigh and said, "I just can't believe that everything we've worked for, sacrificed for, lived for, is all gone in one horrendous accident." He looked down at his wife, and added, "And don't say it was just my dream. She wanted it too."

Pamela leaned back and held her husband's gaze. He had a hard exterior, but she knew, underneath, he cared about those he loved. "You're right. She did want it. I often wondered if she had the intensity that you had, but I know it was her goal too." Squeezing his waist, she added, "But Sam, that's gone, and we need to help her find her way now."

Walking back to the counter, she finished preparing lunch and said, "And I, for one, want to formally meet her new boyfriend."

Placated, Sam disappeared into his office, checking his email to see if the police report from the accident came through. It had. Clicking on it, he read the detailed report, including the illustrations depicting the accident. As he read, his anger renewed.

Pulling up outside of Miss Ethel's house, Jaxon grinned, seeing Jayden's bike there as well. Jogging up the steps, he knocked before entering, hearing voices in the back.

"Miss Ethel," he called out, his feet already taking him to the kitchen. He entered as she was turning from the counter, a slice of pie in her hands.

"Oh, Jaxon," she greeted, her smile wide. "What a lucky day for me to have both of you here."

He clapped Jayden on the shoulder and then sniffed in appreciation. "Peach pie? I did come just in time."

Soon, they were settled with pieces of pie in front of them and the conversation flowed easily as she asked about their jobs and told them what she had been doing.

"So, how is Morgan?" she finally asked.

Swallowing his last bite, he said, "She's doing really good. I took her to the YMCA this morning before I had a shift and she got in the water. She can't swim or even use her left arm in the water now, but she was able to kick her legs and do some walking." He added, "She told me that you came to the hospital, that you know her grandmother."

"Oh, yes, she and I are old friends. I went by the nursing home in a cab and took her to the hospital. I knew she wanted to see Morgan."

Jayden pushed his plate away and leaned back in his seat. "Things gettin' serious between you and Morgan?"

Leaning back, he looked at his twin, unspoken words flowing between them.

"Okay, you two. I might have been able to tell you apart from the beginning, but the silent twin-language was not something I mastered," Miss Ethel joked. "I'd like to know the answer to that as well."

Grinning, he nodded, holding her gaze. "I really like her. I felt something the first time I was around her, but figured we would never have a chance. Now, she's told me that, realistically, she won't be an Olympian, so I know she needs time to figure all that out. She knows better than I do what her chances are of making a comeback, so I'm just trying to be there for her while she works through it. I'm sure of my feelings and I know she cares for me too…I just hope she wants this to go the same place I want it to."

"Does she have any idea what she wants to do?" Jayden asked.

Shaking his head, he replied, "No, and all I want for her right now is to heal."

"Does she remember anything about the accident?" Miss Ethel questioned.

"Not really. She remembers me helping her after being hit by the truck, but that's all. We don't talk about that day." She raised her eyebrow and he hastened to add, "What good would it be for me to go over the entire episode with her? It would just bring up a time that she'd rather forget."

"Oscar Wilde once wrote, 'The truth is rarely pure and never simple.' He was so right," she responded, standing to take the plates back to the sink. Looking over her shoulder, she said, "Sometimes in life there is no clear right or wrong, simply choices."

"Then how do we know what to do?"

"Instinct will often give you the answers. What does your heart tell you to do with Morgan?"

She smiled and reminded, "I have told each of your brothers this at different times. The true measure of a man is not in the mistakes he makes but in how he handles those mistakes."

Shaking his head, he remained silent, his mind churning. Soon, he and his brother said their goodbyes and walked out of the house toward their motorcycles.

"You decide?" Jayden asked, his helmet in his hand.

He stared at his twin, knowing what was in his mind and that he was asking about Morgan. Nodding slowly, he replied, "Yeah."

Jayden grinned widely. "Good. Talk to you soon." Swinging his leg over his bike, he headed down the road, leaving him still standing in the driveway.

Hands on his hips, he stared into the neighborhood, his mind traveling back to his childhood and the lessons Miss Ethel taught. *Things seemed so much easier back then.* As he pondered that thought, he realized it was because Miss Ethel was what he described—a soft place to land.

As he drove home, he decided he would talk to Morgan about the day of the accident. *That way there are no secrets.*

Morgan set her bag down on the inside of her apartment, the smallness of it stark after spending time at Jaxon's home. Her arm did not hurt as much, and she had no more fears of banging it on a counter or cabinet, or even the tiny-ass shower walls.

Her heart heavy, she flipped on the light switch and walked into her kitchen. Opening the freezer, she was glad that her mother's pre-cooked meals were still there. A peek into the refrigerator made it obvious that she needed to make a trip to the grocery store. Glad there was one within walking distance, she was concerned with how difficult it would be to do it all one-handed. Blowing out a big breath, she wondered if coming back was the right thing to do.

Walking into the living room, she sunk onto the old sofa, noting instantly that the cushions were not nearly as comfortable as Jaxon's.

Her dad's recent visit stayed with her, his words ringing in her ears. Closing her eyes, she felt a tear slide down her cheek and she leaned her head way back, exhausted.

"He was part of the accident report, Morgan. You slowed down because of his ambulance. It was because of him that your car was out where the truck could hit it. He hasn't told you because he probably feels guilty. It's partially his fault

that your world's been ripped apart. All our dreams have gone away forever because of him."

Her father had come to Jaxon's apartment earlier to show her the police report. She read it carefully and, while it placed no blame upon anyone other than the driver of the truck, it was there in black and white that Jaxon Chapman was in the ambulance that was attempting to move through the intersection when she was hit. He was a witness. *Why didn't he tell me? Why pretend he was just there to save me?*

Unable to come up with the answers, she told her dad that she was still not coming home with him but would be returning to her apartment. He waited as she packed her bag and drove her over after she insisted that it was time for her to take care of herself now.

She sat until the sun set behind the building across the street and her room was cast in shadows. All cried out, she fell asleep on the sofa, her arm not propped up and her head bent to the side.

Several hours later, a pounding on the door woke her up. Jerking awake, she groaned as her neck protested and her arm throbbed. Looking down, she realized she had missed three texts and four calls from Jaxon. Knowing he must be the one pounding down her door, she stood, wobbling slightly as she walked over.

Jaxon leaned his head against the door and lifted his fist, knocking again. When he had come home and found her gone, he had been confused. He called and texted repeatedly, but never received a response. Her stuff was gone from his apartment and he had no idea what had happened. Had she left him? Was this it? For a moment, he had thought back to his aunt leaving he and Jayden without a second thought and his stomach had twisted. Jayden told him that he thought Jaxon had never been in a serious relationship before because he harbored subconscious fears of abandonment, but he had never thought that could be true—not until now. He had to talk to her.

"Morgan!" The door suddenly opened and there she stood, her eyes red-rimmed, her right hand massaging her neck and her left hand balanced against her waist as she flexed her fingers.

"What's going on, babe?" he asked, his frustration peaking. As she stood mute, her eyes pinned on his, he felt a snake of fear slither over him. "Babe?"

"Anything you want to tell me about the day of the accident, Jaxon?" she asked, her voice strangely cold.

He sucked in a quick inhalation and cocked his head, but remained quiet.

"Like how I had slowed down and moved into another lane to get out of the way of an ambulance, and doing so placed myself in the path of an oncoming truck?"

His breath left him in a rush and his shoulders slumped. He lifted his hands and said, "Morgan—"

"What I can't understand is why you didn't tell me. I read the accident report, my dad brought it to me. I know the fault lies totally on the driver of the pickup truck. But why, Jaxon, did you not tell me yourself? My dad's theory is that you have a hero complex and need to be seen as the savior. Is that it?"

"A hero complex? Seriously, Morgan? You know me—"

"I thought I did," she threw back, her eyes flashing.

"You did—you do," he bit out, leaning forward. "Why would I tell you more about that day than you remembered? It was a horrible day for both of us and I know, for you, it represents the day your life changed. I know what that day is to you. Why the hell would I want to drag you through it, giving you a play by play?"

"I don't know!" she cried, her shoulders slumping. "It just feels like I was lied to. You kept something from me about a day that changed my life."

"I never lied to you," he said, his heart aching for her tears. "If you let me come in, I'll talk to you. I'll tell you whatever you want to know."

She stood unmoving for a moment, something working behind her eyes. Finally, with a shuddering breath, she stepped back. Taking the opportunity, he quickly moved past her and into her apartment, being reminded of how small it was.

Turning around, he said, "Can we sit?"

"Sure," she said, her voice no longer laced with anger, but with resigned sadness. She led him to the sofa but sat in the chair.

He looked around and stalked back toward her bedroom, leaving her sitting alone, her brow crinkled in question. Returning with a pillow in his hand, he leaned over and lifted her arm so that it was propped up.

She said nothing, biting her lip as her gaze lifted to his.

He sat down on the sofa, leaning his forearms on his knees. Holding her gaze, he prompted, "What do you want to know?"

Morgan opened her mouth several times, suddenly unsure of her questions now that he was here in front of her.

"How about I tell you what I saw that day?" he asked. She nodded, her gaze dropping to her lap as she wiped her sweaty right hand on her knee.

"We were coming back from a call, heading to the station, when another call came in. I was the usual driver, but we had someone with us who needed to get more hours driving in. Bob was qualified and capable. I was sitting next to him as the call came in and we headed to the new location. He put on the siren and we began to move through traffic as it cleared for us. As we approached the busy intersection, several cars pulled forward, so they could move to the side. Cars on the opposite side of the road, coming toward us, were stopping as well, since we needed to turn. You were one of those cars."

Jaxon observed as her forehead creased but her eyes gave no indication that she remembered. *Good. No matter what she thought of him, he did not want her to relive the horror of the impact.*

"I...I can't...nothing," she mumbled, still staring at him.

"I'm glad, babe. I still have nightmares thinking about it."

She gasped, her eyes widening. "Oh. Not knowing you were there, I hadn't even thought that you would have seen it…heard it."

Nodding, he leaned forward and held her hand, rubbing her fingers. "I had looked back for a second to check on Mary, the paramedic, and heard Bob yell. He saw the truck run the red light. I jerked around and saw the truck hit you, traveling so fast, he pushed you halfway across the intersection."

"When did you know it was me?" she asked, her voice soft and low.

"I jumped out and got to the truck first. The driver's airbag deployed and he was shaken up, but awake and coherent. I ran to your car next and crawled into the passenger side. It wasn't until I moved to get in front of you and leaned your head back that I saw your face."

He closed his eyes for a few seconds, the memory jolting his heartbeat. Letting out a long breath, he opened his eyes and said, "That's the only thing you didn't know, Morgan. I promise. Yes, I was there, and I've played it over and over in my mind, but I can't see that there was anything we did that was wrong."

She dropped her gaze and nodded slowly. "I know, I just…I just don't understand why you didn't tell me that your ambulance was involved, or at least, there."

Scrubbing his hand over the back of his neck, he said, "I didn't think it mattered. You had no memory of the accident and I just wanted to make sure you were all right."

She sat quietly, her head down, staring at her arm.

"Morgan, I felt something for you the first time we

danced, but our lives? Damn, we were not in the same place. After the accident, yes, I wanted to take care of you because you meant something to me and, then, my feelings grew."

He looked around her apartment before bringing his eyes back to her. "So, why are you here? If you don't trust me, why not go home to your parents so they can look after you?"

"I don't want to be there. As much as I'm having a hard time with the curve life has thrown at me, my dad is also struggling. I think the two of us in one house would be the death of my mom."

He snorted ruefully before taking her hand again. "Am I forgiven? I never meant to deceive you. I just wanted to protect you."

She sighed and turned her hand over so that they could link fingers. Nodding, she said, "Yes, you're forgiven. I'm sorry for just leaving and not giving you a chance to explain."

He leaned forward and kissed her lightly. "I'm sorry as well. Can we go back?" Standing, he reached out his hand to assist her out of the chair.

Biting her lip, Morgan replied, "I'm sorry but, no, Jaxon. I really think I should stay here for a while."

He reared back, surprise written in his wide eyes. Plopping back into the chair, he opened his mouth but before he had a chance to argue, she jumped in.

"I need some *me* time. I've never had that and I'm just now figuring out that's what I need." She held on to his hand and explained, "From the time I was small, my dad became my coach and turned my love of being in the water into a goal of becoming an Olympian. I don't want to say it wasn't my goal also, but now that I've had time out of the water to think about it, I can say that there are things I've given up for that. My weekends were spent in swim practices and competitions, not having fun with friends. My college major was about getting into a sports-related field but, honestly? I can't say that was my career goal."

Jaxon sat still, his heart aching for the things she gave up, and also afraid she was breaking up with him. He stared at her face, the tiny freckles beckoning, and fought the desire to pull her into his lap, promising to make all her troubles go away.

"You inviting me to live with you for the past couple of weeks has been just what I needed," she confessed. "A chance to start healing in a safe place with someone who cares about me and wants me to find my way—"

"I do, you know," he interjected. "I do care for you. My feelings have been growing and, Morgan, I feel for you things that I have never felt before. Things I never thought I'd feel." Her lips curved and it warmed his heart to see the smile.

"I feel the same for you," she said. "But I still need some time for me. Time to learn how to do some things on my own. Time to find out what I want out of life. Time to discover a new goal."

"Does this mean you don't want to see me anymore?"

Her long hair swung from side to side as she shook her head. "No, not at all. I just don't feel equal to you right now. I want to come to you as a whole person and not some broken mermaid."

His breath left him in a long sigh, the image of her as the little mermaid who pulled him out of the water when he was little, fully in his mind. "You're not broken. Not to me."

She smiled, her blue eyes pinned on him, and said, "And I'm so glad you feel that way. But, I'd like the chance to be with you in a more normal way. First, we were a one-nighter and, then, you were my rescuer. *I* need to find out who I am now, but you can be on this journey *with* me."

"I can do that," he agreed, but looked around her small apartment. "But does it mean we have to be apart?"

She licked her lips and nodded. "Yes. I need to learn to live on my own. Not with my dad trying to coach my every move and not with a boyfriend trying to make everything all better. I need to find out more about me."

They stood together and he was glad she allowed him to wrap his arms around her, pulling her in tightly. Kissing the top of her head, he said, "I want to hold you tight and take care of you in all ways, but I'll give you the space you need. I'll give you anything you need."

She nodded against his chest and mumbled, "Thank you," into the soft fabric of his shirt.

As he walked out of her apartment a few minutes later, he prayed it was the right decision.

Morgan had only been on her own for three days and she was ready to give up. The trip to the grocery store had been difficult, using her right hand for everything, including carrying the groceries the four blocks back to her apartment.

She had banged her arm three times on the shower door and at least six times against her kitchen counters. She tried binge-watching a few old television shows, since she rarely had the time for such indulgence when in training, but found they did not hold her attention. She added books to her eReader but her mind would wander frequently, so she had to re-read passages numerous times.

Finally, she decided to take a cab over to the nursing home to visit her grandmother.

The receptionist at the front desk dropped her gaze to her arm before sending her a look of pity. Not wanting to discuss her injury with the young woman, she offered a small smile and hurried down the hall. She was surprised to see Miss Ethel walking toward her.

"Oh, Morgan, how nice to see you. I was just visiting your grandmother. She'll be so pleased to have you visit. She's so concerned for you."

Stopping, she accepted a hug, finding Miss Ethel's arms to be strong and sure, and every bit as comforting as Nonnie's.

Miss Ethel smiled at her and added, "I believe you now know the full details of the day of your accident?"

"Yes," she sighed, finding comfort in the older woman's kind, grey eyes. "My father discovered that Jaxon had not told me that his ambulance was right there the whole time and the reason I had pulled out of my lane was to give them room. I know that it was not his fault, but…"

"But, you would have liked the whole truth, none-theless," Miss Ethel finished for her.

"Jaxon and I talked about it and I do understand he wanted to protect me. I'm not angry anymore about that," she hurried to explain, "but I still needed some space to think things through, figure out what I want to do in light of all that has happened, you know?"

Miss Ethel nodded, her smile sincere. "I understand you are back at your apartment. How are you doing?"

Unable to stop the grimace, she confessed, "Not too bad, but I'm finding it difficult to do the most mundane tasks around the house. It was certainly easier when I was living with Jaxon." Blushing, she wondered if she should have admitted her difficulties. "But, it's all good. I needed to do some things myself and uh…"

"Please, my dear, don't feel embarrassed. You are very smart to take time to figure things out. All my boys have a protective streak, which I think is wonderful, but can also be a bit overwhelming."

She held on to Miss Ethel's arm and said, "Jaxon's been nothing but wonderful to me. I think I ran to him at first because of my father. He's been my coach for as long as I can remember…sometimes more of a coach than a father. And now, well, I need to stand on my own."

"Parents can be clueless sometimes," Miss Ethel said, gaining her rapt attention. "All my boys came to me with different situations, but all needed me to be a guiding force in their lives."

"And you did such a good job," she said earnestly, holding her gaze. "Jaxon once told me that his life started rough, but he landed in a soft place. Miss Ethel, I think that is the sweetest thing he could have said about you."

Miss Ethel blinked, her eyes suddenly watery. "I agree. What a beautiful thing for him to say. I simply loved my boys and tried to guide them to find out what they wanted to do with their lives." Touching her cheek, she said, "And I think that is where you are now. Take time to find out what is next in your life." Suddenly, she looked at her watch and exclaimed, "My goodness, I have held you up for too long, you must be ready to go find your grandmother."

Just as she was waving goodbye, Miss Ethel called back to her. "By the way, Eleanor will call you soon. I think she'd like a visit." With that, Miss Ethel walked out the front door, leaving her staring after her.

Blinking, she hurried down the hall. Once at Nonnie's room, she was disappointed to find it empty, but one of the aides told her that her grandmother was in the sunroom painting.

She entered the large room, painted a soft, buttery yellow, that had a wall of windows to allow the sunlight to stream in, warming the occupants. Nonnie sat in the corner at a table with watercolors before her. A vase with a sunflower was in front of her and she appeared to be concentrating as she dipped her brush into the paint.

Nonnie looked over as she approached and her smile brightened. "Oh, my dear child, come give me a hug."

After offering and accepting a deep hug from her, she sat at the table and said, "I love your painting!"

"Well, I like to dabble, you know." She laid the paintbrush down and focused her attention on her arm. "It looks like it's healing well. How are you feeling?"

"Much better," she admitted. "My occupational therapy is over. I can now pick little things up with the fingers on my left hand, can pull up my pants, and can fasten my bra."

Clapping her hand, Nonnie laughed. "Well, then, as long as your panties and bra are in place, what else do you need?"

She settled back in her seat, laughing along, telling her grandmother all about her physical therapy and having moved back into her apartment.

"And the young man? Jaxon, I believe his name was?"

"You don't fool me, Nonnie. I know you and Miss Ethel have talked and I also know you know his name." She sighed and said, "We're kind of on a break. Not a big break, just a little one."

"I don't know the lingo you young people use," Nonnie complained. "In my day, we didn't take breaks. We courted and then we got married." Cocking her head, she reached over and placed her hand on her arm. "What exactly are you doing?"

She picked up one of the little paintbrushes and fiddled with it as she pulled her thoughts together. Finally, shrugging, she admitted, "I felt like I was too dependent on him. I went from being under Dad's thumb to not being able to take care of myself and it was nice to turn it over to Jaxon and let him handle things for a bit."

"And you think that was wrong?"

Shaking her head, she said, "No, not wrong. I definitely needed help and I realized my world was very small. No roommate anymore since she's with her fiancé. Tiny apartment that I couldn't move around in very well. All my friends are in the swimming world and I found that, after the first days in the hospital when they all wished me well, they went on with their lives and I didn't really have good, true, lasting friends."

"And your father…" Nonnie let the statement linger, giving her a chance to respond.

"Yeah. Dad was mostly my coach and his world's been altered as well. He wanted me to be so positive that I'd get back to competitive swimming, and the realization that I won't has been a strain on us. I mean, my arm could make a full recovery, but the lost time, starting from scratch building up the strength again? I don't think I can come back from that."

"How are you coping?"

"Some days, I'm furious that my life was completely changed just because someone ran a red light. Like being lost in a little rowboat in the middle of the ocean. I can't see land and I'm just tossed with the waves." She fiddled with the paintbrush a little more, gathering her thoughts. "I didn't make the Olympics, but I did compete on a national and world level, so it's not like I never met any goals. Then, sometimes, I think that I have actually been given a gift."

"A gift?" Nonnie asked, her eyes wide in surprise.

"A chance to do something for me, besides just swim. There are so many things in life I've wanted, Nonnie. Things that I kept telling myself I'd get to after I made it to the Olympics. Friends…love…find out if I am something besides just what my father always saw."

Leaning closer, Nonnie clasped her hands. "Oh, my dear girl. You can be anything you want to be."

She leaned back in her seat, staring at the half-finished sunflower watercolor and wondered if Nonnie was right…*and how will I ever know what I want to be?*

"I am so glad you let us take you to lunch," Rosalie said, spearing a fat shrimp in her seafood salad.

"It was nice of you to ask me and then come to pick me up," she replied, her smile warm as she stared at the other three women. Eleanor and Regina rounded out the table and, while she had been nervous to begin with, she found the conversation fun.

"So, I just have to ask," Regina began. "Is talking about Jaxon a taboo subject? I mean, I don't want to make things uncomfortable."

Shaking her head, she smiled. "No, he's not a topic to be avoided. I moved out of his place, but that was because I needed to put some independence back into my life." She hesitated for a few seconds and then added, "Okay, to be honest, I was pissed at first. I found out that he had been at the accident and withheld that information from me."

The other women's eyes widened and she hastened to add, "It wasn't his fault, or anything like that, but I felt like it was an omission of information that I should have known."

Eleanor nodded. "I understand. Rafe withheld information from me and it was devastating when I found out the truth."

She stared at the dark-haired beauty and wondered the circumstances but did not ask. Instead, she said, "Well, I can't say I was devastated. More like really ticked off that he was so clueless that it would matter to me."

"Yeah, but that pretty much describes men, doesn't it?" Rosalie quipped, gaining chuckles from the others.

"I hear you two met at Grimm's. On the dance floor?" Regina asked, her smile bright. "That's how I met Cael. We agreed on one night only, no names and no regrets." Shaking her head, she laughed, "And see how that worked out!"

"That sounds like Jaxon and me, only we did share names. But, it was going to just be some fun, I thought. A chance to blow off some steam before the big competitions started. Turns out, we both wanted more almost immediately, but the timing wasn't right."

"Funny how life works sometimes, isn't it?" Eleanor asked, her voice circumspect. "I was a nurse and planned on staying in the Army Reserves. But, a mission gone wrong and being burned changed my life. It took me a long time to understand what to do with my life after that experience, and that was after the long time it took to heal."

She thought of the year long, horribly painful process of healing from the burns that Eleanor had to endure and her heart ached for her new friend. The knowledge that she had it easy compared to Eleanor struck her.

"Perhaps you'd like to see my clinic sometime," Eleanor asked, her gaze warm on her. "We have an indoor swimming pool that has just been built. I'd love to show you around."

A spark of interest filled her, and she grinned. "I would absolutely love to! Jaxon took me to the YMCA last week and it was fun to get back into the water. Well, at least my legs."

"When can you swim again?" Rosalie asked.

"I can't use my left arm for any resistance exercise now, but can easily move about the water."

"That must feel strange," Regina said, her eyes sad as she looked to her.

"I've been in swimming pools my whole life," she shrugged. "It was all I knew. I used to get up at five a.m. to swim before school and then returned to the pool as soon as school was over. My dad was my coach until I went to college and had a college coach as well. I never fully realized how it dominated my life until it was taken away from me. Like, I knew I wanted a relationship and good, sincere friends, but it was easy to give those up not knowing what it meant to have them in the first place. I had friends, of course, but they were all swimmers and they floated away quickly when it became apparent that I was no longer part of their world."

"Floated away," Rosalie giggled, then immediately blushed. "Oh, I'm so sorry. It just struck me as funny that your swimming friends *floated* away."

The irony of her own words struck her and she giggled as well, Regina and Eleanor joining in until their laughter rang out over the restaurant. Feeling lighter than she had in a long time, she looked toward Eleanor and asked, "Would we be able to visit your clinic today?"

Eleanor beamed as she nodded. "Absolutely! It's such a life-changing place for the veterans who come there."

She smiled in return, wondering if perhaps she could find something life-changing as well.

28

"The Bellamy Center was created to give veterans with burns a chance to continue their therapy and learn new skills after their time at veterans' hospitals and facilities. My maiden name was Bellamy and I wanted it to honor my parents and grandparents."

Morgan was so impressed as she walked along with Eleanor, who was offering a running commentary on the beautiful center. The outside was landscaped to perfection with walks lined with flowering shrubs mixed with evergreens. Flower beds dotted the area and, at a distance, she recognized Rafe with a small group standing around him.

With pride in her voice, Eleanor said, "Rafe is a landscaper and he teaches some of the interested veterans the tools of the trade, so they are employable when they leave."

"Wow," she breathed, her eyes swinging around to take it all in. They stepped inside and her attention was immediately snagged on the large, beautifully decorated building. Comfortable chairs and sofas sat in the sun-filled lobby. The walls were painted soft colors with artwork hanging along the halls.

Eleanor explained, "Burn units have to be so sterile and veterans' hospitals often lack décor. I wanted our veterans to feel like they were in a nice facility and not a hospital."

They walked past the offices and peeked into the fitness room, where she watched a few men and women inside working with physical therapists. They continued down the hall, past the kitchen, and she recognized the work of an occupational therapist, who sat with several men and women learning to hold utensils.

"We have a daycare here as well, for some of our clients and employees. But, what I really wanted to show you, is our new indoor swimming pool."

She felt excitement bubble inside as they moved down another hall, the scent of chlorine striking her. "Oh, my," she breathed, excitement filling her blood as she stepped into the room. The L-shaped pool was not large, but it had four lanes for swimming and the smaller portion of the L was shallow, easy to use for standing exercises. "This is fabulous," she enthused, the familiarity of the environment filling her.

"We have a few veterans who have used it, but with many fearful of what they can and can't do, it mostly sits unused."

She walked around the perimeter of the pool and carefully noted the construction of the facility. The walls were insulated and she felt cool, not cold, air blowing in. Large windows allowed the sunlight to shine in, but with pull-down shades, they could also block out the heat of the sun during the middle of the day in the summer, while allowing it to warm the interior in the winter. *Of course. Burned skin would be more susceptible to the sun.*

Eleanor walked along beside her, a slight limp leading her to believe she had burns on other parts of her body besides just her face.

"Do you use the pool?" she asked, hoping the question was not perceived as impertinent.

Eleanor smiled and nodded. "Yes. I find that it helps with circulation and gently stretching of the scarred skin. I have burns down my entire left side, so keeping the scar tissue as pliable as possible is needed."

"Why do you think the pool is not used more?"

Eleanor stopped walking and turned to face her. "To be candid, it's because we don't have an instructor. Oh, there are plenty of people who are qualified to teach swimming. But we need more than that. Someone who truly understands the human body…injuries…the healing process. And, quite frankly, someone who can empathize with the fear of pain and the fear of the unknown."

She held Eleanor's gaze, sucking in a huge breath of air. She felt lightheaded, as though her mind did not have enough room for all of the thoughts that had suddenly taken flight and were swirling around each other.

A spark of interest filled her and she twisted her head to stare at the undulating water in the pool. The crystal-clear water, so clean and pure. So enticing. Giving weightlessness to someone so mired in dark thoughts. Allowing the freedom to work tired muscles in a way that washes the sweat away. She had always loved swimming more than any other exercise, preferring it over the weights in the gymnasium or running on a track.

Sucking in another deep breath of chlorinated air, she wondered if she had *it* in her. The ability to teach someone else. Not coaching them to Olympic greatness, but to something better. A chance to work their scarred bodies in a way that gave them freedom.

She turned back to Eleanor, seeing the hopefulness in her dark eyes and—

"Eleanor!" A voice from the doorway grabbed their attention. "We've called 9-1-1-. One of the men fainted or something!"

Eleanor grabbed her hand and they hustled to the side door, leading to a patio overlooking the grounds. They saw a small crowd gathering and Rafe kneeling on the ground next to a man.

As they approached, Rafe looked up and said, "He just collapsed. I can't revive him."

They watched as Rafe continued basic first aid and her heartbeat pounded in fear. She was so relieved when she finally heard an approaching siren. The ambulance drove from the parking lot onto the grounds, getting as close as they could while Eleanor signaled them over.

Stunned as Jaxon leaped from the ambulance, she stood in shocked silence, watching as he and another man and woman immediately went into action. She remembered he referred to them as Bob and Mary when he was talking about the accident day.

Rafe was giving the man's name to Bob as Mary inserted an IV needle into his arm. Jaxon took his vital statistics, calling in information to a hospital. Eleanor moved the observers back to give them plenty of room.

Suddenly, calling out codes she did not understand, she watched in horror as Jaxon turned and ripped open the man's shirt. He had an automated external defibrillator in his hand and as Bob placed the pads on the man's chest, Jaxon hooked up the AED.

As it began working, she wanted to close her eyes to the frightening scene in front of her but was unable to take her gaze off Jaxon. Calm. Sure. Confident. A life saver.

A sudden rush of love for him hit her and she locked her knees to keep from falling to the ground. He had not noticed her, and she said nothing, not wanting to be a distraction, but her desire was to rush to him, throw herself in his arms, beg his forgiveness, and declare her love was overwhelming.

Holding tight to those emotions, she forced her body to stay in place, letting him continue his work instead.

The man appeared to be reviving and the trio loaded him onto the gurney and rolled him to the ambulance. As Mary hopped inside and Bob moved to the driver's door, Jaxon took a second to shake Rafe's hand and speak to him. His eyes swept back, probably to send assurances to Eleanor, when they landed on her instead. Eyes wide, his mouth opened, but nothing came out.

A smile was the only thing she could offer him at the moment and she watched, raptly, as her unspoken emotion hit him. His lips curved as the back doors were closed and he jogged to the passenger side. The ambulance, siren blaring, took off through the parking lot.

Eleanor walked to Rafe and the couple held each other tightly. Not wanting to disturb their moment, she turned and moved back through the door. Standing at the side of the pool, she stared at the water, so familiar to her. *'You're a little mermaid'*, Nonnie had always said. *Maybe I am...maybe that's what I was always meant to be.*

Morgan walked into her father's house after knocking on the door first. "Dad? Are you home?" She knew her mother was at her weekly book club meeting and had wanted a chance to talk to him alone.

She moved toward the kitchen and observed him sitting at the table in the breakfast nook, staring at the back yard through a large, sliding glass door. His hand rested on the handle of his coffee cup, his empty lunch plate pushed to the side.

"Dad," she called again, surprised when his gaze did not leave the window. "Are you all right?" She slid into the chair angled toward him and rested her left arm on the table, her eyes roaming over his expressionless face before moving to the view outside. The pool was in the center of the yard with a few chairs set under a pergola at one end.

"Your mother used to like to sit and watch you swim," he said, his voice strangely unanimated.

Not knowing what to say, she remained quiet.

He shook his head slowly and said, "She always warned me about being too hard on you." His voice broke as he continued. "From the first moment you were in the water as a baby, you loved it. I would carry you around in my arms and you would kick and splash. You were fearless, swimming underwater at an early age, loving the water more than playing with your toys."

"I did love the water, Dad. I still do."

"I did too. I never made it to the world championship level but, on a national level, I would at least get on the platform sometimes. Mostly, I was just a great swimmer, but not an exceptional one."

Though he was telling her something she had heard numerous times in her life, she still remained silent.

"I just thought that if you had consistent training and coaching, from your earliest years, it would make the difference. And I was right. You were poised to take it all...maybe Gold."

"Dad," she said softly, and he turned his eyes from the pool in the back yard to her face. She held his gaze, noting the lines around his eyes were deeper, the creases in his forehead more pronounced. "You were a good coach. There were times I wished you were more of a dad than a coach, but," she shrugged, "my life was a good one." She thought of Jaxon and Jayden. She thought of Miss Ethel and all her boys. She thought of Jaxon's world starting hard and knew she had never known such difficulty.

Swallowing hard, she said, "But my life is different now. *Our* lives are different now. Our world changed, and we have to change with it."

"I hate that for you," he said, his voice even more broken as his eyes grew watery. "I feel like I failed you. I made you ready for the Olympics but forgot to make you ready for whatever life threw at you."

She leaned forward, her hand reaching for his arm. She felt the strong, corded muscles in his forearm, lightly covered with reddish hair. His strength mixed with the vulnerability shining in his face as he peered back at her. "Dad, you did not fail me. You coached me to be strong and that strength has made my recuperation go faster. You coached me to set goals and I'm finding new ones, from just living on my own with this temporary disability to what a new career might be. Dad, I'm still a winner no matter what life throws at me."

A sob erupted from deep in his chest as he moved to gather her in his arms. The sight and sound of her father's grief hit her, causing her tears to flow as his arms encircled her. Warmth moved through her veins as she felt her father's humanness for the first time.

"What's going on?" her mother's voice sounded from the kitchen door, worry streaking her face.

Letting her father go, Morgan smiled through teary eyes and said, "We're good, Mom. Just having a moment."

Wiping his eyes as well, her father cleared his throat and agreed, "Nothing to worry about. As Morgan said, we were just having a father-daughter moment."

Her mother stepped into the room, her face a mask of surprise, and said, "Well, I'm glad. Quite honestly, you two scared me to death!"

Standing, she hugged her mother, whispering, "We're fine," before turning to both parents and saying, "I've been thinking of a new career possibility, but I'd rather finalize some things before I tell you about it. Cocking her head to the side, she added, "It might be something I can use some help with Dad, but I'll let you know."

"Well, I'm at loose ends now, so if you need me, I'm here," he replied, earning a huge smile from her.

29

With his hand raised, pounding on the door, Jaxon called, "Mrs. Weber? It's the Richmond Emergency Services. We need to know if you're okay. Can you come to the door?"

Standing in the narrow hallway of the old apartment building, he glanced behind him as Mary talked to the neighbor.

"I ain't seen her in two days. She was feeling poorly a couple of days ago and I told her she outta go see a doctor. But, then, I had to work two long shifts and realized this morning I hadn't heard her coming or going."

Bob moved in next to him and asked, "We need to get in?"

"Yeah. I'm going to see if I can pick the lock without breaking her door."

Mrs. Weber was part of the RES residential check-in program for shut-ins. Within a moment, he had the door lock picked, not surprised at how easy it was.

Knowing she would have prescription drugs in her home, he was glad she had not been plagued with robberies. Opening the door, it caught on the chain lock.

"Damn," he cursed under his breath. "Mrs. Weber? Can you come to the door?"

With no response, he stood back as Todd, one of the firemen who had also arrived on the scene, came forward with the chain cutters. With a powerful snip, the links fell to the side and he was able to push the door open.

He stalked inside and immediately knew the news would not be good. Jogging into the bedroom, he saw Mrs. Weber on the bed, her covers still tucked up under her chin as though she were sleeping. Carefully touching her neck, he felt no pulse.

Bob and Todd headed back down the stairs to get the gurney as Mary moved in to stand next to him.

As he stood, staring at the elderly woman, her thin, white hair brushed back from her face and her wire-rimmed glasses on the nightstand, his heart clenched. Blinking, he tried to keep the image of Miss Ethel from his mind, but his breath was ragged as he drew it into his lungs.

Mary said nothing, but placed her hand on his shoulder, and he heard the audible swallowing coming from her and knew she was affected as well.

"It's never easy," Mary finally said. "At least it looks as though she died in her sleep."

He nodded, hearing Bob entering the apartment again. Blowing out a shuddering breath, he agreed. "She just reminds me of…well, someone I'm not ready to lose yet. Hell, I'll never be able to lose them."

Bob and Todd entered the bedroom, and, with dignity, they easily lifted her onto the stretcher. She weighed so little, it was not difficult to take her out to the ambulance. The drive to the hospital was quiet, no one in the mood to talk. At the hospital, they transferred Mrs. Weber to the ER so that a medical doctor would declare her deceased.

He could hardly wait for his shift to be over. As soon as he climbed onto his motorcycle, he roared down the street, his mind filled with only wanting to see one person. Arriving at the house, he jogged up the steps and through the front door.

"Miss Ethel?" he called out, his heart pounding at the similarity of his call now to the call of Mrs. Weber's name. "Miss Ethel?"

Not receiving an answer, he rushed to the kitchen, but did not see her there. About to go upstairs, a movement through the window caught his eye. Seeing her bent over, pruning her roses in the flower garden, his breath left his body in a rush and he clenched the counter to hold himself upright.

Filling his lungs with difficulty, he steadied his heartbeat before stepping through the back door onto the stone patio. Not wanting to scare her, he called out gently, "Miss Ethel?"

She turned, her face creasing into a wide smile as she stood up straight, wiping her hands on her apron. "Oh, Jaxon, how lovely to see you!"

His heart light, he moved straight to her, enveloping

her in his embrace. Her thin frame was swallowed in his arms and he held tight. Her hands patted his back and he finally loosened his hug. She leaned back and stared intently into his eyes.

"What a greeting, sweet boy." She continued to assess him carefully before asking, "How was your day?"

Inhaling deeply, he let it out slowly and admitted, "Rough. We lost someone and I just…I just…well, I…"

"You wanted to assure yourself that I was still here," she finished for him, her gaze resting kindly on him.

"Yeah," he breathed. He watched as she turned and picked up her clippers, gathering the basket of cut roses. "Your flowers are beautiful as always," he noted, looking at the bushes loaded with blooms.

"I thought I would take some to Morgan's grandmother. She's taken up watercolor floral paintings and asked for some of my roses."

The mention of Morgan brought another sigh from him. It had been a couple of days since he had seen her, and his heart missed her as though it had been much longer.

She straightened and, with her head tilted to the side, asked, "How are things with Morgan?"

He shrugged. "I haven't talked to her in a couple of days. She said she needed time to be by herself and figure out what she needed to do."

Nodding, Miss Ethel began walking toward the house, and quoted, "F. Scott Fitzgerald said, 'The loneliest moment in someone's life is when they are watching their whole world fall apart, and all they can do is stare blankly.'" She placed her hand on his arm.

"Morgan has had to watch her world fall apart. To put it back together again takes time and courage."

He nodded, saying nothing, escorting her back into the house. She set the basket of flowers onto the counter and untied her garden apron. Slipping her hand onto his arm, they walked to the front door, where he found himself engulfed in her embrace.

Smiling up at him, she said, "Thank you for checking on me. You boys are always so good to me."

He kissed the top of her head and waved as he walked toward his motorcycle, remembering for the millionth time, how lucky he was that Miss Ethel had been his soft place to land.

Staring at his beer, Jaxon wondered why he thought it would be a good idea to come to Grimm's on a Friday night. The bar was crowded, both at the tables and on the small dance floor next to the jukebox. He glanced around, but the mass of people made it difficult to see.

Zander and Rosalie, having gotten Miss Ethel to babysit for the night, joined him at the table but, for once, watching the two of them interact with each other only exemplified his loneliness.

Jayden walked in, settling down next to him. He looked over but did not say anything and he knew his twin could read his mood. *Hell, a stranger could read my mood right now,* he realized.

His chair jiggled slightly as someone at the table behind him moved their chair. Not looking around, he took another swig of his beer. Thinking it was time to call it an early night, he stood.

"Hey," a sultry voice called out from his left and he looked down as a petite, well-built blonde sidled up next to him. "You wanna dance?"

Not able to summon up a flirty smile, he shook his head. "No, thanks. I'm—"

"Married."

Jerking at the comment coming from his right, his gaze landed on Morgan, standing next to him, a wide smile on her lips. Tall, long-limbed, extremely toned body showcased in tight jeans, boots, and a blue knit top that had little flounces over the shoulders, she was wearing the same outfit that she wore the first night he met her at Grimm's. Her russet hair, hanging over her shoulders, glistened in the lights of the bar. Her blue eyes were holding him captive. She bit her lip before bursting into laughter.

"Sweetheart, sorry I'm late," she said, moving straight to him.

Getting close, without touching her, he locked eyes with her and smiled widely. "Honey…you're here," he grinned, as she threw her right arm around his neck and moved in for a hug.

Wrapping her in his arms, careful of her left arm, he was reminded of how her luscious body lined up perfectly with his. She planted her lips on his and he angled his head for maximum contact.

"Sorry, jeez. Wear a ring," he heard the blonde say, but continued to focus only on Morgan's lips. She tasted of lemon drops.

Hearing a cross between a sigh and a moan, he plundered her mouth as all other thoughts fled his mind.

Her tongue tangled with his and he felt the electricity straight to his cock. The bar noise fell away, leaving only the two of them in the universe. Nothing existed but the feel of her soft lips against his, her body in his arms, and the taste of sweet lemons on her tongue.

After a long, wet kiss, she finally mumbled against his lips, "Ih sheh gah?"

Brow lowering, he tried to clear the lust-fog before looking into her eyes, "Huh?"

Giggling, she sucked in her kiss-swollen lips as an adorable blush covered her face. "Is she gone?" she enunciated, her voice as soft as a whisper.

Shifting his gaze from side to side, he nodded, but kept his arms wrapped tightly. "Yeah."

"Um...you want to let me go now?" she asked, her arms still clutching his shoulders.

"Not particularly," he replied, a grin curving his lips.

"Good. Let's dance," she laughed.

Smiling at her recreation of their first kiss, his brow lowered as he said, "What about your arm? The dance floor is crowded."

She leaned forward, lifting on her toes to call out over the music, "Then you want to get out of here?"

Surprised at her suggestion, he asked, "Whatcha got in mind?"

She licked her lips and, using the same words from their first meeting, asked, "How about a little diversion?"

His grin matched hers as he said, "You lead, I'll follow, Morgan. Wherever you want to go, whatever you want to do, I'll be right here with you."

They walked into his apartment and Morgan immediately moved to the large windows overlooking the city lights.

"I loved this view the first time I was here," she said, a smile playing about her lips.

Jaxon walked up behind her and wrapped one arm around her chest and the other around her waist. He buried his nose in her hair before sliding down to nuzzle her neck. The familiar scent of her filled him and he reveled in having her back in his arms. "I've missed you, babe. I've missed having you here. Seeing you wake up, all sleepy. Seeing you in the kitchen. Piling up with me on the sofa and watching old movies."

She twisted around in his arms until she was facing him, her head leaning back so that her eyes were on his. "I've missed being here also." She blew out a breath, her smile still in place. "I've missed you."

"I always loved being here by myself," he admitted. "But since you entered my life, this world's been lonely without you."

"I know," she agreed. "I wish I could say I have my life all figured out. I don't, but, I feel like I know the direction to move in."

Anxious to hear what she had to say, he slid his hand down to link fingers with her and drew her over to the sofa. As she sat down, he glanced at her left arm and turned to grab a pillow.

"It's okay," she assured. "I don't have to prop it up anymore, just have to be careful. I have the surgery next week to remove the external pins."

Hating the idea of her having more surgery, he nodded before sitting on the coffee table, facing her with his knees on either side of hers. "Tell me everything." His eyes devoured her face, searching for any clue as to her thoughts.

Morgan held his gaze, reaching over to cup his jaw. His eyes, so familiar, held hers and she fought to breathe.

Her brow crinkled and, with his heart dropping, Jaxon asked, "What's wrong?"

Shaking her head slightly, she said, "How is it that I can hold my breath underwater for so long and, yet, looking at you right now, loving you as much as I do, it's as though I can't suck in enough air?"

Her words hit him and he gasped as he moved closer, until his lips were a whisper away from hers. "You love me?"

She smiled a watery smile, a single tear trailing a path over her cheek. He kissed it away before sliding his lips to the corner of her mouth.

"Oh, baby, I love you so much too," he confessed. "My world has been empty without you in it every day. Please tell me you're here to stay."

"I still have healing to do. At least one more surgery. Lots more rehab and therapy—"

"And we can get through it together," he assured.

"I'd like that," she whispered.

His heart soared at the sound of her words and he moved the barest inch so that his lips captured hers, the warm feel of satin against his penetrating the fog he had felt since she left. Plunging his tongue into her mouth, he rekindled the longing he had experienced since she had approached him in Grimm's.

"So, if we're recreating our first night together," she said, her eyes sparkling, "how about we take this to the bedroom. I've got great leg muscles, you know."

Barking out a laugh, he stood and swooped her into his arm, stalking down the hall. Still careful of her arm, they restated their love for one another long into the night.

Jaxon woke the next morning, the feel of a warm body tangled with his sending a smile across his face. He rolled Morgan's way, seeing her eyes open and staring back at him.

"Hey," he said, his gravely morning voice greeting her.

"Hey, yourself," she replied.

"Whatcha thinking?"

"First? That this is a fantastic way to wake up." That answer earned her a long, wet kiss. As it ended, she continued, "Second, I like waking up here, in your place."

"Baby, you say the word," he said, his grin wide, "and it'll become *our* place in a heartbeat."

His reply sent her mouth flying toward his for a longer kiss. After a moment, she leaned back and said, "And, third, I need to tell you about my new job."

Jolted out of his morning lust, he blinked. "Job? You got a job?"

Nodding, she bit her lips and blurted, "I'm going to be working at Eleanor and Rafe's clinic, teaching water exercises and swimming to the veterans that are staying there. And, I've talked to Dad and he'll help occasionally. It'll use my college degree, and my love of swimming, and—umph!"

She grunted as he rolled on top of her, his kiss stealing her breath.

30

Jaxon waited anxiously in the surgery waiting room, Eleanor and Jayden sitting with him, as well as Morgan's parents. Eleanor looked to the side and said, "I know this is agonizing, but this is fairly easy surgery, you know."

He just nodded, feeling Jayden's hand clamp his shoulder in solidarity. Before he had time to respond, the surgeon walked out and, with a big grin, told them that everything was perfect. Breathing easier, he shook his hand and accepted hugs from his friends. They left the room and he glanced nervously toward Sam and Pamela.

He noted as Pamela nudged her husband and Sam walked over, sticking out his hand. "Jaxon, I never fully told you how grateful we were for the care you gave Morgan at the accident. It took a while for that to penetrate, which I know doesn't say good things about me, but we know that having you right there saved her arm and maybe her life."

He felt the firm, but warm, handshake and accepted Sam's words. He had heard them many times over the years in working rescues, but this one meant the world to him. "Thank you, Mr. McAlister."

"And..." Pamela prodded her husband.

Sam chuckled as he wrapped his arm around his wife's shoulders. "And for falling in love with her as well. I've never seen her so happy and, after the accident, I never thought I would see her this way."

"I can't accept your thanks for that," he said, his smile still wide. "She's brought a lot to my world and our love can only make it better."

The surgery waiting room receptionist called for Morgan's family and he hesitated, looking toward her parents.

"Go on in, son," Sam said. "She'll want to see you first. We'll be right here."

With an appreciative nod, he turned and hurried down the hall.

One year later

Jaxon, with Bob and Mary, moved the man onto the gurney, keeping his splinted leg still and straight.

"I told you this was a stupid idea, George," his wife complained, every step of the way. "Why you thought you'd show the grandkids how to skateboard, I'll never know. You haven't skateboarded in forty years. Now, look what you've done!"

"Ma'am, you need to step back, please," he said, hoping she would move out of their way but, instead, she simply continued to yell at her husband, who was writhing in pain. He threw up a prayer of thanks when a policeman escorted her to the side, giving them room to move.

Thirty minutes later, having delivered him to the hospital, the three of them drove back to the station to clock out.

"Got any plans with Morgan tonight?" Mary asked.

"Heading out to see her right now," he grinned.

She placed a hand on his arm and said, "I'm happy for you, Jaxon. Really happy."

He returned her grin and jogged to his SUV. Arriving at the Bellamy Clinic, he parked outside and made his way around the gardens to the entrance of the pool. Waving toward Rafe, he entered the door and his gaze searched for the woman who had captured his heart. Seeing several others, he scanned the pool, not seeing her.

Suddenly, she rose from the depths, her deep red hair billowing out behind her before it sleeked back from her face. Her eyes opened, their blue depths resembling the purest of oceans. She stared at him, her lips curving into a beautiful smile as her arms moved gracefully in front of her, propelling her closer to where he was standing.

Kneeling on the side, he greeted, "Hey, mermaid."

"Hey, yourself."

"You almost finished?"

"Yeah, I just need to—"

"Morgan!"

She rolled her eyes as she twisted her head around to stare at her father. "You don't have to shout, Dad. I'm right here."

Sam had the good grace to appear contrite as he said, "Sorry. Just wanted to say I was heading out. I've been working with John and Karen today. They look healthy. You've done a really good job with them, sweetheart."

Jaxon extended a hand and assisted her out of the pool. Scooping her towel from the chair, he handed it to her. She winked at him before walking toward her father. Standing on her toes, she kissed his ruddy cheek. "Thanks, Dad. Tell Mom we'll come for dinner this weekend."

Sam tossed a wave and goodbye toward him and walked to the locker rooms.

Turning back to him, Morgan smiled. "So, I guess I'm finished."

He looked around at the veterans still in the pool, working on stretching their limbs, and said, "I have to agree with your dad. You're doing a really good job here."

Sliding her arm around his waist, she kissed the underside of his jaw. "What can I say?" she whispered against his skin. "I'm living in the best of both worlds."

Five Years Later

"Grandpa! Look at me!"

Sam grinned at four-year-old Margaret standing on the end of the diving board. "Go on, girl. Impress this old man!"

Margaret looked over at her dad, waving as he stood next to the side of the pool, cheering. Looking back down at her mom in the water, she pinched her nose closed with her fingers and jumped.

Morgan easily caught her daughter in her arms, bringing them both to the surface, supporting Margaret as she swam toward her grandpa at the other end.

Sam took his granddaughter in his arms, held her high and blew raspberries in her neck. Her giggles rang out over the water.

Morgan laughed at their antics then turned and swam to the side of the pool, hoisting herself out of the water with the help of her husband. Standing on her toes, she touched her lips to Jaxon's, her blue eyes holding his.

"Hey, mermaid," he whispered, his arms wrapping around her. "Speaking of a mermaid, looks like Margaret is having a good time."

She twisted her head around and looked at her dad and daughter splashing in the water. Hearing a high-pitched squeal, her attention was snagged by the pack-and-play under the shade of the umbrella. Miss Ethel leaned over, her hands clapping at the toddler, with Pamela smiling nearby.

"And looks like our son just woke up," Jaxon said, smiling as he led her over to the pergola. Scooping up Jack, he kissed the top of his head before ushering her over to sit on the padded chairs in the shade.

She bounced Jack on her knees as her mom slathered him in sunscreen, then walked back to the pool's edge and eased into the water, holding him as he squealed and splashed the surface with his hands, safe in her arms. Her mom snapped numerous photographs with her phone, saving the memories.

Sam and Morgan continued to play with the children as Jaxon sat with Miss Ethel. Her thin hand reached over and patted his arm. He smiled and covered her hand with his much larger one.

"You okay, Miss Ethel?"

Her grey eyes sought his and she nodded. "I just thought that perhaps you were right, those many years ago."

His brow lowered as he cocked his head. "What was I right about?"

She nodded toward the gathering in the pool and replied, "Perhaps the Disney version was the best. After all, nothing can beat a happily-ever-after."

Smiling widely, he nodded silently, turning his gaze back to his family. Still holding Miss Ethel's hand, he could not agree more.

Don't miss the next Heroes at Heart
For all of Miss Ethel's boys:

Heroes at Heart (Military Romance)
Zander
Rafe
Cael
Jaxon
Jayden
Asher
Zeke
Cas

Asher

Zeke

Cas

Lighthouse Security Investigations

Mace

Rank

Walker

Drew

Blake

Tate (August 2020)

Hope City (romantic suspense series co-developed

with Kris Michaels

Hope City Duet (Brock / Sean)

Carter

Brody by Kris Michaels

Kyle

Ryker by Kris Michaels

Saints Protection & Investigations

(an elite group, assigned to the cases no one else wants…or
can solve)

Serial Love

Healing Love

Revealing Love

Seeing Love

Honor Love

Sacrifice Love

Protecting Love

Remember Love

Discover Love

Surviving Love

Celebrating Love

Follow the exciting spin-off series:

Alvarez Security (military romantic suspense)

Gabe

Tony

Vinny

Jobe

SEALs

Thin Ice (Sleeper SEAL)

SEAL Together (Silver SEAL)

Letters From Home (military romance)

Class of Love

Freedom of Love

Bond of Love

The Love's Series (detectives)

Love's Taming

Love's Tempting

Love's Trusting

The Fairfield Series (small town detectives)

Emma's Home

Laurie's Time

Carol's Image

Fireworks Over Fairfield

Please take the time to leave a review of this book. Feel free to contact me, especially if you enjoyed my book. I love to hear from readers!

Facebook

Email

Website

Made in United States
Troutdale, OR
07/26/2023

11565190R00195